D0348529

SHARON SALA

LIFE OF LIES

mira

mira

ISBN-13: 978-0-7783-3035-6

Recycling programs
for this product may
not exist in your area.

Life of Lies

For questions and comments about the quality of this book, please contact us at
CustomerService@Harlequin.com.

www.Harlequin.com

Printed in U.S.A.

People lie. Sometimes it's just a little white lie, meant to save someone's feelings from being hurt. Sometimes it's a big lie, told out of fear or anger, wanting to hurt someone by passing on an untruth.

But what if your whole life was a lie?

What if you had to participate in that lie for someone you loved?

This happens. Oftentimes to children, who grow up without a foundation to stand on, without a way to know good from bad, or lies from truth.

God bless the children who are denied the truth of how they came to be.

How can they find their futures when they do not know their pasts?

LIFE
OF
LIES

One

Dust motes stirred within the sunlight streaming into the hayloft of the abandoned barn. The hay bales that had been left behind were busted and moldy, fit only for the rats that wintered there, and partially hiding the couple making love on the mattress nestled along the back wall.

The heat of the day and the lack of moving air coated their bodies with beads of sweat, but it was the heat building inside them that was out of control.

Alicia groaned, and Jerry slid his fingers through her long dark hair and kept on moving, shifting his body just enough so that the camera in the shadows on the other side of the loft caught the bounce of her breast and the long length of her legs beneath him.

In the midst of their passion, Alicia heard voices approaching the barn. Her eyes widened. They were about to be found out! She grabbed Jerry's arms.

"Someone's coming!"

Jerry froze, then put his hand over her mouth and

motioned toward their clothing in a pile at the foot of the bed. With the mood broken and their affair on the verge of being discovered, they scrambled to get dressed. But their bodies were slick with sweat and their hands were shaking. All they got on was underwear before the men entered the barn below.

Half naked and shaking in terror, they huddled together on the mattress, listening in disbelief to what sounded like a drug deal going down. Jerry turned toward the camera, his eyes widening in horror, then looked back at Alicia just as a gun went off below them.

Alicia clasped her hands over her mouth to keep from screaming as more gunshots sounded, and as hay sprayed around them, she realized some shots were flying into the loft. She buried her face against her knees, trying to make herself as small a target as possible.

The shots ended as abruptly as they'd begun. She heard footsteps running out of the barn and turned with relief to Jerry until she saw him slumped down behind her, blood spilling onto the mattress.

"Jerry! Oh my God, Jerry!" she cried, and knelt beside him, trying to feel for a pulse. But there was none.

He was dead.

She leaned over his body, sobbing uncontrollably at the reality of what had just happened, then rocked back on her heels and screamed.

"Cut!" the director said, and then jumped out of his chair while Sahara Travis pulled herself up from the hayloft as gracefully as if she'd just curtsied before the queen.

She held out her arms as someone from wardrobe came running with a dressing gown to cover her up.

The director was pleased with both actors, and the lilt in his voice showed it.

Bobby French, the actor playing Jerry, stood up, scratching his bare belly and waiting for someone to bring him a robe.

"That was great, Bobby. Absolutely riveting, Sahara. We'll break for lunch now. Everyone back on set in one hour."

Sahara nodded as she began fastening her dressing gown while looking around for her personal assistant.

"Has anyone seen Lucy?" she asked.

One of the cameramen waved toward the craft service area.

"Catering was here. She might have taken your lunch to your trailer."

"Thanks," Sahara said, and strode off the set and then outside into the sunny California heat.

She was halfway to the trailer when she heard someone calling her name.

"Wait a second!" Lucy called, as she ran to catch up. "I was dropping off your lunch, and I got a call from wardrobe. They wanted you to stop in before you get back on set, but I told them to send someone to your trailer for measurements instead."

Sahara frowned. "Thanks, but why do they need new measurements?"

"Your director doesn't like the wardrobe in tomorrow's scenes," Lucy said.

"Whatever," Sahara said, and walked up the steps and into the trailer with Lucy behind her.

The air-conditioning was welcome as she entered. Sahara turned toward the kitchen to wash up and was startled to see a woman curled up on the floor.

"It's Moira," Sahara cried, running to her.

She dropped to her knees beside the wardrobe assistant, assuming Moira must have fainted. But then she felt for a pulse and there was none.

"She's not breathing! Call 911," Sahara shouted to Lucy, then rolled Moira onto her back to begin CPR while her assistant frantically pulled out her phone.

Sahara tilted Moira's head back and ran her finger inside her mouth to make sure the airway was clear, only to realize it was packed with food Moira never got to swallow. She leaned closer, intent on clearing the airway, when she smelled something that nearly stopped her heart. She yanked her finger out of Moira's mouth and frantically wiped it on her robe, then jumped to her feet to wash her hands at the sink.

The tray with Sahara's catered meal was on the counter and it was obvious that the food in Moira's mouth came from that plate. Sahara smelled the food and then shoved it aside, staggering toward a chair to sit down, trembling in every muscle. The ramifications of what she was thinking were too horrifying to accept.

"The police are on the way," Lucy said, as she turned around, and then saw her boss sitting at the table, staring at the body on the floor. "What's wrong? Why aren't you doing CPR?"

"She's dead. I think she's been poisoned."

Lucy gasped. "What do you mean? How do you know?"

"Her breath... I smelled bitter almonds. Someone put cyanide in my food, and she ate it."

Lucy ran toward the counter and lifted the cover off Sahara's lunch. Sure enough some food had been eaten off the plate. She smelled it, then spun toward Sahara with a look of disbelief.

"I smell it, too, but—cyanide? How do you know?"

Sahara was rocking back and forth where she sat with her hands curled into fists, shaking uncontrollably. She ignored Lucy's question completely, focusing instead on the implications of what had just happened.

"Why would she eat my lunch? Maybe she thought I'd never miss it. Who cares—she's dead, Lucy! But if she was poisoned by my food, then... Oh my God! She died because someone tried to kill me! Why? Why?" Sahara cried, and then burst into tears.

Lucy ran to comfort her as the sound of sirens filled the air. By the time the police cars were on the lot and heading for Sahara's trailer, most of the crew was already there.

Tom Mahan, the director, was in a panic, thinking something had happened to the star of his movie. He was relieved to see Sahara sitting at the table in tears, but that ended abruptly when he saw the body.

"Oh my God! Moira! What happened?"

"We don't know. She was here to take measurements, and it looks like she ate some of Sahara's catered meal and...died. Sahara thinks Moira was poisoned," Lucy said.

"I don't think it, I know it," Sahara insisted. "Remember the movie I did with Rhett Coulter? The stalker used cyanide on Rhett's character to get rid of him so he could get to me. It was the medical examiner who smelled bitter almonds and said he'd been poisoned."

"Yes, I remember!" Tom said. "Wow, good call, Sahara."

She looked up at him in disbelief. "Can we please not celebrate my memory right now? Moira is dead."

"Right! Sorry!" he said, and darted out of the trailer. Moments later he was back with a half-dozen uniformed officers from the Hollywood division of the LAPD, followed by a couple of detectives from Homicide who began issuing orders. To the director's dismay, shooting would have to be stopped and everyone would be on lockdown until statements were taken.

A couple of officers were unrolling crime scene tape around the trailer as everyone was sent back to the set. An interview site was set up near craft services by commandeering one of the long serving tables to use as a desk.

Because she found the body, Sahara was called up first. The video camera was on and once again she was being filmed, but this time she wasn't going to have to fake emotions. She was sick to her stomach and scared to death.

The detective doing the interview sat down on the other side of the table and introduced himself.

"Miss Travis, I'm Detective Colin Shaw from the Homicide division. We're going to be filming all of the interviews for our records." He gestured toward the video camera set up on a tripod nearby. "I need you to tell me in your own words what happened, beginning with where you were the hour prior to the discovery of Moira Patrick's body."

Sahara was suddenly aware of how naked she was beneath the dressing gown and pulled it tighter around her neck.

"We were on set. The crew, the director, Bobby, the actor in the scene with me. We were all there filming a rather difficult scene. It was our third take, so I'd guess we'd been there at least an hour and a half? Then Tom called a lunch break. I was going to my trailer and met my assistant, Lucy, on the way. We found Moira Patrick's body inside."

"Why was Moira in your trailer?"

"She's part of...*was* part of wardrobe, and I was told that the director wanted some changes made for tomorrow's scenes. She was sent to my trailer to get measurements," Sahara said.

"What did you do then?" Shaw asked.

Sahara started to shake as she described beginning CPR, then seeing the food lodged in Moira's throat and smelling the scent of bitter almonds.

"How did you know about that scent being linked to cyanide poisoning? Most people don't know that."

She told him what she'd already explained to Tom and Lucy about her previous movie role, then tears began to spill.

"She ate food meant for me. I was the intended victim."

Shaw frowned. "Who would want you dead?"

Sahara grabbed a tissue from the box on the table and wiped her eyes.

"I don't know. Lots of people. You would have to ask my manager, Harold Warner. He keeps track of all my hate mail."

Shaw shook his head. Considering this was Hollywood, hate mail was as common in their business as spam in email.

"Is there anything in particular you've received recently that gave you cause for concern?"

"Nothing that I know of. Harold doesn't usually show me any of it. Why would I want to see those angry letters?"

"Okay, what about your lunch? Where does your food come from?" Shaw asked.

"I don't know the name of the company. Lucy, my personal assistant, might know. She usually picks it up for me and brings it straight to my trailer to put in the refrigerator. Nothing stays fresh in this heat."

"How do you get on with Lucy? Would she have any reason to want you dead?"

"Lucy? No, absolutely not. We get along fine. She's been with me for almost a year, and I pay her very well. I can't imagine a reason why she'd want to end a monthly income."

Shaw continued with the questions he'd prepared, making sure he'd covered every detail with Sahara before finishing.

"Thank you for your cooperation," Shaw said once he'd gotten all the information he could.

Sahara was pale and trembling.

"Am I allowed to leave the set now?"

"Yes, ma'am. Where did you intend to go?"

"Home. I just want to go home. I don't suppose my assistant is allowed to leave with me?"

"Not yet. We'll need to question everyone before they can head out. I can have an officer take you home, though."

She nodded. "Yes, please. Can I go back to my trailer to change clothes and get my purse?"

"I'm sorry, but no. Right now, everything in that trailer is part of the crime scene."

"Lord have mercy," Sahara muttered. "Then I guess I'll clean up in wardrobe and borrow some clothes to wear home."

"The officer will be waiting out front."

"Am I still in danger?"

"Until we get confirmation from the lab that your food was actually poisoned, I can't say."

Sahara shoved a shaky hand through the tangles in her hair.

"Great. Hopefully I won't have to die before someone makes up their mind."

Harold Warner was a Mel Gibson look-alike and a Hollywood veteran. He'd started out as an actor but quickly tired of the casting calls and went to work on the other side of the business as an agent, then later moved to personal management.

He was just about to pull into valet parking for lunch with a friend when his cell phone rang. Still focused on getting into the proper turn lane, he hit the hands-free button to answer in his usual abrupt and impatient manner.

"Harold Warner."

"Mr. Warner, this is Detective Shaw with the LAPD. I need to talk to you about Sahara Travis."

Startled, both by the man and the question, Harold swerved into the wrong lane, barely missing the Porsche just behind him.

The driver honked at him loud and long as he flew past, but Harold was already trying to get off the street.

"What about Sahara Travis? Has something happened to her?"

"Not to her, no. But we are concerned about her safety after the incident that occurred today. There's been a death on the set of her movie, and we think Miss Travis may be in danger, as well. We're still in the early stages of the investigation, but—"

"A death? What the hell? Is Sahara okay? Where is she?"

"I had an officer take her home," Shaw said.

"Did you put a guard on the penthouse?" Harold asked.

"No, sir. Not at this time."

"Talk about leaving the barn door open," Harold grumbled. "I'm heading to her apartment building right now."

"I need to talk to you about the hate mail Miss Travis has received recently. If you've kept it saved, I'll need to see what's come in."

"Okay, send an officer over to my office. I'll have my secretary make copies for you."

"Thank you for your cooperation," Shaw said, getting only a disconnect for his troubles.

Harold was in a panic. Sahara was his paycheck, and a nice one at that, but he also adored her. It would be a tragedy if anything happened to her. He turned around and headed downtown, blowing through yellow lights and cutting corners too close for comfort.

He was sweating by the time he pulled into the parking lot at The Magnolia. He sat there long enough to give his secretary instructions and then ended the call and ran inside. He was sweating and puffing, thinking he probably should've been using that gym membership he kept in his wallet, when he saw Adam, the security guard, in the lobby.

"Afternoon, Mr. Warner."

"Afternoon, Adam. Is Miss Travis in?"

"Yes, sir. She came back about thirty minutes ago. You go on up. I'll ring her for you."

Sahara was still rattled by the events of the day and was about to make herself some hot tea when the house phone at her elbow suddenly rang. It startled her enough that her heartbeat hit a hard, solid thud before it went back into a normal rhythm.

"Good Lord," she muttered, as she picked up. "Yes?"

"Afternoon, Miss Travis, this is Adam. Mr. Warner is on his way up."

"Thank you, Adam."

Moments later there was a knock at her door. She

looked through the peephole and felt a huge sense of relief at seeing Harold's familiar face.

"Come in," she said, as she opened the door.

"Are you okay?" he asked, shutting the door behind him.

"I am not physically injured in any way, if that's what you're asking. If you want to know how I feel inside, I'm sick to my stomach. A friend ate food meant for me, and it killed her. I can't describe how sad that makes me feel. Who the fuck wants me dead this week, Harold? What do you know that I don't?"

"Nothing new on that front. I promise. You're on the upswing with marriage proposals. Your hate mail won't amp up again until this movie comes out. You know how people feel about women who cheat on their husbands…"

Sahara rolled her eyes. "Does no one understand the meaning of fiction, and that acting means it's not me, it's me being a character in a story?"

"It's all part of the life, you know that. Now tell me what happened, and don't leave anything out," Harold said.

"Do you want some tea?" Sahara asked.

"No, I want answers," Harold said.

"Then come into the kitchen, because I want tea."

So she talked as she worked, making and pouring her tea while telling him everything from the moment she got to work until they walked into the trailer and found Moira.

Harold was used to her cool demeanor, but today he

could tell his ice princess was cracking. By the time she finished her story, her voice was shaking.

She sat with her hands in her lap, staring down at the petit four on her plate. She'd taken one bite before the memory of the food inside Moira's mouth flashed in her mind and she had to put it aside. It took half her cup of tea to wash down the bite she'd taken.

Harold knew she was bothered. Hell, he was bothered, too.

"I'm getting a bodyguard for you."

She looked up. "No."

"Don't be hardheaded, girl. Someone wants you dead."

Her chin jutted in defiance, even as her eyes filled with tears.

"I don't need a bodyguard. They've shut down filming until the crime scene is released, so it's not like I'm going anywhere. I won't let anyone in the penthouse, so there's no need for a guard, and that's final."

"But—"

"No buts, Harold. I'm serious. Lucy can run errands for me. You're running interference for me. The media is going to be all over this when it breaks, but I'm not talking and I'm not budging from my home. I get that I need to stay safe, but I can do that by staying here—alone."

He sighed. "Okay for now, but if anything else happens, you're getting one whether you like it or not."

"Nothing else is going to happen. I'll even cook my own food. I can cook, you know."

He sighed. "Actually, I didn't know that. Good for you."

She glared at him. "That sounded patronizing."

"Sorry," he said.

"No, you're not," she said.

Harold's voice was rising. By the time he got to the end of his apology, he was yelling.

"You're right! I'm not sorry. I'm frustrated. Part of my job is taking care of you...making sure you're okay at all times, and you won't let me do my job."

She got up and carried her dirty dishes to the sink, dumped everything down the garbage disposal and turned it on, grinding out the sound of his disgust. When she turned around, he was still there.

"I'm sorry I yelled," he said.

Her shoulders slumped. "You should be. Go home, Harold. If something happens I need to know, you will call me."

"Fine."

She walked him to the door.

"Remember the code to go down?"

"Yes, I remember the damn code."

She grinned. "Your Texas roots are showing, Mr. Warner. Stop cursing."

He took her by the shoulders and kissed her forehead, then left her standing in the doorway as he crossed the hall to the elevator and punched in the code on the keypad. The doors opened. He stepped in and then turned around to wave at her, but she'd already gone inside and closed her door.

"Damn hardheaded woman," he muttered, and rode the elevator down.

* * *

Four hours later Lucy arrived at Sahara's apartment with Sahara's clothes, purse and a six-inch Italian meatball sub from the drive-thru of a deli she'd stopped at on the way over. It was just past four o'clock when she rang the doorbell.

Sahara opened the door to her personal assistant and was surprised to see that Lucy had her purse.

"My bag! How did you get that? I didn't think we could remove stuff from the crime scene," she said.

Lucy shrugged. "That's why you pay me the big bucks, right?" She smiled. "I took it with me when I left the trailer and put it in my car. The sandwich, on the other hand, is fresh. Have you eaten anything?" she asked.

Sahara shook her head. "No, I can't get anything down."

"Well, yes, you can and will," Lucy said. "I bought it on the way home, so we know it's safe. It's a meatball sub—your favorite."

Sahara eyed the short, dark-haired woman and sighed.

"My Achilles' heel. Thank you, Lucy. You know me too well."

Lucy eyed Sahara closely, the worry obvious on her face. "You took a shower. That's a plus. Now, why don't you sit down, and I'll bring you something cold to drink to go with your food."

Sahara's heart hurt. She kept picturing Moira's body on a slab in the morgue and wondered if her parents had been notified. If only this day would be over.

She followed Lucy to the kitchen and slid onto a bar stool at the end of the counter, thinking, as she watched her assistant work, that Lucy knew the kitchen better than she did even though Sahara had lived here for more than three years.

She put her head in her hands and closed her eyes, wishing she was anywhere but here, wishing she hadn't even accepted this role. The character of Alicia Lewis was like nothing she'd ever done, and now it felt tainted—the whole shoot felt tainted—as if it wasn't supposed to happen. If it hadn't, Moira would still be alive and working on some other project for another director, maybe sneaking bites of someone else's food.

"Here you go," Lucy said, as she set a plate in front of Sahara with the sandwich cut into thirds, a handful of chips on the side and a tall glass of sweet iced tea.

"Thank you so much," Sahara said. "Have you eaten?"

"No, but—"

Sahara pointed at the bar stool beside her. "Sit. I can't eat all of this anyway. We'll share."

Lucy blinked, unsure of how to respond. It wasn't that Sahara didn't treat her well, but she'd never done anything so…friendly.

"You want me to eat from your plate?"

Sahara looked startled. "I'm not sick. You won't be catching anything, but if you don't want to, it's—"

Lucy shook her head. "No, no, that's not it. I was just surprised, I guess."

"I won't share my tea, though. You'll have to get your own," she said, and grinned.

Lucy laughed, a little embarrassed. This was the first time since she'd started working for Sahara that she'd been this open.

"Yes, I'll get my own drink," she said, and poured another glass of sweet tea before she sat down.

Sahara pushed the plate between them, then reached for one of the pieces and took a bite. The thick red sauce permeated the meatball in spicy perfection while the toasted bun provided a crunch of texture.

"It's so good," Sahara said, and picked up a chip to chase the bite. "Thank you for thinking of me."

"You're welcome," Lucy said, and took a piece for herself. She wouldn't let herself think of how weird this felt, and hoped her boss didn't regret the familiarity tomorrow.

Two

Sahara walked the floor after Lucy left. Every sound startled her. Every siren outside made her feel hunted. By the time sundown came, she was exhausted, but she couldn't sleep. She tossed and turned for almost an hour, then gave up and turned on the lights. There were only two things that helped her relax. One of them was sex with a willing man, but since she was missing a partner, she opted for the other option and headed for the kitchen.

She opened the freezer and then leaned forward, welcoming the blast of cold air against her heated skin as she scanned the choices.

Butter Pecan, Rocky Road or straight Vanilla Bean.

"It's been a rocky day. I think this fills the bill," she said, reaching for the pint of Rocky Road ice cream. She closed the door with her elbow as she reached for a spoon and crawled back up on the bar stool to take off the lid.

The first bite was sweet salvation…chocolate, marshmallow and walnut bits.

Sex on a spoon, Sahara thought, and sighed as the cold treat slowly melted on her tongue.

She flashed on Moira again, but this time remembering what a sweet, funny girl she'd been and how she did love to eat. Her eyes welled with tears as she scooped up a bite and lifted it in a toast.

"To you, sweet Moira," she said aloud in the empty kitchen. "May you have ice cream forever wherever you are."

The killer was walking the floor and pissed beyond measure. This should have been an easy kill, and yet it had gone horribly wrong. Who the hell could have known that anyone would have the gall—the daring—to eat food off Sahara Travis's personally prepared plate?

He finally headed for the bathroom to get ready for bed and paused at the mirror, eyeing his reflection. He was a long way from the years when his mother called him Bubba, but every time he looked in a mirror, that was who he saw.

Whatever. The plan had failed, but he wouldn't let himself be discouraged. This didn't mean anything except that there would be a next time.

Sleep was as frightening as the day had been. Sahara was up before daylight, exhausted and heartbroken. She stayed in a hot shower until her skin felt raw, trying to wash away yesterday's horror, then dressed in old gym shorts and a T-shirt and went barefoot to the kitchen. She disliked the one-cup coffee makers and quickly started a full pot to brew, then toasted an English muffin while she waited and ate it with strawberry jam.

Soon, the scent of freshly brewed coffee was permeating the room, and it was just the wake-up she needed. After pouring herself a cup, she opened the sliding door leading out to her balcony, intending to take her first sip along with a breath of fresh air.

But the moment she stepped out on the balcony, a roar erupted from the crowd of people that had gathered below, startling her to the point that she splashed hot coffee on her bare foot and then cried out in pain.

She hobbled back inside to get ice on the burn and then called downstairs to the lobby to ask Adam what the hell was happening.

"Good morning, Miss Travis," Adam said.

"Good morning, Adam. What's going on outside?"

"Seems to be a gathering of fans and the media, I think."

"Because of me?"

"Yes, ma'am. News broke about what happened on your set yesterday."

"The vultures are already descending," she muttered.

"Yes, ma'am."

"That's great, just great. So much for a trip to the ER. What do you have on hand that's good for burns?"

"Oh no—are you okay?"

"Not the end of the world. Just hot coffee on the top of a bare foot, but looks like it's going to blister and hurts like hell."

"Keep ice on it, and I'll have a doctor here shortly."

Sahara winced at the pain shooting up her leg.

"Thank you, Adam. Sorry to be a bother."

"No, ma'am. This is no bother. This won't be the first time we've had to call a doctor to this building. It shouldn't be long. I'll call right now," he said, and disconnected.

Sahara hung up the house phone and then hobbled into the kitchen for more ice just as her cell phone signaled a text.

It was Lucy, asking if she needed anything and saying that she was on her way over.

She responded with a text to bring some bananas, a box of cook-and-serve vanilla pudding mix, milk, a box of vanilla wafers and anything else that looked good. Might as well stock up if she was going to be stuck here for a while.

She got a thumbs-up and a laugh emoji from Lucy, then disconnected and put some more ice on her burn.

Lucy came out of the supermarket with a whole extra sack of groceries above what Sahara had asked for. She already knew about the media chaos. She'd seen it on the early-morning news, which meant it was time to prepare for a lockdown. No way could Sahara go anywhere without bodyguards today, and Harold Warner was in charge of all that.

Lucy blew a lock of hair from one eye as she put the bags inside her car. It wasn't quite 9:00 a.m., and it was already hot. If only her boss had a place up in the hills, one with a big pool and an even bigger wall around it, work would be so much better. She didn't understand why an actress as famous and rich as Sahara Travis insisted on living in the middle of such a huge city, even if it was at The Magnolia, and even though she owned the penthouse. Sure, this place had a pool, but it was on the roof opposite the helipad at the other end, and it was even hotter up there—closer to the sun. Technically, the other residents of The Magnolia were on the same social level as Sahara, but it just didn't fit Lucy's idea of Hollywood glamour.

She upped the air-conditioning to frigid as she drove and breathed a sigh of relief as her car finally began to cool. She knew the media was already on-site, but upon arrival, it suddenly felt as if she was driving into a riot.

"Oh good Lord," she mumbled, then honked loud and long to move a group of paparazzi as she took a quick turn into the adjacent parking garage.

She got out, unfolded a portable cart she kept in the trunk and transferred the two sacks of groceries into it before heading into the building.

Adam saw her coming. "Do you need any help, Miss Lucy?"

"No, I've got this, but thank you," she said.

"All right, then. You tell Miss Travis that the doctor is on his way."

Lucy frowned. "Doctor? What doctor? Is she hurt?"

"She burned the top of her foot with hot coffee."

"Oh no," Lucy said, and began hurrying toward the elevator.

"I'll ring her and tell her you're coming up," Adam said.

Lucy waved to indicate she'd heard him and kept on going.

* * *

Sahara was in misery when she got word that Lucy was on the way up. The burn was worse than she'd thought. Nothing was alleviating the pain, not even the ice. She stumbled to the door and opened it just as Lucy came off the elevator at a fast clip, dragging the grocery cart behind her.

"Adam said you burned your foot."

Sahara pointed down at the top of her left foot as Lucy raced in with the groceries. She locked the door and then knelt to look closer at Sahara's burn.

"It's making a blister. Oh wow. That looks really painful."

"Ice isn't helping," Sahara said. "I don't suppose you know how to treat a burn?"

"No, but Adam said to tell you the doctor was on his way over. He should be here soon."

"Thank God. I'm going to lie down. Will you listen for the doorbell and let him in?"

"Of course," Lucy said, following Sahara into the kitchen as she got another handful of ice cubes, wrapped them in a dishcloth and left.

Lucy began putting groceries away, wondering what else this day would bring.

As she washed her hands a few minutes later, she heard the doorbell, so she dried them quickly before she hurried to answer.

The man at the door was not exactly what she was expecting, but he was carrying a black bag and properly identified himself with photo ID.

"Dr. Barrett to see Miss Travis?"

Lucy frowned at the jeans, sandals and casual cotton shirt hanging loose over his pants, and then eyed the three-day beard and sunglasses pushed up on the top of his head.

"You don't dress like any doctor I ever saw."

"Well, this is my day to spend at the free clinic, and I try not to outdress my patients. They seem to trust me more this way," he said.

She smiled at him. "Sorry for jumping to judgment, but we can't be too careful right now. I'm Lucy, by the way."

"No problem, Lucy. I heard about what happened on the news this morning," Barrett said.

"Sahara went back to her room to lie down. Follow me."

Chris Barrett had been to this complex before and was used to treating the wealthy, but he had to admit the idea of seeing Sahara Travis in person was exciting. She was one of the most beautiful women in Hollywood, and also one of the most secretive. She didn't follow the party circuit and was rarely seen other than at red-carpet events.

He followed Lucy through the elegant living area to the door ajar at the end of the hall.

Lucy knocked twice and pushed it inward.

"Dr. Barrett is here," Lucy said.

Chris walked into the suite, expecting to see a diva in silk and satin. Instead, he was met with bare feet, old shorts, a ragged UCLA T-shirt and a face of exquisite beauty completely devoid of makeup.

"Miss Travis, I'm Chris Barrett," he said, and fell head over heels in love.

"He's dressed like this because it's his day to work at a free clinic," Lucy offered.

Sahara rolled her eyes. "And I'm dressed like this because it's comfortable. Hello, Dr. Barrett, I'm Sahara," she said.

Chris grimaced when he saw her foot.

"What happened here?" he asked, as he lifted her foot onto an ottoman.

"I spilled hot coffee on it. It was a fresh pot, so it was scalding. Do you have something to make it quit hurting...like a pill, or a shot, or a magic wand? I'm not picky."

Now he was entranced by her deprecating humor.

"I left the wand at home, but I'm pretty sure I have stuff that will ease your pain."

He took a bottle of disinfectant out of his bag and stood up. "May I use your bathroom?"

Sahara waved a hand toward the door behind her and then leaned back in the chair and closed her eyes.

Lucy caught the glimmer of tears on her lashes and was impressed by Sahara's stoic manner. Somehow she'd always thought Sahara Travis was a pampered woman, but there was obviously a backbone to go with all that beauty. She knelt beside Sahara's chair and laid a hand on her arm.

"I'm so sorry you're hurting. This is the last thing you need right now. Can I get you anything? Something to drink maybe?"

Sahara grasped Lucy's hand and gave it a quick squeeze.

"No, I'm fine, but thank you for asking."

The doctor returned, properly disinfected, and was all business as he gloved up and began working on her foot.

When the house phone began to ring, Lucy got up to answer, leaving Sahara alone with the doctor.

Chris wanted to talk to her, to get to know her, but this felt like the wrong time. He might never get a chance like this again, but he was a doctor first, and she was obviously in too much pain to chitchat.

Sahara leaned back in the chair and closed her eyes, letting her mind drift as the doctor worked so that pain was not at the forefront of her consciousness.

Finally, Chris taped the last piece of gauze around her foot and then gave her leg a quick pat.

"There you go, Miss Travis. This should keep you comfortable for a while."

Sahara opened her eyes to see Lucy sitting nearby watching the process and then saw the white gauze wrapped around her foot.

"Thank you for coming here. I didn't know how I was going to get out of the building without drawing attention to myself."

"I can only imagine," Chris said. "Now, don't get it wet. Change the bandage once a day, and when you take this one off, make sure nothing looks infected, then apply some more of this salve and wrap it back up with more gauze." He motioned to the assortment of supplies he was leaving behind. "I'll stop by and check on you in a couple of days, if you'd like."

She nodded.

"How long does the stuff last that you applied to the burn? Can she apply more or will over-the-counter pain meds help?" Lucy asked.

He handed her a prescription.

"If you'll get this filled, she can take as needed. The main thing is to take it easy. Don't be up on it too much right now and take the chance of reinjuring it."

"Okay," Sahara said.

"Well, I'd better be going. I'm sure there are patients waiting at the clinic," he said. "I'll see you in a couple of days unless you need me sooner."

"I'll see you to the door," Lucy said, thus ending whatever else Chris Barrett wanted to say.

He looked back just as he was walking out the door, but Sahara was already out of the chair. So much for following doctor's orders.

Sahara made it back to her bedroom before she burst into tears. Between the pain of the burn and Moira's death, life had finally overwhelmed her. She hadn't felt this lost since she was a child.

She eased down onto her bed and then turned onto her side away from the window and closed her eyes, trying to focus on anything but the pain.

Think, Sahara, think. Best day of your life?

That's easy. The day I left New Orleans. It was a freedom I'd never known.

Best friend growing up? Susan, no, Emily, yes, Emily.

First time you had sex? The night of my sixteenth birthday with the boy across the street. What was his name? Larry? Harry? Well, shit. How did I forget the name of the first guy I had sex with? Bad me. Bad, bad me. It's not like there were dozens afterward. Three, maybe four semiregular guys in my lifetime, but no one in over a year. I need to get laid.

Sahara groaned. The fact that she looked at life in this way made her sad. She'd always dreamed of sex meaning something between two people who loved each other, but she didn't believe in Santa Claus anymore. Maybe there was no forever love, either.

Nix the pity party, Miss Travis. Some people pay good money for this kind of PR.

Lucy knocked on the door and came in, tiptoeing toward the bed.

Sahara kept her eyes closed, letting her believe she was asleep. She felt the afghan at the foot of the bed being pulled up and over her shoulders and sighed.

Lucy heard it, feared she was going to wake her up and quickly left.

Sahara waited until the door closed, and then she reached for the edge of the afghan and pulled it tight beneath her chin to keep the bad juju away. Someone had tried to kill her. It hadn't worked, so they would likely try again.

Please, God, don't let that happen.

It was the last conscious thought she had before she fell asleep.

* * *

Tom Mahan had been on the phone with the investors all morning. They were concerned about the delay in production and wanted answers the director didn't have.

"Look, Fenton, I am aware that you have a big investment in the film, and we scored big when Sahara Travis came on board. But I called the detective in charge of the case this morning to see if he had any news for me, and he confirmed her food had been poisoned with cyanide. She's still alive, but the young woman from wardrobe is not. Her name was Moira. Her parents are devastated. We're all devastated by this, so we're not going to resume filming at this time. I'll know when it feels safe enough."

Fenton Whiteside sighed. He knew Mahan's hands were tied. Murder was always a messy situation.

"I'll let the other investors know. Just keep in mind that you get a bonus if this film comes in under budget, and you'll be kissing that goodbye if we're shut down long. Paychecks still go out, whether they report for work or not."

"Yes, yes, I know. This isn't my first rodeo, but it's damn sure the first time someone was murdered on one of my sets. I'll be in touch," he said, and disconnected.

He needed to go check on Sahara but dreaded the crowd he'd have to go through to get to her apartment. It had been all over the news this morning, so he had no doubt the Hollywood media machine would be in full swing. He made a quick call to her apartment, but when the call was answered, it was her assistant, Lucy, who picked up.

"Hello?" Lucy said.

"Lucy, it's me, Tom. May I speak to Sahara, please?"

"Sorry, she's still sleeping. The pain in her foot has knocked her out, and I don't want to wake her. Can I have her call you?"

Tom was in shock.

"What's wrong with her foot? Why is she in pain?"

"Oh, I guess I thought you knew. She accidentally spilled hot coffee on the top of her foot this morning. She has a second-degree burn. The doctor has been here and is treating her."

"Son of a bitch! Why wasn't I informed?"

"I couldn't say, but I'm guessing that since filming has been put on hold, she didn't think it mattered. She'll heal and be back at work when you need her, and if she's not healed, you can shoot around the fact that she's going to be barefoot for a while. And don't curse at me again."

Tom sighed. "I'm sorry. It was just a surprise, that's all. I sincerely apologize. Give Sahara my condolences on the accident, and if there's anything I can do for her, anything at all, please let me know."

"Yes, sir. I will," Lucy said, and heard the line go dead.

"Prick," she muttered, and went back to the pudding she was cooking. One of Sahara's favorite comfort foods was banana pudding, and while she usually made it herself, Lucy knew that wasn't happening this time around. The least she could do was have it ready.

A short while later she set the pudding aside to cool a little before putting the dish together, and as she was cleaning up, her cell signaled a text. When she saw who it was, she grinned. Wiley Johnson was who she thought of as her part-time lover...like in the song. He made her feel special. When they were together, she felt as beautiful in his eyes as Sahara Travis was to the world. It was a good way to feel.

The text was an invitation to dinner. She responded with a yes, but only if she didn't have to work late here. The thumbs-up he gave her made her smile, and she shivered just thinking about the sex they always had for dessert.

Lucy was in the living room with the TV on mute and her laptop on her knees. Her fingers were flying on the keys as she worked while listening for sounds that Sahara was waking up. She glanced up at the clock. It was almost noon.

She set aside her work and went down the hall to check on Sahara. She could hear a television playing, so she knocked once, then opened the door into the suite.

Sahara was sitting in a window seat, looking out into the city.

"Hey," Lucy said softly.

Sahara turned and smiled. "Hey, yourself."

"Are you getting hungry? I made some lunch for us."

Sahara swung her long shapely legs off the seat and stood.

"We could have ordered delivery, but I'm sure not going to turn down anything homemade."

"Don't get too excited," Lucy said. "I'm not the Martha Stewart type. How's your foot feeling?"

"Better after that stuff he put on it. It still hurts and certainly gives me a whole new understanding of people who suffer serious burns."

"Life is like that," Lucy said, as she led the way into the kitchen. "Do you want to sit in here or take the food to the living room so you can put your foot up?"

"Eat in here," Sahara said. "I always ate in the kitchen with Billie when I was growing up."

"Who's Billie?" Lucy asked.

Sahara hesitated, then finally answered. "The woman who cooked for my parents."

"You didn't eat with your parents?" Lucy asked, and then watched all expression leave Sahara's face.

"No," Sahara said, but she didn't elaborate. "What did you make? I'm suddenly starving."

"I have cold shrimp with red sauce…heavy on the horseradish, a little pasta salad, and I made your banana pudding."

"That sounds lovely!" Sahara said.

Lucy was pleased that her efforts were appreciated and quickly made their plates and carried them to the counter.

She poured iced tea for their drinks and then got the cutlery and napkins.

Sahara already had a cold shrimp in her fingers and was liberally dunking it in the red sauce as Lucy finished setting their places.

"I didn't wait for you, but it's your fault because

it all looked so good," Sahara said, as she swallowed her first bite.

Lucy pointed at Sahara's lips.

"You have a little sauce just there."

Sahara dabbed a napkin against her mouth and then plucked another shrimp from her plate.

"There's likely to be more there before I'm through."

A siren sounded as a police car sped past out on the street below. Sahara sighed.

"God bless whoever is in need," she said, and then took a drink of iced tea.

Lucy gave her a strange look. "Why did you say that?"

Sahara looked up. "Say what?"

"About someone in need," Lucy said.

"I don't know. Sirens always give me the shudders. Somewhere, someone is in need or there wouldn't be sirens, so I say a prayer."

Lucy frowned. "Are your parents religious? Oh, maybe that's too personal. I'm sorry."

Sahara forked up a bite of pasta salad.

"No, they're not religious. The only thing they ever worshipped was each other."

Lucy smiled. "That is so sweet."

Sahara shrugged and put the salad in her mouth.

"Mmm! This is so good! I love the little pepperoni pieces in with the pasta and veggies. I want to remember that."

"Thanks," Lucy said, and the rest of the meal passed with casual conversation and ended with two bowls of banana pudding.

Sahara scraped the last bite of pudding from her bowl and then licked the spoon.

"Oh my Lord, but this was good. I'll be on the tread-mill for a week. Thank you, Lucy. Thank you for doing this, even though it's not in your job description."

Lucy paused as she was gathering up dirty dishes.

"It has been a weird week. Sometimes change is good for what ails us. I'll clean up here. You get off your foot."

Sahara could already feel it throbbing and wasn't going to argue.

She hobbled out of the kitchen, taking her iced tea glass with her, and went into the living room. She was all the way to the sliding doors to go out onto the patio when she remembered the paparazzi. She wasn't going to give them an opportunity to make a nickel off her face if she could help it and went to her bed-room instead.

Three

The house phone rang as Lucy was wiping off the counters. She tossed the dishrag back into the soapy water as she went to answer it.

"Hello?"

"This is Detective Colin Shaw, Homicide. May I speak to Miss Travis?"

"Just a moment, please," she said, and hurried out of the kitchen and through the house to Sahara's bedroom suite. The door was open. Sahara was stretched out on the sofa and staring out the window with the television on mute.

"Sahara, Detective Shaw on the phone for you," Lucy said.

"Thank you," Sahara said, and sat up as she reached for the phone.

"Hello, this is Sahara."

"Miss Travis, Detective Shaw here. I have some information for you. Do you have a minute?"

"Yes, of course," Sahara said. "What's up?"

"Lab tests are back. You were right. It was cyanide in the food that killed Moira Patrick. We don't have any leads at the moment, though we've been through the hate mail your manager sent over. We're still studying everything, but I need you to try to remember if there's anyone you can think of that you've recently had words with?"

Sahara closed her eyes. So nothing was supposition anymore.

"No."

"Maybe someone you work with who seems envious of your position, or resents your success?"

"I'm telling you, Detective, there's no one. I mean, it's believable that they exist. No one escapes that in this business. But there hasn't been anyone who's said anything of the sort to my face."

"When does filming resume?" he asked.

"I haven't heard."

"Well, then, be careful and remember that familiar faces do not necessarily belong to friends."

Sahara shivered. "I'll keep that in mind," she said, and then hung up the phone and immediately called Harold.

Her manager was in the middle of quarterly tax reports and started to let it go to voice mail until he saw who was calling.

"Hey, honey, how are you doing?"

"Oh, I'm all right," Sahara said. "I just got word that the food was, indeed, poisoned with cyanide. I need a favor from you."

"Anything. What do you need?"

"The address and phone number of Moira Patrick's parents."

"Why?" Harold asked.

"Because I need to express my sympathies and let them know I intend to pay for her services."

"I'll do that for you first thing in the morning," Harold said.

"No. No, you won't. This is my job. I want to call them before the night is over, so please get it for me now."

He sighed. "Yes, of course," Harold said. "Give me a few minutes and I'll get what you need."

"Thank you, Harold. I appreciate this."

"No problem. It's part of the job."

He disconnected and called Detective Shaw, rattled off what he needed and why, then sent the info to Sahara in a text and returned to doing taxes.

Sahara got the text and then stared at the number, trying to muster the courage to make the call. Basically, it came down to doing what was right, so she called, then waited.

A woman answered in a weak, shaky voice.

"Patrick residence. This is Amanda."

"Hi…" she replied hesitantly. This call wasn't going to be easy. "This is Sahara Travis calling. I'd like to speak to either one of Moira Patrick's parents."

"Oh, Miss Travis. I'm Moira's mother."

Sahara took a deep breath. "There are no words for how sorry I am about what happened to her."

"Thank you, thank you," Amanda said, weeping

across the line. "Moira loved her job, and she admired you so much."

"Thank you for that," Sahara said, wiping a tear from her cheek. "I'd do anything to bring her back. She was a wonderful person. This is a nightmare, and we still have no idea who is responsible. But I want to let you know that I'll be paying for the services myself. Not the company. Me. I wish with all my heart this had not happened."

"That's very kind of you but not necessary."

"It's important to me that I do this," Sahara said. "I insist. I just need the name of the funeral home and I'll cover the cost of whatever you choose for the arrangements."

"Well, all right, then," Amanda said. "Just a moment while I get the card to make sure I relay the proper address."

"Why don't you just send me a text with the information when you have time," Sahara said.

"Yes, all right, and thank you again for this kindness."

"It is the least I can do to honor a young woman I greatly admired. I can't show up in person to the services—I wish I could, but between the mobs of people and the media…it wouldn't be appropriate and you deserve peace when you have to say goodbye to Moira. But I want you to know my heart will be with all of you."

Sahara waited for the text, then forwarded it to Harold with a note to cover the cost of everything from her personal account.

* * *

The next morning she got a call from Dr. Barrett's office, asking for an update on her burn. Sahara informed them that the pain was lessening, but that she hadn't taken off the bandage to look.

"Would you be available today for Dr. Barrett to stop by to check the injury?"

"Yes."

"Great. He'll be there within an hour or so."

The moment the call ended, she went to the bathroom to get a towel and shampoo and quickly washed her hair at the kitchen sink. Then she hobbled back to the bathroom and toweled it dry. The thick, long curls were a menace to control, but that was what professional hair and makeup teams were for. She was fine with it on a day-to-day basis, and there was always someone around to fix it if it didn't please the people who wrote her checks.

She was wearing pink shorts and a white T-shirt, her ode to a California summer, and as usual she was barefoot. She'd sent Lucy on an errand to get makeup and her brand of toiletries, so when Lucy Benton's name popped up in caller ID, she answered without caution.

"Hello."

"Who is this?" a man asked.

The male voice startled her. Her heart started to pound. Was this the man responsible for Moira's death? Did he do something to Lucy? She didn't want to be the reason people were dying.

"Where's Lucy?" she demanded.

"Who's Lucy?" he asked.

"She's a friend, and you just called me using her phone."

"Look, lady, I just found the phone in a shopping cart at Whole Foods and called the first name on the contact list. Just trying to help out."

"Then please drop it off at the customer service counter. They'll page her."

"Yeah, all right."

"I'm her boss, and I already took a picture of your face, so if you don't turn in the phone, I will turn you in to the cops," Sahara said, bluffing completely, but he didn't have to know that.

"Well, hell, lady. How did you—"

"I see where you are, and it's nowhere near customer service."

"I'm going, I'm going there right now," the guy said.

Sahara could hear him panting as he ran and then heard him turning the phone over at the counter just as she heard Lucy's voice in the background.

"That's my phone!"

"It was just in my basket, lady. I was on my way to turn it in, that's all…"

"Oh! Then thank you very much," Lucy said, as the manager at the counter took the phone, verified the info and handed it over.

Lucy pulled out a ten-dollar bill and gave it to the man who'd turned it in.

"Not a lot of honest people in the world anymore. I appreciate you turning this in."

The guy took the ten, then waved it in front of Lucy and the phone.

"Turn the phone around...let that woman on the phone know that I did the right thing."

Lucy frowned.

"What are you talking about?"

"Well, uh...I called the first number on your contact list trying to find out who owned the phone, and the woman said she took a screenshot of me talking to her and was going to turn it in to the cops if I didn't hand over your phone. I mean, I was gonna do that anyway, but...well, you must be pretty important to have a boss who'll do something like that."

He walked away, poking the ten-dollar bill into his pocket, and the manager looked at Lucy in confusion.

"I've never heard of a phone that could take a picture of the person you're talking to unless you were FaceTiming or something."

Lucy grinned and put the phone to her ear.

"Hello, are you still there?" she asked.

Sahara was grinning. "Yes, I'm here. I heard it all."

"Many thanks. I don't know if I believe he would have brought it back if it hadn't been for the story you sold him."

"Are you okay, otherwise?" Sahara asked.

"Yeah, I'm fine. It must've slipped out of my purse when I was paying, I guess. Be there soon."

"Good to know. Gave me quite a scare to hear a man's voice calling from your number. Just for a moment I was afraid someone else had been targeted because of me. Be careful."

"Of course," Lucy said, and disconnected as she hurried outside and got into the car.

The sun was bright. It would be another hot day. She missed the changing weather from back home and, not for the first time, wished Sahara Travis lived in the hills.

By the time Lucy got back to the penthouse, Sahara was on the phone with Tom.

"I understand you have a burn on your foot," Tom said.

"Yes, but it's getting better. The doctor is coming by in a bit to change the dressing and check it out."

"So if we resumed shooting soon, you'd be able to come to set?"

"Yes. You may have to shoot around a bare foot or something for a while, but I'm not bedridden by any means."

"That's good. Yes, yes, that's good," Tom said. "The investors are on my ass, so—"

"Don't worry, Tom. Just send my car and the pages and tell me when to show up."

"That's great!" Tom said. "You're a real trouper, Sahara. I've been trying to get a new trailer moved out for you, but—"

"There's no need for that," Sahara said. "I'm not superstitious, and I don't intend to run from this creep. The trailer is fine as long as they've cleaned up the crime scene."

"Of course," Tom said. "Absolutely. See you soon."

Sahara rolled her eyes at Lucy as she disconnected.

"That was Tom. He's getting antsy. Sounds like we're going to resume shooting soon."

Lucy nodded. "Good. The sooner this is behind us all, the better."

Sahara turned around and stared at Lucy a few moments and then walked out of the room. There were a whole lot of things she could say about how callous that sounded, but she wouldn't. It had been a stressful experience for all of them. Maybe this was just how Lucy dealt with the strain of what had happened.

"Any death threats in my email?" she asked, changing the subject.

Lucy shook her head. "No, thank goodness."

"Well, that's good news. Oh, the doctor is coming here soon to change the dressing on my foot."

Lucy pushed back from the computer and ran to catch up with her boss.

"Do you want something cold to drink? Raspberry tea maybe?"

"That sounds good. Yes, thank you," Sahara said. "Do we have hummus and pita chips?"

Lucy grinned. "Does a bear—"

Sahara laughed. "I am in something of a rut with snack choices, aren't I?"

Lucy grinned. "I'll bring your snack. You get settled in wherever you want to receive the doctor."

"In the living room," Sahara said. "But not the one in my suite. The one we never use."

Lucy went one way while Sahara went another. When Sahara reached the formal living room, she had a purpose in mind. She sat down at the baby grand, adjusted the seat and the pedals, and then ran her fingers up and down the keys. It was slightly out of tune, but it had been ages since she'd played, so maybe it wouldn't matter.

She sat for a few moments with her fingers on the keys and her eyes closed, and then followed the music she heard in her head.

Lucy brought the snack and left it on the piano, but Sahara was lost in the song and didn't look up.

Chris Barrett was about to ring the doorbell at Sahara Travis's penthouse when he realized he was hearing piano music. He paused in the hall, smiling. Last time he'd heard music like this had been in his grandparents' house when he was a kid. "Sentimental Journey" was a song out of their youth, and so were pianos.

Curious as to who was playing, he quickly rang the bell.

The personal assistant let him in again, but this time without criticism.

"Good morning, Lucy."

"Morning, Dr. Barrett. Sahara is waiting for you in the living room."

"Where's that music coming from?" he asked.

"Oh, that's just Sahara. She's always playing grandma music."

Chris was surprised, and when they reached the living room, he stopped and put a finger to his lips. Lucy left him alone to watch as Sahara played all the way through to the end. The moment she dropped her head and put her hands in her lap, he began to clap.

Sahara looked up. "Dr. Barrett!" she said, startled. "I

didn't realize you were here." She stood and motioned toward the sofa. "Should we sit?"

"Sure," he said, then waited until she crossed the room and plopped down on the sofa.

She smelled like the tropics, and Chris thought about what it would be like to come home to a woman like this every day.

"How has your foot been feeling? Any problems?" he asked, as he began removing the bandage.

"It hurt a lot the first night, but not so much now. We're going to resume filming soon. I'm hoping it's not going to present a problem."

"Let me get the rest of this off so we can see what we have going here," he said, and as soon as he had the bandage off, he gloved up and began examining the injury. "It looks better than I would have expected," Chris said. "Healing quickly."

"Family trait," she said, and leaned forward for a better look. "The blister broke. That skin is coming off. What's going to happen there?"

"We would expect the skin beneath to already be in a stage of regrowth, and it appears that it is. I'm going to remove a bit more of this dead skin, and then we'll redress it and bandage it back up. Don't wear any kind of shoe that rubs against the burn area."

"How much longer before you would call it healed?"

"It's hard to say."

He heard her sigh. It obviously wasn't the answer she wanted. He glanced up, fully intending to keep talking, but she was so stunning—even without a hint of makeup—that it caught him off guard.

Sahara frowned, then leaned forward and snapped her fingers in front of his face.

"Paging Dr. Barrett!"

He jumped. *Well, damn it.*

"I'm so sorry," he said, embarrassed. "But, uh, I have an excuse. I left my sunglasses in the car and... was blinded by your beauty?"

Sahara threw her head back and laughed.

"Oh Lord. Where did you hear that one?"

"My pool boy...on the phone yesterday...trying to talk his girlfriend out of being mad at him."

Sahara laughed again. A doctor with a sense of humor. That was a nice change of pace.

"Did it work on her?" she asked.

Chris grinned. "Nope."

"And yet you thought you could pull it off?" she said.

"I thought since I had age and this pretty face going for me, it might work."

Sahara shook her head. "Nope. It's a no go from me, too."

"Well, it never hurts to try," he said with a smile, and began packing up his bag. "As usual, I'm on the way to somewhere else. Take care, Miss Travis. I'll check back in on you in another couple of days."

"When can I get it wet?" she asked.

"When the skin isn't so new and tender. Probably still a few days."

She sighed again. "Not ideal, but thank you."

Lucy appeared in the doorway as if by magic, just

in time to see him out. She met Sahara on her way into the kitchen.

"Your timing is impeccable," Sahara said.

Lucy shrugged. "I was eavesdropping in the hall."

"At least you're honest about it," Sahara said with a grin.

"I didn't sense a connection in the making. Was I wrong?" Lucy asked.

"No, you weren't wrong at all," Sahara said. "Do we have any shrimp left?"

"Yes. How does a shrimp cocktail sound?"

"Sounds delightful. And some iced tea. I don't care what kind."

Lucy nodded and began assembling plates and pulling food from the refrigerator.

"So, what did the doctor say about your foot?"

Sahara looked up and grinned. "You didn't already overhear that, too?"

Lucy giggled. "No. Seriously, are you healing okay?"

"Yes, it's just going to take time for the new skin to toughen up, but it will happen soon enough."

"Okay, then," Lucy said, and dug out the deli-made red sauce that Sahara liked and began assembling the tasty appetizers.

"Double up on that shrimp, please," Sahara said. "This is lunch…not an appetizer."

Lucy smiled and squeezed some more shrimp into place around the rim of the dish. She was digging in the pantry for poppy seed crackers when the house phone rang.

"I'll get it," Sahara said, and slid off the bar stool to pick up. "This is Sahara," she said.

"Afternoon, Miss Travis. This is Adam. I have an envelope here for you from the studio."

"Is the messenger still there?"

"No, ma'am."

"I'm getting a little stir-crazy. How about I ride down to meet you at the elevator. You won't have to leave your post, and I'll pretend I just went on some lavish shopping spree."

Adam laughed. "Yes, ma'am. That would be great. I'll be there when the doors open."

"On my way," Sahara said.

"Pages already?" Lucy said.

"I think so. Tom certainly didn't waste any time. I'll be right back and I'll let myself in."

"Okay," Lucy said, and continued assembling lunch as Sahara grabbed her keys and left the penthouse.

Just getting out into the hall between her apartment and the elevator felt like she was escaping. It angered her that she'd let some faceless coward run her to ground, hiding like a criminal. She punched in the code on the keypad. The doors opened. She walked in and rode down. Adam was waiting with the envelope as promised.

"Thank you, kind sir," she said.

"My pleasure, Miss Travis. How's your foot?"

"Slowly healing, and thank you again for being my knight in shining armor and getting a doctor to make a house call."

He beamed. "Yes, ma'am. My pleasure. Have a nice day."

"You, too," Sahara said, and rode back up and let herself in.

She laid her keys on the table by the door and headed for the kitchen, opening the envelope as she went. Sure enough, it contained pages of the script with all of the dialogue and costume changes marked.

"We're back in business, I guess," Sahara said, as she laid the pages near her place setting and slid back onto the bar stool.

She scanned the memo on top and then leaned back with a sigh.

"It's an early call tomorrow, and they're sending a car for me, so you can just meet me on set."

Lucy carried the food to the island.

"Sure thing," she said. "I'll stop by that little French pastry shop that you like and pick up some croissants, and I'll also pick up your lunch. No need taking a chance on someone getting to your food again. It's going from my hands to yours."

"I appreciate that," Sahara said.

"And I am happy to do it," Lucy said. "So, what's going on in the new scenes that required wardrobe changes?"

"I don't know. Let me see," Sahara said, and she plucked a cold peeled shrimp from the bowl and dredged it in the spicy cocktail sauce before popping it in her mouth.

After waiting to see if Sahara Travis would ever come back out of that penthouse, Bubba was getting antsy. Right after he learned that the wrong woman died eating the poisoned food, he'd begun preparing the next wave of attack. His plan? Bomb the elevator. It had to work because it was the only way she could leave her apartment.

He got the name of the company The Magnolia used for mechanical repairs and set the next step in motion. That meant finding someone to build and place the bomb. Once that happened, there was nothing he could do but wait.

It was midafternoon a few days later when he learned Sahara would be leaving the penthouse the next day. He contacted the bomber he'd arranged for with one text message.

Go fix the elevator. It needs to be in place this evening. She'll be leaving the penthouse by 5:00 a.m.

The bomber reacted calmly. Everything was ready. He put on the disguise, slipped the bomb into a big yellow toolbox and then carefully covered it with tools and headed to The Magnolia. He circled the building several times before he saw a service vehicle pull around to the back. He waited until the vehicle left, then parked, grabbed his toolbox and headed inside.

There was a small hallway that led to a check-in window. He walked up, quickly eyeing the security camera in the far corner of the room behind the receptionist's desk. He tapped on the counter to get her attention.

She looked up, recognized the uniform, saw a company ID tag from where she was sitting and smiled.

"How can I help you?" she asked.

"Got a call to check brakes and cables on the penthouse elevator."

Her brow furrowed. "I don't know anything about that."

"I go where they send me," he said with a shrug.

The receptionist was hesitant. It was Magnolia policy to never bother the residents. Their job was to make life as private and luxurious as possible, so calling to confirm a repairman who wasn't going anywhere near the penthouse itself could mean a black mark against her work record.

"Well, I guess it's all right. Sign in on the clipboard and sign back out when you leave."

He signed in, then tapped the counter once more.

"Which way from here?"

"Down the stairwell to the basement. The residential elevators are on the west wall. The single one on the south is the penthouse."

The bomber nodded, picked up his toolbox and shuffled off.

Once in the basement, he went straight to work. Someone had obviously come down in the elevator earlier, because the car was on the first floor, and it didn't take long for him to get to the controls to bring it one floor farther down. At least he didn't have to climb up the ladder inside the shaft to get to the car, although he'd been prepared to do so, if needed.

After a quick glance around, he climbed up on top

of the car to set the bomb, fastening it right against the cables, then set a small camera on top of the emergency exit in the ceiling, aiming it down into the car so that when the Travis woman got in, he could see her and detonate. If she didn't die in the blast, she certainly would when the car crashed into the basement.

Once he was done, he gathered up his tools and headed for the stairwell. Now that this was done, he needed to disappear. His only witness was the woman in the office, which concerned him some. However, when he got back to the office to check out, there was a sign on the window.

Back in Fifteen Minutes.

He signed out and left. A simple trip to the bath-room had saved the woman's life.

Four

By the time Sahara went to bed that night, she was comfortable with the new lines and mentally immersing herself back into the role. She was a little sad, a little bit afraid and definitely uncertain what tomorrow would bring, but it felt good to be resuming normal activities.

When her alarm went off the next morning at four o'clock, she had just enough time to shower and dress for the day before the car would arrive to take her to the set.

While she was getting ready to leave, the bomber was in the parking lot of The Magnolia watching the video feed inside the elevator car from a remote control camera, waiting to hit a button and blow her to kingdom come.

Oblivious to the impending danger, Sahara moved through the penthouse with comparative ease, opting to wear some loose terry-cloth slippers to work. Adam had just called to let her know her car arrived, so she headed out the door wearing gym clothes and a lightweight zip-front hoodie. She was carrying a small purse barely big enough for credit cards, her phone in one hand and her coffee in the other as she punched in the code to send for the elevator.

And up it went.

When the bomber saw the doors open and his target step onto the elevator, he grinned. He didn't waste any time. He took a quick breath and detonated the bomb.

But Sahara had realized she'd forgotten the pages with all of her notes and comments for the day's shoot and had jumped out of the elevator with her key card in hand before the doors had closed. She was already running back across the hall to get them.

She was three steps from her door when the bomb went off. It blew the elevator doors into the hall only feet from where she was standing, immediately filling the hall with flying debris and a cloud of white billowing dust.

The impact knocked her to her knees and sent the key card sailing out of her hand. She was down on all fours screaming and crying for help when she heard the elevator car fall. It slid down the shaft in a horrible screech of metal against metal, and the faster it fell, the louder the screech until it was a constant, unending scream.

Sahara had lost her sense of direction in the thick, billowing dust and smoke, and all she could hear was that shriek as she frantically crawled from one side of the hall to the other, screaming for help, trying to orient herself with where she was. When she finally felt the ornate carving on her front door, she scrambled to her feet.

The light in the hall was off, leaving her in solid darkness. When she finally felt the keypad, she sobbed with relief as she began trying to key in her code. But the feeling was short-lived, because the floor began shaking beneath her feet. The car had become its own missile, rocketing down the shaft until it passed the ground floor and smashed into the basement in a second explosive blast, filling the shaft with even more smoke and debris.

Out in the parking lot, the bomber drove away convinced he had succeeded, and while most of the other tenants thought it was an earthquake, Sahara feared it was no accident. She was ninety-nine percent sure that a second attempt had just been made on her life.

When she finally made it back into the penthouse, she locked herself inside and then sank to her knees, sobbing. Too weak to stand, she fumbled for her phone, then groaned when she realized it was somewhere in the hall, and she wasn't going back into that choking smoke.

Slowly, she struggled back to her feet and then stumbled to the nearest bathroom, desperate to get the grit and dust from her face and eyes. Once she could see, she ran through the rooms to get to her bedroom suite, locked the door and then ran for the house phone at the end of the wet bar.

Her heart was hammering so loud she could barely think, and her hands were shaking as she called the lobby, waiting for the dear and familiar sound of Adam's voice.

The lobby downstairs was in chaos.

Certain Sahara had gone down with that elevator car, Adam was already in tears as he dialed 911.

The driver who'd been waiting for her heard the commotion and ran inside, only to find out the woman he was supposed to pick up was inside the elevator that had crashed. In a panic, he called his boss, who immediately called Harold Warner.

Harold had business to tend to all over the city this morning and had hired a car so he could work as he traveled from appointment to appointment.

He was making a notation of a dinner meeting the day after tomorrow when his cell phone rang. He hit Save to his Notes and answered the call.

"Harold Warner."

"Mr. Warner, this is Lou from Hollywood Limo."

"Yeah, hello, Lou. What's up? No problem picking up Miss Travis, I presume?"

"I'm sorry, sir, but my driver just called and said that while he was waiting for Miss Travis to come down, there was an explosion inside The Magnolia, and that the penthouse elevator came down and…crashed with her in it. I knew you needed to know. I'm so sorry to be the bearer of such news."

Harold froze. He couldn't believe what he was hearing.

"No! Oh my God, no!" he cried, then hung up on the limo service and called the phone in the lobby of Sahara's building. It rang and rang, but no one answered. He hit the intercom and buzzed the driver.

"Get me to The Magnolia as fast as you can."

"Yes, sir," the driver said, and immediately turned

them around and headed in the direction of the well-known building.

Harold was in shock. For a few moments, he couldn't think what to do or who to call and then realized he needed to let the director know his star wasn't going to make it to the set this morning—or any morning.

Adam had Fire and Rescue coming in the front door and the Hollywood PD outside directing traffic, plus he was fielding calls from all of the other residents of the building while trying not to break down completely at the loss of one of his favorite residents. He was a grown man who wore a weapon to work every day. He had been hired to do a job—keeping the residents of The Magnolia safe and seeing that their privacy stayed intact. But he'd known Sahara Travis for years and liked her as a person. Knowing that she'd died on his watch was tearing him up. He'd just watched a team of firefighters heading up the stairs floor by floor to escort any reluctant residents down while another crew was making its way down to the basement.

Behind him, the phone began to ring again. He sighed, blinking back tears as he reached to answer, then froze.

Seeing her name on the caller ID was like a message from the grave. His hands were shaking as he lifted the receiver.

"Hello?"

"Adam, it's me."

Adam let out a shriek. "Lord have mercy! Oh sweet Jesus! Sweet Jesus! You are alive!"

She started crying all over again. "Yes, but by the grace of God. I forgot something and went back to get it. The elevator is empty. Tell rescue I'm alive but stranded up here. And please call the LAPD and ask for Detective Shaw. Tell him someone just tried to kill me again. I need to find a way to get out of here. I can smell smoke, and I don't want to survive all this to end up dying in a fire."

Harold Warner's driver pulled up a full block away from The Magnolia.

"I'm sorry, Mr. Warner, but police have the streets blocked off down there. I can't get you any closer."

Harold's heart was pounding. He was about to walk into a truth he didn't want to face.

"Yes, okay. Just pull into this parking lot and wait. I have to get down there."

"Yes, sir," the driver said, and turned into the parking lot and killed the engine.

Harold got out, mopping the sweat from his face as he started down the street at a swift pace. He'd been thinking about Sahara ever since he'd gotten the call, remembering the first time he'd seen her. She'd come into his office, a little-known actress with two indie movies to her credit and seeking a manager. Before the meeting was over, he'd not only taken her on but felt like he'd been the one applying for representation. She'd grilled him about his education and even asked to see his résumé—she'd wanted to know what he could do for her that she couldn't do for herself. He'd initially laughed at her audacity and then realized she was serious and he needed to be. Twelve years later, their story and the success of their working relationship was an industry fairy tale.

A police car came rolling up on the street beside him and honked at him to move over, yanking him back to reality. He turned and glared at the cop who was driving, then kept on moving. He was already walking on the sidewalk. The cop could keep his ass and the cruiser in the street.

Harold swiped his handkerchief across his cheeks to dry the tears that were streaming down his face. His chest hurt. He couldn't believe she was gone.

Police were everywhere, rescue and fire trucks maneuvered their way closer to the building as residents were slowly being ushered out. The crowd was already gathering, most curious gossip-seekers uncertain about what was happening, but wanting to be in on whatever bloody details they could see.

He got stopped at one checkpoint, identified himself to the cops as Sahara Travis's manager and was allowed to pass. Once he got closer, another cop escorted him into the lobby.

He choked up again when he saw Adam, and then all of a sudden the ex-linebacker picked him up in his arms, laughing.

"She's alive, man! She's alive!"

Harold gasped. "What are you saying?" he asked, as Adam put him back down.

"She just called down here! She *was* in the elevator, then realized she forgot something and jumped out at the last minute to go get it. The elevator fell without her in it! She's trapped in the penthouse, though. Police are organizing a rooftop rescue right now."

"Oh my God! Oh my God," Harold muttered. "You talked to her? This is for sure?"

"Yes, I said—she just called! What's happening right now?"

"Detective Shaw is outside somewhere. You'll have to talk to him. That's all I know."

Harold couldn't believe what was happening. He'd already buried her in his mind, but, just like in the movies, she was alive again.

Sahara stayed on the landline inside the penthouse until Fire and Rescue had given her instructions on how her removal from the scene would go, and all the while her apartment continued to fill with smoke. She didn't know if the fire was spreading or contained for now within the elevator shaft, but she wasn't waiting around to find out. Following the orders she'd been given, she ran through the penthouse and took the stairs leading up to the roof.

The sun was a blast of white heat as she pushed the door open. It was like running out into a natural spotlight she could have done without. The streets below were gridlocked from the crowd and the rescue vehicles. The wind whipped her hair into her face and tugged at her clothing as she ran toward the helipad at the far end of the roof.

Seen from the crowd below, her rescue was like a scene from one of her movies, and the crowd was riveted by the sight of the famous actress running through the billowing smoke coming through the roof vents toward a landing helicopter.

The second the skids touched down, a man leaned out, grabbed her outstretched arms and swooped her up into the chopper. A cheer went up from the crowd as the helicopter lifted off and quickly flew away.

Sahara looked back once and then covered her face with her hands, her body trembling uncontrollably. One man threw a blanket around her shoulders while another handed her a bottle of water. She took a big drink and then used part of it on her face. The heat and smoke were still burning her eyes.

An EMT was taking her blood pressure and pulse while the other EMT, who happened to be a female, reached out and took Sahara's hands and just held them.

It took Sahara a few minutes to get past the noise inside the open cabin to realize the danger was over, but when she took a breath, she choked from emotion and relief. Someone squeezed her fingers. Sahara looked up into the darkest, kindest eyes she'd ever seen and took comfort in the woman's calm, steady gaze. Slowly, slowly, the shaking stopped. She began to realize she had these people to thank for her life, and did so, one by one.

They smiled as they gave her a thumbs-up, then one of them pulled the blanket tighter around her chin and scooted her up against his chest for more stability. It was like being buckled into a car seat, and the security she felt in the EMT's arms lulled her into a sense of safety that abruptly ended when the chopper landed and he released his hold on her.

Once more, she was transferred to another set of strangers. And again, she had to trust they had her best interests at heart.

Bubba was furious, then frustrated, then in disbelief when he learned Sahara Travis was still alive. But he knew something she didn't know. She was going to be on her way to New Orleans soon, which would complicate everything. So he paced the room, cursing his failures until he'd given himself a headache, then sat down and made himself focus. He wanted to take her out before she left LA, but how could he make that happen?

And then it hit him. Her plane. The private jet. It would mean one more bomb to build, but this time they'd be in the air before it went off and she'd have nowhere to go to escape.

He called the bomber, relayed his displeasure with the failure and then gave him further instructions.

"And don't fucking fail me this time! Do you hear?"

"I hear you, but I *didn't* fail. She got on that elevator, and I pushed the button. Who the hell could have predicted that she'd jump out at the last second?"

"Whatever, I don't need your excuses. This time, do what you have to do. Understand?"

"Yes, I understand."

Sahara was in the ER when Harold arrived. He pushed past a nurse in the doorway and went straight to the bed where Sahara was lying and took her in his arms.

"I thought you were dead. The entire drive over to The Magnolia I thought you were dead. Sweet Mother Mary, Jesus and Joseph…you are a miracle," he said, hugging her and patting her over and over again.

"What are you saying? You're Jewish," she muttered, wrapped her arms around his neck and burst into tears.

"Well, you're not, and I thought it best to thank your people first," Harold said, and blew his nose.

"Excuse me, sir," the nurse said, as she moved him aside.

"I won't leave you alone," Harold said when Sahara began to look anxious again.

"I'm not hurt," Sahara said. "All of this is just dust from the explosion in the shaft. Nothing actually hit me."

"You're still getting the whole run-through, so settle back and deal with it," he said.

"I have no place to live. I don't know who wants me dead. I feel like a target on a gun range. What's happening, Harold? *Why* is this happening?"

"Don't know yet, honey, but we will. You will not spend another day alone until this danger is behind you."

"I'm not moving in with you," she muttered.

"Of course you're not. But I have a bodyguard on the way over here. He's an ex–Army Ranger, and he'll make sure you're safe until we get this lunatic behind bars."

"A bodyguard?"

The whine in her voice made him frown.

"After all of this, what did you expect?"

"I didn't think it through," she said, fiddling at the dust that kept falling out of her hair and onto the hospital gown and trying to brush it away.

Harold eyed the nurse who was trying to dodge Sahara's fidgets as she struggled to get her blood pressure taken.

"Sahara, just be still and let the nurse do her job. I'm going to sit in that chair. Trust that I will not let anyone get close enough to hurt you again."

She leaned back and gave in to the prodding and pulling, the lab tech taking blood, the X-ray machine that came and went.

"What happened to your foot?" a nurse asked, as she removed the dirty gauze around it, cleaned the burn and replaced the bandages.

"Burned it with hot coffee," she said. "I've had a doctor—Chris Barrett—who's been treating it."

"Good man," the nurse said, tossing the gauze in the trash, then cleaning Sahara's foot and replacing the bandage.

An hour passed and then another. They were well into the third hour, and Sahara had finally calmed down enough that she was dozing and waiting to be discharged when she heard Harold shuffling around and then talking. Eyes still closed, she assumed he was on the phone thanking someone for taking the job on short notice, until she heard a man's deep rumbling voice in reply.

"Happy to help," he said.

She opened her eyes to see a giant of a man standing between her and the door, and she blinked again. Was he real?

As if sensing he was being watched, he turned toward her. She flashed on warm tan skin, thick dark hair and eyes the color of coal before he nodded politely and resumed his conversation with Harold.

Well...hello to you, too, whatever your name is.

Harold promptly filled in that blank.

"Sahara, this is Brendan McQueen. He will be your bodyguard until the person responsible for trying to kill you is caught. Brendan, meet Sahara Travis. I'm depending on you to keep her safe."

As Brendan moved to the side of her bed, Sahara felt his gaze take note of everything about her within two or three seconds, including her filthy hair, the hospital gown and the bandaged foot, before he shifted it straight to her face.

"Sorry to meet you under these circumstances, Miss Travis. Know that from this moment until I am released from duty, I will be standing between you and trouble. I am pledging my life to keep you safe, so I ask only a few small things from you in return."

"And those are?" she asked.

"That you never lie to me about anything and never leave my sight."

She frowned. "You're not coming into a bathroom with me, buddy."

"I don't have buddies, but you can call me Brendan. If you don't want me in a bathroom with you, then I'll make sure you're the only one in it, because if you go into a public bathroom with multiple stalls, rest assured I will be standing inside that room until you are ready to exit."

Her eyes narrowed, but she knew this was for her own good.

"Deal. Do we sleep together, too?"

His face remained stoic, ignoring her attitude.

"No, Miss Travis. I'm good with the floor."

"You can call me Sahara," she said, and then shifted her focus to her manager. "Harold, we need to talk."

"What about?"

"The movie. I need you to get me out of the role. There's no way to keep other people safe while someone's after me, and I don't want another Moira on my conscience. If I hadn't told Lucy to meet me on set this morning, she would have made sure I had my pages when she picked me up, and we would have been in the elevator together—and on adjoining tables in the morgue by now."

Harold flinched. "You're going to lose a lot of money."

Sahara glared. "I already have too much money, and

none of it is worth a life, so I'm going to pretend I did not hear you say that."

Harold flushed. "You're right. I'm sorry. It was the businessman in me. I'll tend to it immediately. But what are you going to do? Where do you intend to go?"

She pointed at the bodyguard. "Ask him where a safe place would be. I'm open to anything."

Brendan frowned. "Let's backtrack. Who's Lucy?"

"My personal assistant," Sahara said.

"Where is she? Why isn't she here?" he asked.

As if on cue, Lucy came flying into the exam room, her hair in tangles, a coffee stain on the front of her blouse, a bloodstain on her elbow, another on the knee of her pants, and her purse clutched beneath her chin.

"Oh my God," she wailed, heading straight for Sahara's bedside when someone grabbed her by the back of her pants and stopped her in place. "Let me go!" she screamed.

"Who are you?" Brendan demanded.

"That's Lucy! Turn her loose," Sahara said.

Lucy lunged to Sahara's side and began apologizing as she put her belongings onto the chair beside the bed.

"I was on set when word came that you were dead. All hell broke loose. Look at me. I look like I was run over by a pack of wolves. People were running amok, heading for their phones, turning on televisions, watching the director losing his mind. I ran to your trailer to get my stuff. I just couldn't believe it was true and was going to go to The Magnolia to see for myself when someone knocked me down as he came running out of the trailer carrying one of your silk nightgowns. It's probably for sale on eBay right now."

Harold couldn't believe what he was hearing.

"Why was there so much chaos?" Sahara asked.

Lucy shrugged. "Oh, you know. Everyone figured they'd try to sell their story about working with you on your last movie to the media. I heard some idiot on the phone with *TMZ*, another was calling *Entertainment Tonight*…someone was calling the *National Enquirer*. Those money-hungry bastards."

Sahara hid her shock and was glad she'd already made the decision to quit the movie. She wouldn't be able to go back without wondering who had tried to profit from news of her death.

"Are you okay?" Sahara asked. "Your elbow is bleeding a little and so is your knee. Sit down and I'll call a nurse. You need some first aid."

"I'm all right. I just can't get over all this. First the poisoned food and now this! It's for sure God's will that you are still alive," Lucy said.

Harold belatedly introduced Lucy and Brendan.

"Lucy, this is Brendan McQueen. He's Sahara's new bodyguard. Brendan, Lucy Benton, Sahara's personal assistant."

"We've met," Lucy snapped.

Brendan didn't respond.

Sahara rang for a nurse, who soon had Lucy's scrapes cleaned just minutes before Sahara's discharge papers arrived.

"So you really can't get back into the penthouse?" Lucy asked.

Sahara shook her head and turned away, not wanting any of them to see her tears. But Brendan saw them and filed away the knowledge that she wasn't nearly as tough as she pretended to be.

"You'll need clothes," Lucy said. "Give me an address, and I'll go get the essentials and have them to you before dinner."

"I don't have an address," Sahara said.

Brendan handed Lucy his card. "You go shop and text me when you're finished. I'll send you an address, which I trust you will not share."

Lucy took the card and turned her back to him. She didn't like him—she was used to being the person who took care of Sahara, whom she relied on, and this guy had jumped in and taken her place. She put a hand on Sahara's shoulder.

"Do you want me to stay with you?" Lucy asked.

"There's no need," Brendan said.

"Yes, I'd like that," Sahara said, ignoring her new bodyguard. "If I keep you close, then I'll know you aren't being targeted in an effort to get to me."

"I'll bring a suitcase when I come," Lucy said.

"You'll have to buy new luggage for me, too. Everything I own is in that death trap," Sahara muttered.

"I'll take care of it. And I'm going to assume you want comfort and low-key in your wardrobe?"

"You know me."

"Then I'm out of here, and thank you for the first

aid." Impulsively, she leaned down and kissed Sahara's forehead. "I'm so grateful you are alive." The affection surprised both of them, but it wasn't unwelcome.

She gathered up her purse and left, limping as she went.

Brendan gave Sahara a wary look but stepped aside as a nurse came in with discharge papers. Twenty minutes later Sahara was buckled up in the front seat of his black Hummer, waving goodbye to Harold as they drove away from the ER entrance.

"Where are we going?" she asked.

"A hotel for tonight. I have access to a remote cabin up in the mountains. Easy to see if anyone comes or goes, and it's teched out with radar and satellite security systems. It has an indoor pool, a full gym in the basement and a screening room for movies should the urge occur. We'll go there tomorrow."

Sahara sighed. One place was as good as another until the police figured out who was doing this. She leaned back against the seat and closed her eyes.

Brendan navigated traffic smoothly while keeping an eye on his passenger, who seemed to have fallen asleep. So when she suddenly spoke, it startled him.

"This is so awful," she said quietly.

He heard so much in her voice, but most of all regret.

"Have you ever been stalked before?" he asked.

"Sort of. But no one was ever hurt like this. I can't quit thinking about Moira."

"Was she the woman who died on set?"

Sahara nodded. "In my trailer. She was twenty-four

years old—worked in wardrobe and had a crush on one of the grips. He didn't even know it."

He glanced at her again as he braked for a red light. She was crying—a quiet grief he would not have expected from someone with a diva reputation. He was beginning to wonder if that reputation was all hype.

"I'm sorry for your loss," he said.

"Do you have any tissues?" she asked.

He pointed to the glove box.

She found some individual tissue packs, pulled one from the packet to wipe her eyes and then blow her nose. A few minutes later he moved into an exit lane and turned off the street and up the drive into a chain motel.

"A Motel 6? Are you serious?" she asked.

"It is not Motel 6, but it is the last place anyone would expect a star like you to be in, and it's only for one night. Sit tight and don't move. No one can see inside, so they won't know you're here."

"Don't forget to get an adjoining room for Lucy," she said.

"I forget nothing," he said. "I'll be locking you in, so don't fiddle with anything or you'll set off the security alarm."

He got out without waiting for an answer and strode toward the office.

Sahara watched in spite of herself. He had a nice tan and was certainly good-looking, which meant nothing in a city full of pretty people, but she liked the set of his jaw and the straight line of his nose. And his eyes.

Despite the gruff tone in his voice, he had kind eyes. His head was bare, as were his arms in deference to the heat of a California summer. His stride was long and his shoulders almost as wide as the door he entered.

Once he disappeared inside, she glanced at the interior of the Hummer and crossed her arms across her breasts, making sure she didn't bump anything that would earn his ire, and swallowed past the lump in her throat.

Five

Lucy was properly horrified at the bodyguard's choice when she reached the motel, but said nothing. She brought in all the purchases she'd made, and after Sahara's bath and shampoo, they spent the next hour in Lucy's room trying on everything, removing the tags and then packing the suitcases.

The door was ajar, and they were still folding clothes into the new luggage when Brendan knocked once, then walked in with his phone in his hand. He made no apology that he'd walked in on her while she was dressed only in a bra and a pair of shorts, her still wet hair already tangling into curls, but his conscience pinged when she reached for a blouse and held it in front of her.

"Your manager is on the phone. He needs to talk to you," he said.

Sahara was reaching for the phone when she caught a look of pity on his face. It scared her.

"You already know what he means to tell me, don't you?"

He laid the phone in her hand.

Her fingers were shaking as she put the phone to her ear.

"Hello? Harold?"

"Sahara! Sweetheart…" He hesitated. "I don't know how to tell you this."

"Tell me what, Harold? My God! Spit it out. You're scaring me."

"The New Orleans Police Department has been trying to locate you all day. Your mother… Sahara, I'm so sorry. She's dead. They found her in the garden of your parents' home this morning. She's been murdered and your father is missing."

The phone dropped from her grasp as Sahara fainted into Brendan's outstretched arms.

Lucy gasped. "What's wrong? What's happened?" She lunged at the phone Sahara had dropped. "Harold, what the hell! She fainted! What did you tell her?"

"The truth. Her mother has been murdered and her father is missing. I think your next stop is going to be New Orleans."

The shock of the news took the edge off spending the night in a low-brow motel with a bodyguard sleeping in a sleeping bag at the foot of her bed, but the morning had barely begun when the first argument between Brendan and Sahara erupted.

She was standing in front of the single bathroom mirror in scraps of nylon passing for underwear and an oversize T-shirt elongating her already long, slender legs. She was brushing her teeth as she argued with him, and Brendan was having a serious problem remaining objective.

He'd never had a client like her before. He was used to demanding divas in silk and satin, or male actors with massive entourages and even bigger ego problems. And then there was Sahara Travis in a basic T-shirt, slinging toothpaste and icy glares without caution and managing to look damn sexy while she was at it.

She spit, rinsed her mouth and then pointed the bubbly bristles of her toothbrush at him.

"I don't want to fly commercial. Harold has already notified my pilot. I have my private jet fueled and ready. It's the one I always use."

"How many people know you have a private jet?" he asked.

She shrugged. "It's probably common knowledge."

"Then you're flying commercial, which is what no one would expect."

"Surely you don't think—"

He waited for her to finish the sentence, then saw the moment it clicked. If someone would go to the lengths required to bomb her private elevator, why wouldn't they also try to destroy her jet? She stopped talking, rinsed out her mouth and toothbrush, and put the toothbrush away.

"We don't have tickets," Lucy said.

"Yes, we do," Brendan said. "All three in first class."

"This is going to be a nightmare," Lucy muttered from the bedroom, having overheard their new plans.

"It's already a nightmare," Sahara said, now fully on board with Brendan's plan. "Don't argue. Brendan, I'm going to get dressed, so look away."

"What time is the flight?" Lucy asked.

"It boards in a couple of hours. We have time. Trust me," he said, and then stood in the doorway between the two rooms with his back to theirs while Sahara dressed.

When she was finished, he loaded them and the bags into the Hummer before sliding into the driver's seat to buckle up. Sahara looked years younger than her thirty-three years. Her hair was dry, and she'd piled a fierce tangle of dark curls on her head. The expression on her face was somewhere between anger and despair. He hated to see the usual fire in her tamped down so early in the morning.

"Hey."

Sahara looked up, thinking not for the first time that her bodyguard looked like a giant-size version of Channing Tatum. Then she realized he was asking her a question and tuned back in to what he was saying.

"Breakfast will be compliments of a McDonald's drive-thru. What's your poison? Biscuits and gravy, or breakfast burritos?"

"She doesn't eat that greasy fast food," Lucy snapped.

"Yes, I do," Sahara said. "My trainer doesn't like it, but yes, I do. I'll take a sausage-and-egg burrito with hot sauce and a Diet Dr Pepper."

Brendan stifled a smile. Dr Pepper for breakfast was not something he'd imagined a woman like Sahara would order.

"How about you, Miss Lucy?"

Lucy sighed. "A bacon-and-egg biscuit and orange juice."

"Harold sent me new ID and credit cards. Use mine to pay," Sahara said, as she dug them out of her new purse.

"No, ma'am. Too easy to find you that way," Brendan said.

Sahara blinked. "Oh. I didn't think..." she mumbled, and dropped them back into the purse.

"Don't worry. It's all covered and often part of the job," he said.

Sahara glanced at his profile and the size of his hands on the steering wheel and wondered if everything about him was supersize, then looked away and closed her eyes and chided herself for thinking it. No one knew the toll it was taking for her to go home. The only plus side to any of this was that her mother was no longer able to hurt her. Maybe she should feel guilty for thinking that, but she didn't. It was the truth.

Brendan parked his Hummer in airport parking, which meant they were now carrying their own bags into the terminal to check-in. Sahara was pulling her carry-on and often running a couple of steps to keep up with his pace.

When they reached check-in and then the security checkpoint, she was recognized almost instantly, and they were forced to rush through the process to beat the chaos that followed.

Once they were headed for their gate, Brendan took her carry-on as well as Lucy's. People began calling out Sahara's name and taking pictures at random, even trying to stop her for autographs. It was all business as usual for Sahara, but this was why she preferred to take her private jet when she traveled.

Word spread to the usual paparazzi, who were always present at Los Angeles International, that Sahara Travis was in the building and on the move. But it didn't stop Lucy's intent when she held up progress long enough to get water and magazines before they were off again.

Brendan saw them first, but when Sahara noticed the paparazzi coming toward her like rats escaping the sewers to feed, she moved closer to him. He glanced at her face and saw panic.

"Sahara, you just keep moving. I've got this. Lucy! Flank her and don't stop walking."

"Okay," Lucy said, and moved even closer to her boss as they headed for their gate.

The first photographer made the mistake of getting too close and then wouldn't give way. Brendan's hands were full of carry-on luggage when he bumped into him, knocking him to the floor.

"He pushed me!" the photographer yelled, and in that moment, Sahara lost her cool.

She spun on the lot of them, shouting.

"His hands are full, so just get out of the way. He never touched you. You all know someone is after me, everyone's heard. Is it one of you? Is it you?" she cried, looking down at the photographer who'd gotten dumped onto his ass. "You didn't have to get that close to take a picture. What were you trying to do? Someone call the police! I want him arrested. He might be the man trying to kill me."

A look of horror spread across the man's face. This wasn't going as he'd planned.

"No, no, it's not me. Hey, I'm sorry. I'm sorry. I just wanted a good shot—"

But it was too little, too late. Airport security arrived and took him into custody as the other photographers quickly scattered.

Sahara grabbed her own carry-on and glanced up at Brendan.

"Okay to go now?"

He arched an eyebrow and grinned. "I believe so, and…thanks. I feel so much safer now."

Sahara grimaced. "I'm tired, I'm scared, I really don't want to set foot back in New Orleans, and I don't have time for lawsuits, so I lost it, okay?"

He was shocked by her admission. He couldn't hug her, so he took back her carry-on with his last two free fingers and curled them tight.

"Follow me, boss. We're almost there," he said.

Sahara followed, willing herself not to cry.

Lucy saw the flush of emotion on Sahara's face and knew enough to stay silent.

They finally reached the gate, and when the people at check-in recognized her again, they hustled her little entourage through the line and boarded them early.

"Thank you," Sahara said, as the flight attendant seated them.

"You're welcome, Miss Travis. As soon as we get the passengers loaded, I'll be back to take your drink orders." Then she glanced at McQueen. "Sir, can I help you stow your luggage?"

"I've got it, but thanks," Brendan said.

A calm settled over Sahara as she took the window seat and buckled herself up. Lucy was in the seat directly in front of her and Brendan was in the aisle seat beside her. For the first time in days, she felt safe.

Lucy got up on her knees and looked over the seat at Sahara, still intent on doing her job to keep her comfortable.

"I brought magazines. Do you want something to read?" she asked.

"Not right now," Sahara said.

"Did you take your Dramamine? You know you have a tendency to get a little airsick."

"Damn. I forgot," Sahara said.

"I have some. Just a second," Lucy said, and dug through her carry-on to find the little tube of pills. She shook one out in her hand and handed it to Sahara, then pulled a small bottle of water out of the same bag, opened it and handed it over the seat.

Sahara downed the pill, then put the lid on the water and set it in her drink holder.

"Thank you for taking such good care of me, Lucy."

"You're welcome," Lucy said, then handed her a neck pillow.

Sahara put the pillow around her neck, thought of where they were going and closed her eyes. She'd promised herself she would never go back there again.

Broken promises. Broken dreams.

Her life was full of both.

She could hear tiny little clicks in her right ear and guessed Brendan was sending someone a text. First class was being seated now, and it didn't take but seconds for Sahara to be recognized.

A well-dressed fortysomething woman had the seat beside Lucy, and when she paused to put her bag in the overhead bin and recognized Sahara Travis, Brendan saw the look of the hunt in her eyes. She was going to be pushy enough to try to introduce herself, he knew, so as her gaze went to Sahara's face and her lips were parting, Brendan shook his head.

"No, ma'am," he said quietly.

The woman blinked, then quickly sat, intimidated by his size and the deep rumble of his voice.

More people were filing past them now, but Sahara kept her eyes closed. She wanted this day to be over, and they still hadn't left the ground.

Her name was on everyone's lips. She could hear the whispers and excited undertones of people thrilled to be on the same flight as a star like Sahara Travis.

The rumble of voices grew like the wild kudzu vines from home, choking out everything in its path and taking all the air and energy out of the cabin. She wanted to hide, but damn it all to hell she was stuck on this commercial flight just to stay alive.

She was under no misapprehension that her mother's murder and the attacks on her life weren't connected. She thought there was surely a law of coincidence in the universe, and this hell she was living in no way came from serendipity.

Thankfully, by the time the passengers were seated

and the flight attendants were stowing last-minute luggage and urging people to buckle up, the Dramamine tablet had put her to sleep.

Brendan glanced at her. She was buckled in and safe. So far, so good. The plane began to taxi. As it did, Sahara's head rolled toward his arm, coming to rest just below his shoulder. He could smell the motel shampoo in her hair. When the plane finally left the runway, he was holding her hand.

When Bubba saw a news flash about a movie star on her way to New Orleans because her mother had been murdered, accompanied by a brief video clip of her, her assistant and one great big man he took to be a bodyguard moving through the airport, his heart skipped a beat. It was also apparent that Sahara had flown commercial. Once again, through no fault of his own, his plans had failed. But it was just as well. She was coming to him. He'd get her on his own turf.

Sahara woke up hours into the flight and took the cold soda she was offered, sipping it slowly while ever conscious of the looming presence of the man beside her. He was remarkably quiet. The only time he spoke was to dissuade passengers from stopping to talk or to ask for autographs. Another hour passed before Sahara finally tapped his arm.

"I need to use the restroom," she whispered.

"Yes, ma'am," he said, and stepped into the aisle to let her pass, then followed her to the front of the plane.

He looked inside the cramped bathroom cubicle before he let her in, then turned around to face the people in the plane with an emotionless expression. Within a few minutes he felt a hand on his back. He glanced over his shoulder to nod at her and then led the way back to their seats.

"Everything okay?" Brendan asked once they were seated.

She saw the genuine concern on his face and nodded, grateful that Harold had the foresight to choose a man like this.

Another hour passed, and the closer they got to New Orleans, the more anxious Sahara became. By the time they began preparing for landing, she was so tense it felt like she was vibrating from the inside out.

Fifteen years.

She hadn't been here in fifteen years and had never planned to come to this city again. Now she would have to play the role of her life by pretending to be the grieving daughter. It wasn't going to be easy. How did you grieve for someone who'd never loved you—never wanted you in her life? And the fact that her father was missing made her extra anxious. If he showed up and she was forced to face him down again, she didn't know if she would survive it.

Brendan knew she was bothered—she was radiating tension. He suspected there was some history that she was going to have to deal with in coming here, but mistakenly thought most of it right now had to do with having lost her mother. When the plane finally touched down and began taxiing toward the airport, Sahara grabbed his hand.

"I've got this," he said. "Just trust me." He reached for his phone to check messages. "Well, hell," he muttered, as he read one particular text.

"What's wrong?" Sahara asked.

He wouldn't say it aloud but leaned over and let her read the message on his phone. He saw her eyes widen and the shock spread. Her voice was shaking when she dropped the phone back into his hand.

"Well, damn, McQueen. I owe you one. You were right about the plane. It wouldn't have cleared the runway, would it?"

"No."

"Do the police think the bomber killed the mechanic they found in the Dumpster?"

"Probably," he said.

Her shoulders slumped. The bodies on her conscience kept piling up.

"So how do we navigate the awaiting madhouse?"

"I've got a car waiting, and help will be at the gate to get us through luggage pickup and out of here."

"What kind of help?" Sahara asked.

"One of my buddies. His name is Will Sherman. He's ex–Army Ranger, too."

Within minutes they were at the gate. A tall, lanky man in blue jeans and a New Orleans Saints T-shirt stepped out of the crowd and took part of the luggage Brendan was carrying. He nodded at Sahara.

"Will Sherman at your service, ma'am," he said, and then fell into step behind both women.

They made their way to luggage pickup amid stares, double takes and the constant clicking of people snapping pictures on their phones. She stayed as close to Brendan as she could get and let Lucy and Will retrieve the bags.

The media she'd been expecting was outside the terminal, and there was no way around their presence. But Brendan was adept at keeping them at bay, and Will Sherman sent the stragglers behind them scurrying with a sharp "get the hell away from her" command.

"Hey, Will, where's the SUV?" Brendan asked, as they reached airport parking.

"Follow me," he said, and led the way through the parking garage.

When Brendan saw the man standing beside a big red SUV, he dropped the luggage and hugged him.

"John! Long time no see, brother!"

"Good to see you, Brendan."

"You, too. Help me load all this up ASAP. Time is critical here," he said, and then cupped Sahara's elbow and guided her toward the front seat.

"Sahara, this is my younger brother John. He rented the vehicle for us under his name, and it's been in his sight ever since he picked it up, so it's safe. John, this is Sahara Travis."

"Very nice to meet you, John McQueen, and thank you for helping," she said.

John nodded as he clasped her hand.

"Please accept my sympathies on the loss of your mother, and I hope they soon find the person behind all of this. Allow me to help you into the vehicle while Brendan loads up the luggage. He's picky about stuff like that."

Sahara was quickly seated inside the SUV. The engine was running, the air conditioner on high. John gave her a thumbs-up and then shut her inside while Lucy climbed into the back seat.

"Oh my God, it's hot in this city," she said.

"Summer in New Orleans."

Lucy eyed the pallor of Sahara's expression.

"Are you feeling okay? Is there anything you need?"

"There's nothing that will fix this," Sahara said.

Lucy sighed. "I'm really sorry about your mother. I assume we're going straight to your home?"

"Yes, that's where we're going."

Lucy leaned back and shut up. It seemed the wisest thing to do.

Moments later, Brendan got in. "Will is following us from his vehicle. Unless there's a security system already in place at your parents' house, he's going to set one up for me once we get there. It's what he does for a living. The housekeeper knows we're on the way. I called. Her name is Billie. Do you know her?"

Sahara stifled a gasp and then clasped her hands against her heart.

"Billie is still there?"

"Yes. I take it you know her?"

Sahara's eyes welled. "I know her."

"Okay, then, we're off," he said.

Stunned by this news, Sahara sat back without comment, blind to the city as they passed through it. This place was already dead to her. She just had to bury what was left before she could escape it a second time.

She didn't question how Brendan knew where he

was going, but he was taking all of the right streets to get to the family home. She glanced at the side-view mirror and assumed the gray SUV behind them was Will Sherman's.

When they paused at a Stop sign to let a delivery van pass, she recognized the business logo. Devereaux's Pralines. Her mouth watered, thinking of the sweet, buttery, brown sugar candy.

Some things never changed.

Within twenty minutes of leaving the airport, Brendan turned into a driveway and paused at the iron gates. He lowered the window, punched in a code and then waited for the gates to open.

"How did you know what to key in?" Sahara asked.

"Billie told me."

"Oh yes, Billie," she said, and made herself look at the two-story redbrick house as they drove around to the gatehouse and parked.

Six

Will pulled up behind them and got out to help carry luggage inside.

"Sit tight a second," Brendan said, then rang the delivery bell by the back door and waited for it to open before he let Sahara get out.

A tall, slender woman with a pretty face and graying hair opened the door, looking anxiously toward the red SUV.

"Brendan McQueen," he said. "Are you Billie?"

She nodded.

"Be right back," he said, and ran back to get Sahara.

"Let's go," he said. "I don't want to scare you, but I also don't want you out in the open here."

Sahara reached for his hand as he helped her out, and then let him hurry her inside.

When Billie Munroe saw Sahara coming, she opened her arms wide and grabbed her the moment she crossed the threshold.

"Sahara! Sweetheart! I didn't think I would ever see you again," Billie said, and hugged her close.

Sahara was still reeling from the fact that Billie was here.

"When did you come back?" Sahara asked.

Billie frowned. "Back from where, child? I never left."

Sahara staggered backward into Brendan, who steadied her for support.

"No, no, no," Sahara whispered. "They said they paid you off and you left. I looked in your room. It was empty."

Billie's eyes welled. "You should have known better. The night you left, I was in the hospital having my appendix removed. When I came home, your parents told me you ran off, but I knew better. I knew they'd done something. I just didn't know it had involved me, or I would have pushed my way into your life and told you."

Sahara was sobbing. "I'm sorry," she said, and threw her arms around Billie's neck.

"Hush, girl, we're fine. We'll always be fine," she cooed, and handed Sahara a handful of tissues to wipe her eyes. "And this must be Brendan McQueen…the man who called."

"Yes, ma'am. Thank you for helping us get Sahara here safely."

"Anything for my girl," she said.

Lucy and Will came in carrying bags as Sahara was mopping up tears. She quickly introduced them.

"Billie, this is Lucy Benton, my personal assistant. Lucy, this is Billie Munroe, the woman who kept me alive and safe beneath this roof."

Billie was still wiping her eyes as she cupped Sahara's cheek.

"Brendan said you needed a bedroom with two beds, so I put you in the blue room. I didn't think you'd want to stay in your old room anyway."

"And you would be right," Sahara said.

"Follow me," Billie said, and led them through the house and up the stairs.

Lucy eyed the elegance of the home and its decor as the housekeeper led the way to the bedrooms, imagining what it would have been like to grow up in such opulence. They put her in the green room across the hall from Sahara, and as soon as she deposited her luggage, she went to help Sahara unpack.

Sahara kicked off her soft slip-on shoes and sat down in a white wingback chair to check the bandage on her foot.

Billie saw the wound and gave her a worried look.

"What happened to you?" she said, as she dropped to her knees beside Sahara's chair.

"Oh, it's fine. Sloshed hot coffee on it. It's healing."

"I have something that will heal it quicker," Billie said. "Leave that bandage off a minute."

"Yes, ma'am," Sahara said, watching the older woman leave the room, then glancing up at Brendan. "I've been gone fifteen years, and she picks right back up as if I'd never left."

"She's seems like a good woman," Brendan said.

"The best," she said, and then pointed at the beds. "So, I assume you're going to take the one by the door?"

He went to look out the window to make sure there

was no exterior access to this room. Satisfied that twenty feet straight up the side of an ivy-covered brick wall should be safe enough, he nodded.

"Brendan, please tell me this is all a bad dream. Please tell me if I open my eyes this will all go away," she whispered.

Brendan didn't respond. He wished it were true, but they all knew it wasn't.

"So, Will," he said, "what's the scoop on a security system here?"

"Not one."

Brendan scowled. "Seriously?"

Will nodded.

"Then load this place up inside and out," Brendan said.

"You got it, boss," Will said, and left the room.

"I'll unpack for you, Sahara," Lucy said, and proceeded to hang up the new clothes while Brendan did a sweep of the room, checking every access in and out.

Sahara lay flat on her back, staring up at the ceiling.

Brendan grabbed her by her ankle and dragged her to the side of the bed.

"This is happening, and the sooner you get up and face it, the better we're all going to be."

Sahara was shocked by such rude behavior.

"Damn it! Why don't you tell me what you really think?" she said, as Billie came back with a little basin of water and some salves to put on her foot.

Brendan sidestepped Billie, still pressing his point.

"Look, Miss Travis, you can sit there and sulk about the extra security measures I'm taking, but murderers have already been on this property. They killed your mother and got away, and I don't intend for that to happen again."

The word *mother* rolled off her back like water as she leaned over to watch Billie doctoring her foot. She reached out and laid a hand on Billie's shoulder.

"Katarina Travis was not my mother. Billie Munroe is my mother, and I thank you, Mama. It already feels better."

Billie looked up and smiled. "You're welcome, baby. I guess the old secret no longer matters, does it?"

Sahara slipped off the side of the bed and got down on her knees to hug her.

"It never mattered to me. I hated that Katarina made us live that lie."

Brendan didn't know what was happening.

"What the hell are you talking about?" he asked.

Sahara touched Billie's cheek as she began to explain.

"Katarina Travis was not my birth mother. Billie is. Katarina couldn't have children, but she denied my father nothing. He loved Katarina, but he couldn't keep his dick in his pants. When he got Billie pregnant, Katarina decided she would pass me off as hers. Don't ask me why. She didn't love me, didn't pretend to care what happened to me, but in the eyes of the world, I was their love child…conceived when they were in Egypt, thus the origin of my name. Then they kept Billie on as a nursemaid."

"Damn," Brendan said. "When did you find all this out?"

"I've always known."

"So what happened here that made you leave?"

"The night of my high school graduation I came home and found my clothes packed, the keys to an old car sitting on top of the luggage, five hundred dollars in an envelope and Leopold and Katarina standing at the top of the stairs arm in arm. It wasn't a pretty scene, but the bottom line was Katarina didn't want me beneath their roof another night. I asked where my mother was, which made Katarina livid. They told me they'd paid her off and she was gone, and they wanted me gone, too. They told me I was smart enough to figure it out. I didn't believe them about Billie—I knew she would never abandon me like that—and went to look in her room, but it was empty. I thought I would die. I didn't know what to do or where to go, but they kicked me out, so I got in the car and drove away."

Billie's voice was shaking as she picked up the tale.

"When I woke up in the hospital to be told my girl was gone, I was devastated. They told me an ugly lie… that you'd turned your back on all of us. My shame is that I believed it."

"They were evil, and I'm not sorry she's dead," Sahara muttered.

McQueen's head was spinning.

"So how many people knew this secret?" he asked.

Billie shrugged. "Leopold and Katrina. Sahara and me."

"To the rest of the world, Sahara was their daughter?"

"Yes, to be paraded out when they were entertaining,

because she was so beautiful…even as a child," Billie said. "Katarina took the praise as her due, by claiming the child's beauty was inherited from her."

Lucy shook her head. "Hollywood will have a field day with this, so you better figure out if you want this news public."

Sahara had forgotten Lucy was there, but she didn't mind her knowing—and Lucy was right. This secret would blow up the media coverage on her, which would only serve to confuse what was already happening.

"I'm the housekeeper," Billie said. "I raised Sahara. That's already common knowledge, and that's how it will stand until she wants it told another way. I have prepared food. Please refresh yourselves, and Sahara will show you the way to the dining room when you're ready to eat."

"Thank you. We won't be long," Brendan said.

"This hell is all worth it just to have you back," Sahara said, and hugged Billie again.

She cupped her daughter's face and kissed both cheeks before leaving them on their own.

Sahara was unpacked, and she had sent Lucy back to her room to unpack her own luggage. She was moving about the bedroom, poking into corners, looking for familiar objects. There was a phone ringing somewhere in the mansion, signaling a conversation yet to be had.

Sahara watched Brendan from the corner of her eye. When he wasn't pissing her off with his overbearing ways, he intrigued her. So he had a brother. She wondered about the rest of his family—if he had children, if he had a significant other...not that she cared.

"Hey, Brendan, can I ask you something?"

He closed a dresser drawer and turned around.

"Yes?"

"Do you work out?"

One eyebrow arched. "What? You think I popped out of my mama's belly like this? Of course I work out. It started in the army and now it's part of what keeps my clients safe."

She grinned. "My apologies to your mama for alluding to an unnatural birth."

"Well, there are four of us. She's probably felt we were all unnatural at one time or another," he said with a laugh.

"All boys?"

He nodded. "I'm the oldest, then John, then Carson, then Michael. They're all married. They all have kids. I'm the holdout, but I'm also the favorite uncle."

She couldn't imagine him playing—with kids or anyone else, for that matter. So, there was more to him than a pretty face and body.

"You see where I grew up. What about you? Where did you grow up?"

"Wyoming."

"In a city?"

"Nope. A ranch outside of Cheyenne. My family still lives there."

"Is it a big ranch?"

"You'd think so, but about standard for the state.

They run about five hundred head of cattle and a small herd of horses on about ten thousand acres."

Her jaw dropped. "Are you serious?"

He grinned. "Yes, ma'am. It's called a lack of good grazing land. Takes a lot of land to sustain one steer."

She tried to imagine him as a cowboy but couldn't really picture it.

The house phone in Sahara's bedroom started ringing, and she picked it up.

"Yes?"

It was Billie.

"The police know you're here. They want to interview you. I told them to give you at least an hour so you could eat. The food is ready when you are."

"Thank you, Mama. I should have expected that. We'll be right down."

She hung up.

"Billie said the police will be here in an hour. They want to interview me. I suppose they're going to look for a way to pin the murder on me. That's what they do in the movies."

Lucy was still feeling giddy from the call she'd made to Wiley as she walked back into Sahara's room. He was shocked she'd gone to New Orleans with Sahara and was upset he hadn't known, then got an earful of sweet talk in the process. But she was pulled back to reality when she heard what Sahara was saying.

"Why would they do that, assume you're guilty?" Lucy asked.

Sahara shrugged. "It's where they always start, isn't it? Blame the family—especially the rich, estranged family? Now, excuse me while I take a bathroom break. Be right back and we'll go downstairs. My mother made us something to eat." She smiled a genuine smile. "After finding out she still lives here, my shitty life has finally taken a good turn. I'm actually sort of hungry. How about you guys?"

"We're with you," Brendan said.

"Excuse me. I'm going to wash up, as well. I'll meet you in the hall," Lucy said.

Brendan tried to get a read on the assistant as she left the room, but she was a hard one. Polite, emotionless, rarely laughed, but competent. She wasn't the usual Hollywood kiss-up employee, but then Sahara wasn't the usual Hollywood diva, so there was that.

They trooped downstairs in tandem without talking, Brendan leading the way down the stairs with Lucy and Sahara following.

There was an immense portrait of a very handsome couple hanging in the hall. Lucy pointed. "Is that them?" she asked.

Sahara didn't bother to look up. "Yes, that's Leopold and Katarina Travis…my so-called parents."

"But this place is stunning. You got to grow up here," Lucy said, a hint of awe in her voice.

Sahara stopped, her eyes blazing with sudden anger.

"No. I was *forced* to live here, trotted out when it suited their purposes to put me on display, and stuck in the kitchen with Billie to play by myself when I was not. I told you I ate in the kitchen with the help. That's because *the help* was my family. That's where I lived. Not in this godforsaken tribute to excess." She took a deep breath and tried to let go of the anger. "Now, enough about them. I can smell Billie's good cooking already."

Brendan could tell by the stiff set of her shoulders as she walked off that some old wounds had been opened. He lengthened his stride to catch up.

The kitchen was a little warmer than the air-conditioned hallway, but in a comfortable way.

Sahara couldn't believe fifteen years had passed since she'd been in this room. Except for a couple of new appliances, nothing had changed but Billie. She was a little older and a lot grayer. Sahara wondered how much of that gray hair came from the grief of losing her daughter.

It made her want to cry all over again, thinking how they'd both been lied to. She wanted this killer to be caught so she could have her life back, and wondered if Billie would ever consider coming to live with her in LA.

She slipped up beside her mother and whispered in her ear.

"Mama, can we please eat in here?"

Billie beamed. "Of course."

Brendan scanned the room as he entered, eyeing the curtained windows and the clear glass window on the back door, and then looked out into the garden, making sure there were no sharpshooters waiting for a kill shot. He saw the crime scene tape outside where Katarina's body had been found, then turned to watch Billie setting out food. Sahara must have talked her into serving them there, rather than the dining room. He understood why. This was where she felt safe, loved and welcomed.

"The food looks wonderful," Sahara said, and reached over Lucy's shoulder to snag a blackened shrimp from a platter of shrimp and rice. "Taste this, Brendan."

He took the shrimp from her fingers and popped it in his mouth, then gave her a thumbs-up.

"That's some good seasoning."

"Thank you, Mr. McQueen. Everyone, please sit. Would you prefer wine or sweet tea with lunch?"

"Oh, sweet tea for sure," Sahara said.

"And for me," Lucy said.

"And for me, and please call me Brendan," he said, then thanked her as she filled his glass.

"Aren't you going to sit with us?" he asked.

Sahara looked up to realize there were only three plates at the table.

"Mama! Good grief. Come sit down with us. There's so much about this mess that we need to talk about."

Billie sat.

Sahara frowned, got up and got a plate and flatware, and plopped it down in front of Billie, then poured her a glass of sweet tea, as well.

"Now, then. We eat," Sahara said, satisfied that Billie was already putting food on her plate.

So they ate and they talked.

Billie had already heard about the attacks on Sahara's life and was worried.

"Brendan, how are you keeping her safe?"

"As you already know, she goes nowhere without me, and I'm good at my job. We'll just leave it at that."

"He's ex–Army Ranger," Sahara said.

"So is Will, the man installing security outside right now. When he's finished, he'll be putting security up inside, as well," he said.

Billie nodded. "Okay, then. Whatever it takes to keep my girl safe."

"Yes, ma'am. I fully intend to do that," he said.

"Did anyone save room for dessert?" Billie asked once they'd cleaned their plates.

"Not unless there are beignets," Sahara said.

"There are beignets," Billie said.

Sahara groaned with pleasure.

Lucy gave her a disapproving look. "You won't fit into wardrobe at this rate," she said.

"I don't have wardrobe. I'm not going back to finish the film. I told Harold to get me out of the contract."

Lucy looked stunned. "Why would you do that?"

"Because people are trying to kill me, Lucy! Because other people are dying because of me," Sahara snapped. "Why would I continue to put them in danger?"

Lucy paled. "Right. I was just…surprised is all."

"I'm sorry. I just forgot you didn't already know."

"Who found Mrs. Travis's body?" Brendan asked, deciding it would be better to change the subject and avoid any more arguing.

"I did," Billie said. "I got up to begin breakfast at my usual time, which was just before 6:00 a.m. The back door was ajar. I thought someone had broken in to rob us, and then I saw Mrs. Travis lying on the walkway between the rosebeds. She was in her night-gown. She'd been shot. I called the police and then went to look for Mr. Travis, and that's when we discovered he was missing."

"Do they suspect that he's the killer?" he asked.

Billie shrugged. "I don't know what they're thinking, but they'd be crazy to take their case in that direction. He worshipped the ground she walked on."

"Where are the beignets?" Sahara asked, clearly uninterested in discussing the Travises any further.

"In the butler's pantry. You'll see them."

Sahara got up and disappeared into a room off the kitchen.

"I'll help," Lucy said, and followed.

Brendan got up so that he could see them, then watched the casual ease with which the movie star was digging through a two-hundred-year-old butler's pantry for deep-fried dough. He stifled a grin when she did a little pirouette because she found them, then directed Lucy to bring what looked like a big salt shaker with her as they came back to the table.

"Prepare yourselves. These are the best beignets ever," Sahara said.

Billie distributed dessert plates, and Lucy poured more sweet tea. For a short period, they set aside the ugliness of why they were there and were able to just enjoy each other's company and some delicious food.

Sahara put a beignet on her dessert plate and then took the shaker Lucy had carried to the table and liberally sprinkled her beignet with cinnamon sugar on top of the powdered sugar already there.

Brendan hid a smile as she literally licked her lips before taking that first bite.

When a little cloud of powdered sugar shook loose from the beignet, Sahara mopped it up with her finger and kept eating.

"Where's the paparazzi when you need them?" Lucy said, and giggled. "A shot of you covered in cinnamon and licking up sugar would be worth a year's wages."

Sahara shrugged.

Billie smiled. "It's also on your nose and your chin."

As soon as Sahara finished, she grabbed a paper napkin and cleaned herself up.

"Wouldn't want the cops to think I wasn't grieving here," she said.

There was a knock at the kitchen door.

Sahara jumped.

"It's Will," Brendan said, and answered the door. "How's it going?" he asked, as Will entered the kitchen.

"Good. I called my crew. They just arrived, so I wanted you to know there will be six of us in here for a while, because this place is huge. Tell me what you want covered."

"All of the doors and windows on the first floor. Motion detector lights on both front and back doors, and I want two control panels. One on the ground floor near the front entrance, and one in the hallway upstairs so that the security system can be armed or disarmed from either site."

"I'll get the guys and we'll get started."

"The police are going to be here soon. Just so you know," Brendan said.

"We'll stay out of their way," Will said.

On cue, the doorbell rang.

Billie got up. "All of you, into the library. I'll bring them to you."

"And I'll bring my men in through this door, then," Will said, and hurried out.

"This way," Sahara said, and led the way through the maze of hallways to the other side of the house, then into a room with dark cherrywood paneling and two walls of floor-to-ceiling books. The odor of tobacco lingered. It made her shudder. Leopold smoked a pipe. She wondered where the hell he'd gotten off to, but then let it go. As long as he wasn't here, she'd cope.

She paused in the middle of the room.

"Stay away from the windows, please," Brendan said.

"Oh, right," Sahara said, and chose a chair out of the line of sight. "Lucy, I doubt they'll talk to you, but if they do, don't be nervous. And just for the record, I'm sorry you're caught up in this."

"No, it's okay," Lucy said, and took a seat in one of the overstuffed chairs.

Instead of sitting, Brendan moved closer to Sahara.

"You can come hold my hand if it will make you feel better," she said, her sarcasm obvious.

His eyes narrowed, but he didn't respond.

She sighed. She was just trying to lighten the moment, but she'd pissed him off—again.

"I'm sorry. I'm just nervous," she said.

"I know. It's okay. Chin up. Here they come," he

said, and then just like that, he watched the famous Sahara Travis stepping into character as she wiped her face of expression and lifted her chin.

Seven

Billie felt the weight of suspicion as she led the police commissioner and two homicide detectives into the library. They'd stared at her as if she'd pulled the trigger herself, even though she'd already been through this when the body was found.

"Sahara, this is Police Commissioner Murtaugh and Detectives Julian and Fisher. Gentlemen, Sahara Travis. Ring if you need me," she said, and left the room.

Sahara waved them toward a long leather sofa.

"Please have a seat. Commissioner. Detectives. This is Brendan McQueen, my bodyguard, and Lucy Benton, my personal assistant."

Sahara was vividly aware of where Brendan was in reference to where she was sitting and was grateful for his presence, something she hadn't expected to feel.

"First let me say how sorry we are for your loss," the commissioner said.

Well aware that the police commissioner did not

attend crime scenes or make these kinds of calls, Sahara knew he was here solely because of her fame.

"Thank you," she said, and then eyed the detectives. "I assume you're working my mother's case, so can you tell me what you know? Are there any suspects? Does anyone know where my father is?"

Fisher was pushing thirty and wore his light brown hair in a ponytail. He looked enough like Adam Levine of Maroon 5 that they could have been brothers.

Julian was a handsome thirtysomething local, born and raised in the Ninth Ward in New Orleans.

Fisher spoke first. "At this time, we don't have any suspects, and we're waiting on the autopsy report. We have a BOLO out on your father, that means—"

"I know what it means," Sahara said. "Be on the lookout. So are you looking at him as a possible suspect?"

The trio of men looked at each other and then back at her.

"If I may be so bold, you don't seem to be grieving much for your mother's death," Commissioner Murtaugh said.

Sahara crossed her legs and folded her hands in her lap.

"I was not particularly welcome here and have not been home in fifteen years. It's horrible, how she died. But it's not like we were a part of each other's lives."

Fisher frowned. "Short of seeming callous, we'd be lying if we said you weren't a person of interest in this case. You must know that you're their heir. You stand to inherit nearly a million dollars from your mother's death."

This was exactly what Sahara had been waiting for—an accusation based on inheritance. It was so damn easy to blame a family member and close a messy case instead of looking into their business. She stood abruptly.

"Don't be ridiculous. I am the highest paid actress in Hollywood right now. I have ten times a million dollars just in my *checking* account. I own the penthouse in The Magnolia in downtown Hollywood, and according to Forbes, counting investments and endorsements, I'm worth more than five hundred million dollars. So *I* don't mean to sound callous, but you'd look absurd to even pretend to pin this on me over a measly million-dollar inheritance. Just so you know, Brendan is here as my bodyguard for a reason. There have been three attempts already made on my life back home. One woman is dead, having eaten some food meant for me that had been poisoned. The elevator to my penthouse was sabotaged and dropped twenty-five floors. I escaped by a fluke."

Brendan interrupted. "The third attempt was made to her private jet, and there is another body there to add to the count. A mechanic found in a Dumpster. I received a message after we landed that the men I had check it out after we left did find a bomb. Her plane would never have cleared the runway before it exploded."

Lucy gasped. "What? Are you serious! I didn't know that!"

Sahara sighed. "Sorry. I forgot to talk to you about

it. I didn't find out until we had landed, and then there was all the mess about getting through the airport."

"We'll certainly take all that into account, Miss Travis, but we're still obliged to investigate all possible leads, which means I'll have to ask you some questions. Let's start with the circumstances around your leaving New Orleans. Why did you not come home at any point in the last fifteen years?" Fisher asked.

"Because when I graduated high school, my parents gave me an old car and five hundred dollars, and told me they'd done their part to raise me and to leave, so I did."

Murtaugh frowned. "That doesn't sound like the charming couple I knew."

"I guess you had to be me," Sahara said. "Unfortunately, I can't help you find your killer because I know nothing about the last fifteen years of their lives, and I am here only because Leopold is missing and the responsibility of burying her is left to me."

"You call your father by his first name?"

"At their request, yes, and I also called my mother Katarina. Like I said, you had to be me. Is there anything else?"

"Who besides you stands to inherit?"

"No one I know of," Sahara said. "You should talk to their lawyer. If he's still practicing, it's Chappy Farraday."

"We already did. You're the only one mentioned in the will. Do you have extended family?"

Sahara shook her head. "There's no other family that I'm aware of."

The phone rang on the desk and the detectives looked to her, waiting for her to answer it.

"Billie will get it," Sahara said. "Is there anything more?"

"Not at this time," Fisher said. "You'll be staying here for a while, I assume?"

"Unless the killer takes me out, in which case someone will be burying me, too."

"That's not going to happen," Brendan said.

"Then we'll be leaving. Again, my condolences," Murtaugh said.

"Thank you," Sahara said, and rang for Billie, who showed them to the door.

Their footsteps were still audible when Sahara spoke.

"I'm so damn tired I want to crawl in bed and sleep until tomorrow, but I think I'll just go change my clothes. I have a horrible, horrible feeling that front doorbell will be ringing off the wall within a couple of hours."

"Why?" Lucy asked.

"People will be coming to gawk at a movie star with the pretense of paying their respects, and then they will all go home and say, 'She looks prettier on screen than she does in person.'"

"Don't say that," Lucy said. "I'll come up with you. I'll fix your hair and help you dress."

Sahara's shoulders slumped as she gazed at the both of them.

"I know what you're thinking. That I am a cold-hearted bitch for not caring about Katarina being gone, but that could not be further from the truth. It's this house. It's them. This brings back too many ugly memories."

The phone rang again.

Sahara was trying not to cry. She turned to Lucy. "Well, if you're going to help me, then come on. Billie won't be able to put them off much longer."

Brendan had an urge to hug her as they left the library, but he stifled it. Tonight he was going to do some background research on the Travis family. There had to be an answer somewhere in their past that would make sense of what was happening. And he wasn't so sure anymore that what was happening to Sahara had anything to do with her being an actress. It was starting to seem more to do with her being Leopold and Katarina Travis's daughter.

Will Sherman and his work crew finished installing the security system just after the visitors started to arrive. They'd explained the system to both Billie and Sahara, as well as Brendan, showing them how to arm and disarm. At Sahara's instructions, Brendan told them to send the bill to Harold Warner and gave them the address in LA.

Billie set up the formal living room, the one they called the white room, for Sahara to receive the guests, and people began coming and going most of the day. They were all good friends of the Travises and considerably more distraught than she was, but she was cognizant of what was expected and dressed to match the white and gold furnishings, wearing a white strapless sundress with a gold bib necklace that looked like it had been looted from an Egyptian pharaoh's tomb.

She'd thanked Lucy twice for having the foresight to get dressier clothes, even though she'd told her not to. The gold sandals she'd picked out had a strap across the toes and open backs, leaving the healing area of her foot unencumbered. Her long black hair was loose and in a controlled curl around her face. Her lips were a dark, vivid red, the startling contrast she intended to the white-and-gold room.

Brendan had changed into light-colored slacks and a white, short-sleeve shirt hanging loose outside his pants. It accentuated his tan to perfection. She knew there was a pistol at his waist beneath the shirt, but he looked damn good, like he belonged in the islands somewhere, though she wasn't about to tell him.

She wouldn't have to—the women who'd come to pay their respects were mutely telling him how hot he was in a myriad of ways. Sidelong glances, out-right flirting and what seemed like an epidemic of hot flashes. She'd never seen so many women of a certain age fanning themselves at one time in an already air-conditioned room.

Lucy was in the back of the room, a silent witness to this part of the ritual of burying a loved one. Sahara knew she was there—available if needed.

The women were obviously enamored being in the company of such a famous star, but there were a few who'd known her most of her life and kept referring to all the times Katarina and Leopold had taken her out into social situations to insinuate themselves into her personal space.

"Oh, Sahara, darling, do you remember that New Year's Eve when Katarina dressed you up like an angel for her masquerade ball? You sat on a little gold throne and sprinkled gold dust on the dancers as they passed by you."

Sahara remembered being so tired that she'd fallen asleep sitting up, and Katarina had slapped her so hard after everyone left that her lip bled.

"Yes, ma'am. I remember," she said.

"Is it true someone is trying to kill you, too?" another woman asked.

She just nodded. They wanted the gory details, and she wasn't going there.

"That's awful. Just awful. Do you think the man trying to kill you got angry because he failed, and killed poor Katarina out of spite?"

Sahara was appalled that anyone would insinuate it was her fault Katarina was dead and was struggling with a way to answer without screaming at her when Billie came in with a tea trolley of petit fours and cold drinks, left it against the wall and pushed out the trolley that was already empty. It was the third trolley in four hours.

The elegant, blue-haired dowager sitting in a chair nearest to Sahara looked straight at Brendan and lifted her empty glass, then tapped it gently on the arm of her chair.

Sahara flinched.

The bitch. She knows Brendan is not staff.

Without saying a word, Sahara got up and took the glass out of her hand and refilled it from the trolley, then carried it back and put it directly in her hands with a fresh napkin to catch the condensation.

"I didn't intend for you to wait on me, dear. I thought staff would—"

"There is no staff in this room, Mrs. Haley. Just the man keeping me alive and the lady who makes my world a simpler place to be."

Lucy felt a little teary. She hadn't expected that kind of acknowledgment.

Brendan swallowed past a sudden lump in his throat and kept his gaze on the view through the windows. He'd paid little attention to what was being said in the room, but he was touched that once again Sahara had taken offense on his behalf.

The blue-haired dowager smiled, but it never reached her eyes.

"I see… Well, then. I want you to know how much I thought of Katarina. We lunched together at least two or three times a month, and there wasn't a time when your name didn't come up. She was so proud of your accomplishments, as was Leopold."

"Really? I had no idea," Sahara said, and knew if she didn't get a break she was going to come undone.

She glanced up at Lucy, unaware of the desperation on her face, but Lucy saw it.

All of a sudden she was coming toward Sahara from the back of the room in a purposeful stride.

"Sahara, I am so sorry to interrupt, but there's a call for you that you have to take." She gave her phone to

Sahara as if the call was on hold, then she turned to the half-dozen women who'd already been there an hour past proper, and shrugged as if all of this was out of anyone's control. "Ladies, may I be your escort out while Sahara takes her call?"

They all immediately stood as Sahara got up to leave the room.

"Of course. Our sympathies. We'll see you at the service. If I can help, please don't hesitate to call," the blue-haired lady said.

Sahara heard them all and kept smiling and nodding as they gathered up their things.

"My apologies, ladies. Duty calls," she said, and glanced once at Brendan, who followed her out of the room. But instead of going upstairs, she headed straight for the kitchen.

She was trembling and didn't even know it until she stumbled. All of a sudden she was in his arms and the weight of her world was now on his shoulders. She covered her face, trying to stop the tears.

"Just cry, damn it," he said gruffly, and so she did.

Billie saw them coming into the kitchen.

"Is she hurt?"

"No, ma'am. Just had enough."

"This way," Billie said, and led them to four small rooms at the back of the house where she lived. "Put her on the sofa," she said, and pulled aside an afghan as Brendan put her down.

Billie passed her a handful of tissues while Brendan pulled down the window shades.

"Sorry, but it's necessary right now."

Billie brushed the hair from Sahara's forehead and then leaned over and kissed the side of her cheek.

"I am so sorry, my sweet baby. I'm sorry I let Leopold ever have you. I thought I was doing the right thing by knowing of the luxury in which you would live while I was close by to care for you, but I was wrong, and I'm sorry that you've had to live the past fifteen years alone. I should have been a stronger woman for you. For my girl."

Brendan turned away. The more he was around Sahara Travis, the more he saw the woman beneath the star. The hell of it was, he was attracted to her in a way he'd never been to a client before. She was a constant surprise, smart as a whip, sexy as hell, and there was a huge part of her that broke his heart.

Sahara scooted over to make room for Billie and then wrapped her arms around her mother's neck and sobbed.

Lucy reclaimed her phone, but the phone calls to the house continued up until the dinner hour. She took down all the names and messages and in turn thanked them on behalf of Miss Travis, and then in proper Southern fashion, at the dinner hour the calls immediately ceased. In the South, there was, after all, a time and a place for everything and this was no exception.

Dinner was cooking at the Travis mansion, and the four people in residence were all in the kitchen behind curtained windows helping with the preparation.

Sahara was back in shorts and a T-shirt, her eyes still a little red from crying, but barefoot without the bandage and focused on making a pot of Cajun rice. Lucy was setting the table, and Billie was stirring a pot of gumbo that had been cooking all afternoon. Even Brendan had been given a task and was holding his own as a bartender, making predinner martinis for the cooks. It was one of his easier gigs.

Finally, Billie announced that dinner was served and insisted they sit. She brought the plates of food to the table, still steaming, and then finally her own.

"It is a blessing to have all of you here with me," Billie said. "Enjoy."

And so they did, eating with thanks for the company and the food. Nothing was said about the murder or why Sahara had come home, until they were beginning to clean up.

"I'm not entertaining company again," Sahara said. "They can call me whatever they choose…uppity, rude, unfeeling, but it's their fault. I have never been asked so many rude questions at once in my life. I don't have to do it, so I won't."

"Works for me," Lucy said.

"I'm on your side," Brendan said. "You don't know how close I came to searching every woman who paid a call. I was already going to warn you that if the procession continued, that's what was going to happen."

Billie grinned. "I would have loved to see that happen."

Sahara shook her head. "It would have been the height of rudeness and talked about for years."

Brendan grinned as Sahara continued.

"Anyway, Lucy, whoever calls wanting to come over

tomorrow, the answer is no. Tell them I've taken to my bed out of grief, or else I'm busy organizing the funeral service—which is the truth. It's not a job I want, but the only way I'd get out of this is if Leopold shows up to do it, and that's something I don't want to face."

Billie furrowed her brow. "I can't imagine what's happened to him. He would never leave Katarina behind like this. It's not like him at all."

"Has there been a ransom call? Anything to suggest he was kidnapped?" Brendan asked.

Sahara's eyes widened. "I'd never thought of that."

"The police also asked that, but so far the answer is no," Billie said.

There were a few moments of silence.

"So, what's on the agenda for tomorrow?" Lucy asked.

"Figure out what to do with Katarina. There's a family mausoleum, so I know where she'll be interred. I guess I'll have to speak to whoever is pastor now at their church."

"We'll need to get the grounds done," Billie added. "I'll contact the landscaper we use."

"What about that crime scene tape?" Sahara asked.

"I'd guess the whole scene has been released by now, but I'll find out if it can be removed before I call the landscapers," Billie said.

Lucy had been rudely staring at Brendan through most of dinner when she suddenly cried out.

"I just now figured out why you looked familiar when we met. You look like Channing Tatum…older and a whole lot taller, but there's something about the shape of your face that reminds me of him."

"Since I'm older, it would be a fairer assessment to say he looks like me," Brendan said.

Lucy grinned. "I guess you're right."

Sahara had first noticed that, too, but no longer thought about it. Brendan was himself and like no one else she'd ever known.

"Does anyone want dessert?" Billie asked.

"Not me. Not tonight," Sahara said.

"I'm good," Brendan said.

"No, thank you," Lucy said.

"Then I'll just make some coffee while I clean up. It will be done soon, and if anyone wants a cup, you'll know where it is."

A clock in the library began striking the hour. Ten chimes. Ten o'clock.

Sahara was too wired to watch television, but when she began to help clean up, Billie ran them all out of the kitchen.

"This is my world. Out you go…all of you."

Lucy sighed. "Sahara, if you won't be needing me anymore, I think I'll go to bed. I'm exhausted."

Sahara turned and hugged her.

"What's that for?" Lucy asked.

"For saving me from the blue-haired bitch today."

"Oh, right," Lucy said, and grinned.

"Sleep well," Sahara said.

"Thanks," Lucy said, then pulled out her phone and began checking her messages as she walked away.

Sahara glanced at Brendan, suddenly wishing for a

change of scenery. If only they were both at a cocktail party where they could flirt all night and wind up together in bed. Maybe it wasn't a bad idea...

"So, Mr. McQueen," she began with a smile, "I know where the music is playing on Beale Street."

"Maybe another time," Brendan said.

She shrugged, knowing it was impossible—knowing she'd said it in jest.

"Then I'm going to head upstairs and take myself a long hot bubble bath, and I'm not coming out until the ends of my fingers are all puckered up and my bones have melted away."

He saw the flash in her eyes and the way she'd arched her back just a little as she turned toward the stairs. That was a blow-to-the-gut come-on, and she'd done it on purpose. She just wanted to play, but sex wasn't a game to him.

He followed her up, making sure to keep his distance, but keep her in sight. Right now, she felt caged up and restless, and he didn't trust her any farther than he could throw her.

Sahara wanted him, but she already knew he wasn't the messing-around kind. She rolled her eyes at what she'd just said, chiding herself for teasing him. She wasn't like that and she didn't want him thinking it, either. She hit the door with the flat of her hand and disappeared inside.

Brendan walked in a few minutes behind her to give her some privacy, but he still caught a glimpse of one bare butt cheek and a long bare leg as she disappeared into the bathroom. Every stitch of clothes she'd had on was on the floor by the bed.

He took a deep breath and shoved a hand through his hair.

"Son of a bitch," he muttered, and stretched out on his bed, turned on the TV and turned up the volume.

He didn't want to hear the water running. He didn't want to hear the silence. He didn't want to think about that long sleek body slick with bubbles and growing more and more mellow from the heat, so he got up and ran downstairs to let Billie know he was setting the security alarm.

As instructed, Will Sherman and his crew had installed a security panel in the foyer and one in the hall upstairs. Brendan ran back upstairs and set it from the hall, adding one more way to keep her safe.

Sahara fell asleep on her belly with one arm hanging off the side of the bed. Her voluptuous mouth was puckered slightly, as if waiting for a kiss.

Brendan could have watched her like that all night, but instead he locked their bedroom door, then took his gun to the bathroom with him while he showered. Normally, he slept in the nude, but when on the job, he always slept in a pair of gym shorts.

He left the door open as he showered and shaved so he could hear any movement in the adjoining room, and left the night-light on in the bathroom when he came out. The last thing he did was put his gun beside his pillow before he turned out the lights.

Sahara was on her side now, rolled up as tight as she could be, with the covers pulled up beneath her chin.

He frowned. That was too reminiscent of the way a frightened child slept. He'd seen it too many times, in too many war-torn countries. He couldn't help but wonder if being back here had resurrected old ghosts. He couldn't do anything about unsettled spirits, but he could make sure no living, breathing people messed with her again.

Eight

The next morning Brendan was dressed and watching the traffic passing by outside the bedroom windows when Sahara woke. The first thing she saw was his silhouette against the window, and she lay there quietly, wondering what it would be like to have a man like him to love.

Then he turned around and caught her staring.

"Good morning," he said.

"Good morning to you, too," she said. "What's the weather look like today?"

"It's supposed to rain."

She threw back the covers, and the moment she got up, he pulled the shades.

"I'm going to dress, and then we can go down to breakfast," she said.

"Good. I'm hungry, but I'll wait out in the hall," he said. "Just stay away from the windows."

"I will," she said, and headed for the bathroom as he stepped outside.

She hurried, knowing he was waiting for her.

Lucy was already in the kitchen with Billie and carrying butter and syrup to the table as they walked into the room.

"Waffles! She's making waffles," Lucy crowed, as she set the condiments on the kitchen table and went back for silverware.

"Good morning, Mama," Sahara said, as she walked up behind Billie and kissed her on the cheek.

Billie beamed. "Good morning, my darling. I made your favorite breakfast."

"I see that," Sahara said. "I don't suppose there are strawberries on the premises."

"I made strawberry compote with some frozen ones. You will like it."

Sahara did a little twirl and then hugged her.

Brendan grinned. He was trying not to be enchanted by this woman, but it was becoming more and more difficult. Who danced with delight at strawberry compote?

"Go sit," Billie said. "I have enough in the warming oven to start with."

"What about you?"

"No. Not this morning. I am the waffle maker today. They aren't good cold and you know it, so please begin. I want you to enjoy."

Brendan was filling coffee cups when Sahara sat down at the table.

"Thank you! You're as handy as a pocket on a shirt," she said.

He grinned. "That's what my grandpa used to tell me."

She was intrigued that she and his grandfather shared something so random.

"Really?"

"Really," he said.

Billie brought the warming tray stacked with hot, crispy waffles, then came back with a small bowl of strawberry compote and a ladle for dipping.

While Brendan and Lucy opted for butter and syrup, Sahara ladled hot strawberry compote onto hers. The first bite brought back a flood of memories from her childhood. This was always her birthday breakfast.

The silence that fell around the table was a testament to the good food, and when the last waffle came off the waffle iron, Billie put it on her plate and slipped into the chair beside her girl.

Sahara scooted the butter and syrup toward Billie and then got up and refilled coffee cups for everyone.

"I should have done that. I'm sorry," Lucy said.

"Ridiculous! You're not a waitress, and for what it's worth, this is my home, which makes you my guest."

Brendan's phone rang as he was carrying his dirty dishes to the sink.

"Hello...Yes, she's right here. Just a second." He handed his phone to Sahara. "It's Harold, for you."

"Good morning, Harold. What's up?"

"Just checking in," he said. "I got you out of the contract with no problems. In fact, the investors were grateful for your consideration of the time schedule and the safety of the others and intend to mention you in the credits in some way."

"That's nice," Sahara said. "Especially nice that they aren't angry. It's never good to aggravate investors."

"Absolutely," Harold said. "Also…just wanted you to know that the repairs have begun on the elevator to the penthouse and Adam said to tell you hello, and he misses your smile."

Sahara smiled as she leaned against the counter.

"That's so sweet of him."

Brendan wondered who was sweet and what he'd done to put a smile on her face like that.

"Oh, Harold…one other thing. As soon as the elevator has been repaired, would you please get my cleaning service into the apartment and have them clean it thoroughly? Last time I saw it, there was a gray cloud of dust and smoke in every room."

"I'll get right on that," Harold said. "Anything else? How are things going there? Any news on what happened to your mother?"

"No updates here. What about the police in LA? Do they have any leads on who was after me?"

"All I know is what Detective Shaw told me. They have security footage from The Magnolia of the so-called repairman who likely placed the bomb and have cleared the woman who let him sign in. They have footage of the same man at the airport dumping a body in a Dumpster, then carrying a package into the jet and coming out without it."

"Do they know who it is?"

"No. It's the same man, but the fingerprints they recovered aren't in the system, so that doesn't help."

She relayed this information to Brendan, who

reached out to take the phone from her. "Harold, it's Brendan. Ask the police to send copies of the security footage to my email. Got a pen?"

"Yes, go ahead," Harold said, and wrote it down. "I'll call them as soon as we're done. Ask Sahara if there's anything else she needs me to do."

"Harold wants to know if there's anything else you want him to do."

She nodded, so he handed back the phone.

"Harold, there is one more thing. I want to sell the penthouse. There's no way I could live there now."

"I thought you might say that. Not to worry. I'll get a Realtor on it as soon as everything has been cleaned and repaired. Do you know what you want for it?"

"Get it appraised, see what the Realtor thinks, and then I'll make a decision."

"Can do. Listen. I'm so sorry for all that's happening. If there's anything else I can do for you, just let me know."

"Oh, my phone! It was in the hall outside my apartment. I'm going to assume when it and my purse are found, they'll put them in the penthouse, so if you can find them and FedEx them to me, I would so appreciate that."

"You could just buy a new phone, you know," Harold said.

"That one has all my contacts. I don't want to start over unless I have to."

"Okay. I'll see what I can do. Let's hope that dust didn't screw it up."

"Don't say that," Sahara said.

"Stay safe. I'll be in touch," Harold said.

"Thanks," she said, and disconnected, then gave Brendan the phone.

"Everything okay?" he asked.

She nodded.

He didn't want to freak her out, but this was her life and she had to know everything he did.

"There's one thing I haven't heard mentioned, although I'm sure the police in both locations have already considered it."

"What's that?" Sahara asked.

"Based on the evidence, there's either more than one perp, or he's hiring out his hits."

Sahara frowned. "Why do you think that?"

"Because Katarina was murdered before sunrise on the same day that your elevator fell. And…she was likely killed about the same time you got on the elevator. So that's one body in New Orleans. Almost one in Los Angeles. At the same time."

"Well, shit," Sahara said, and sat down with a thump.

Brendan empathized. "Indeed," he said.

Lucy was obviously horrified. The shock on her face said it all.

"This makes no sense, and, to my embarrassment, I have just discovered I have syrup on my blouse. I must have been wolfing that wonderful waffle down. I'm going to go change. I'll be right back."

"No hurry," Sahara said. "We have all day to figure out what to do about Katarina's memorial service."

Lucy left the kitchen just as the phone rang.

"That's the landline," Billie said. "I'll get it."

She took the call on the phone in the kitchen. "Travis residence...Yes, it's all right. See you soon."

She disconnected. "And so it begins," she said.

"What?" Sahara asked.

"Floral deliveries. The florist asked if it was too early to deliver, and that he had multiple arrangements."

"I never even thought of flowers," Sahara said. "Why will they be bringing all of them here?"

"Because Katarina's body is in the morgue, so there's no funeral home handling the body, and no viewing room to hold the flowers."

"Oh. Then where should we put them?" Sahara asked.

"We'll take off the cards, and then I guess just put the arrangements wherever there's a place for them to be."

"Okay," Sahara said. "I'll get a tea cart and put it in the foyer. We'll move them that way," she said.

"Show me where the carts are. I'll move them for you," Brendan said.

"Sahara knows where they are," Billie said. "Get to it. They'll be here before we know it. And I need to unlock the front gate so I can buzz them in and out."

"Why don't you just leave it open?" Sahara asked.

Billie and Brendan both looked at her as if she'd just lost her mind.

"Because the famous actress Sahara Travis is in this house, and there are any number of fans who would happily trot up to this door and ring the bell on the off chance you might answer it. Even the killer," Brendan said.

Her expression blanked. "I can't believe I forgot. Coming back here has clearly rattled me," she said softly. "Follow me, Brendan. We'll get this set up before I have to go hide."

A few minutes later the tea carts were ready and a guest book had been placed on the hall table just as Sahara heard the buzzer signaling a car at the gates.

"Billie's got this," she said. "Time for me to disappear."

"Where do you want to go?" Brendan asked.

She shrugged and walked away as Billie came down the hall toward the front door.

Billie saw the dejected expression on her daughter's face, but there was nothing to be done about it.

Brendan followed her into the library. He was a little surprised when she headed for the wet bar, but then relaxed when he saw her go for a cold soda from the mini-fridge.

"There's Coke, Pepsi and ginger ale. Want one?"

"Not right now, but thank you."

She unscrewed the cap on her ginger ale, added some ice to a glass and poured in the soda, then wrinkled her nose as she took her first sip.

"I like the fizz. It always tickles my nose," she said, took a second sip and then carried the glass and the rest of the ginger ale to a chair.

"Talk to me, Brendan. Tell me about Wyoming. I met John. Tell me about your other brothers... Carson and Michael, right?"

"Well, I don't remember the details when John was born, because there's only three years' difference in our ages, but I was five when Mom brought Carson home from the hospital. I was a little worried that he would grow up and mess with my stuff like John was beginning to do, and I was eight when she came home with Michael. That's when I locked my bedroom door and wouldn't come out."

Sahara laughed.

Brendan moved toward the windows, checking to make sure there was no one on the grounds who didn't belong, but Sahara was intrigued by his happy family. She wanted to know more.

"Are you the only one who was in the military?"

He nodded.

"Why did you go?" she asked.

"It seemed like a good idea at the time," he said.

She sat there a minute watching his smile fade and suddenly jumped to her feet.

"It was a girl, wasn't it? What did she do, break your heart?"

He shrugged, willing to spill his guts if it helped her pass some time.

"We had a fight. She slept with my best friend to get back at me. I realized my choice in girlfriends and best friends left a lot to be desired, so I decided they deserved each other and joined the army. Best thing I ever did."

Sahara immediately regretted what she'd said.

"I'm sorry, Brendan. That was an appalling thing

to happen to anyone, and I apologize for making a joke about it."

Her hand was cold against his skin from holding the glass. Her eyes were shimmering in sympathy.

"Hey, no harm, no foul. That was years and years ago. Truth is, they both did me a favor or I might never have left Wyoming."

"You ran away from home and so did I. How about that? Something we actually have in common," she said, and flopped back down in her chair.

"Hard to believe," he said, his eyes narrowing as he watched a van coming through the gates.

"What do you see?" she asked.

"A florist's van."

She toed the carpet beneath the chair while condensation ran from the glass onto the coaster.

"What's the name on the side?"

"Beloit Blooms. Marcus Beloit, owner-designer."

She jumped up.

"Marcus? I went to school with a Marcus Beloit. I want to go see if it's him."

"I doubt the owner will be doing delivery," Brendan argued.

"I still want to see. We were friends. I just want to check."

"Then lead the way," he said.

Sahara lengthened her stride as she headed for the foyer, anxious to get there before the deliveries were finished.

Billie was putting one arrangement on a tea cart while the deliveryman went back for more.

"Who delivered these?" Sahara asked.

"Beloit Blooms."

"Was it Marcus?"

Billie smiled. "Yes, do you remember him?"

"Yes, yes," Sahara said, and when she saw a blond-haired man wearing white shorts and a pink print shirt coming back up the steps with a large potted fern, she started to go out to meet him.

"Wait inside," Brendan cautioned.

"Oh, right," Sahara said, and smiled and waved from the shadows of the foyer. "Marcus!"

A huge smile spread across his face.

"Sahara, darling! Let me put this down," he said, as he handed the second arrangement to Billie.

He started to lean in and kiss her when Brendan thrust his arm between them and brought Marcus Beloit to a halt.

Marcus gave him the once-over. "Oooh, girl! Who do we have here? He is absolutely gorgeous."

"He's my bodyguard," Sahara said. "It's okay, Brendan. We went to school together. He's a friend."

Brendan dropped his arm but didn't relinquish his stance. She could hug whoever the hell she wanted, but he wasn't yielding space to make it easy.

Marcus gave Brendan a big smile.

"I didn't mind a bit," Marcus said, and winked at the bodyguard, who calmly ignored the gesture.

"We need to visit and catch up," Sahara said. "Can you come to dinner tonight? Say around seven o'clock?"

"Why, I'd love to, honey, but let me first say, I am so sorry about your mother. It's just terrible what happened to her, and I want you to know we're all praying for you and for a resolution to this tragedy."

"Thank you," she said.

"I'd better get back to the shop. My deliveryman is out sick today, which is why I'm pulling double duty. So, I guess I'll see you later." Then he eyed Brendan again. "Will he be dining with us?"

Sahara laughed. "Yes, and so will Lucy, my personal assistant."

"What fun!" He pointed up the hall behind them. "Is that your Lucy?"

Sahara turned around. "Yes, that's Lucy Benton. Lucy, this is Marcus Beloit, an old friend from school. He'll be joining us for dinner tonight."

Lucy nodded politely. "Nice to meet you."

"Absolutely! See you at seven o'clock if not before. There may be other orders for delivery here, and if so, I'll be back," Marcus said, then he hurried down the steps and leaped into the van before driving away.

Sahara grinned at Brendan. "You sure caught his eye."

He was completely unperturbed. "Yeah, it happens a lot. It's the muscles."

She laughed as they closed the door and turned to Billie, who was at the tea carts, pulling cards from the flowers and making note of who they were from and what they'd sent.

"So, one more for dinner tonight?"

Sahara grinned. "Yes, please."

"Do you have a preference for what is served?"

"Something yummy."

"Then I say pecan-crusted sea bass, cheese grits, braised artichoke hearts and, for dessert, Ponchatoula strawberry shortcake with Chantilly cream," Billie said.

When Brendan's stomach growled out loud, everyone laughed.

"I second McQueen's vote," Sahara said, "but I also think it might be time to stir up a little lunch. Lucy can man the door and pull the cards from deliveries until it's ready, and Brendan and I will find somewhere to put all these flowers."

Billie showed Lucy how she was tracking the deliveries, then headed for the kitchen while Sahara got a tea cart loaded with flowers and started to push it up the hall.

"Let me check them first," Brendan said.

"Really? Flowers? For what?" Sahara asked.

"All kinds of things," he said, and methodically went through everything that had already been delivered. As soon as they'd been declared "clean," she pushed the cart toward the table in the middle of the foyer, set the largest arrangement on it, while Brendan picked up two large ferns and set them on marble pedestals on either side of the doorway into the formal dining room.

He saw movement through the windows. Three men were moving around the garden, pulling up the crime scene tape.

"Hey, do you know who those people are?" he asked.

Sahara set a flower arrangement on the sideboard inside the room in case Billie wanted to use it for dinner tonight.

"Probably the grounds crew. Billie was going to call them, remember?"

Brendan hadn't moved. "Where's Billie?"

"I'm right here," Billie said, as she entered the room.

"Who are the people outside?" Brendan asked.

"Oh, that's Sutton and his work crew. They do the landscaping here."

Sahara looked closer. "Miss Barbara's son, Sutton?" Sahara asked.

"Yes. He owns Davidson Landscaping. Leopold gave him money to get started about seven or eight years ago."

"Who's Sutton?" Brendan asked.

"Miss Barbara worked here with Billie for a time," Sahara explained. "Sutton is her son. We used to play together as kids."

"First the florist, now the gardener. This is turning into reunion week," Brendan said.

"Well, they still live here. I'm the one who came home," she snapped.

Brendan pulled her away from the window.

"I'm not trying to keep you from seeing old friends, but I can't make this any clearer. The killers couldn't get to you in Hollywood, so they lured you to a place that will make you easier to get to. You're vulnerable here. Like it or not, you're a sitting duck. We don't know who's behind these attacks, and we don't know why, which gives them a very big edge. Understand?"

He was so close to her face she could see her own reflection in his eyes and the muscle jerking at the corner of his mouth.

She shrugged out of his grasp. "I told you Marcus was a friend, and I'm telling you so was Sutton when we were children. If you don't like the answers I give you, then stop asking questions," she snapped.

Billie frowned. "Stop it, both of you. Settle this peacefully now or go somewhere else to argue. I do not want this room filled with negative energy when we're going to be dining in here tonight."

Brendan stepped back.

Sahara threw up her arms and stomped out of the room, but he followed close behind.

Billie's eyes narrowed as she watched them walking away, then she began getting out the good china and silver to set the table, muttering to herself as she worked.

"All that fussing. That's nothing but sexual tension. They need to get all that over with before they really lose it on each other. That's what I think. Yes, I do."

Sahara didn't know why she was mad. She knew he was right. She'd been careless again. He was doing the job Harold was paying him to do. And then the moment she thought that, it hit her. That was what was bugging her. He wasn't with her because he liked her, even though it sometimes felt like he did. She was just another job to him. He didn't care, so why should she?

She stopped in the middle of the hall and turned around so fast Brendan nearly stumbled over her.

"Truce?" she asked, and held out her hand.

That was the last damn thing he had expected.

"Truce," he said.

"We have to shake on it," she said.

His fingers curled around her hand, engulfing it. She tightened her grip and pumped his hand once and then turned him loose.

"Done," she said. "My apology. I'm not normally a bitch. It's coming back to this place that's making me crazy. Forgive me?"

He sighed. "I work for you. I'm sorry if I upset you, but I take my job seriously. I have never lost a client, and I would sincerely appreciate any help you can give me to ensure you don't become the first. Understand?"

"Understood."

The doorbell rang.

"More flowers."

"Do you want to go see them?" he asked.

"No. I think I should avoid silhouetting myself in any more doorways."

She was serious, and he suddenly wanted to kiss her. *Crap, McQueen. Where did that come from? She's off-limits, and you know it.*

"I need to make some phone calls. Want to go back to our room?"

"After you," he said, and then heard Lucy shouting.

"Sahara! Wait!"

Lucy came toward her carrying a giant arrangement of flowers in a large ceramic pot.

"It won't fit on the tea carts. Where would you like me to put this one?"

Sahara eyed the colorful arrangement.

"It can go in my room," she said, then looked at McQueen. "If he says so."

Brendan took it out of her hands.

"I'll carry it," he said, and followed her up the stairs while Lucy went back to man the deliveries.

"Where do you want it?" Brendan asked, as they reached the bedroom.

"Oh, on the table behind the little love seat."

He set it down, gave it a cursory inspection and then moved to the windows. Just traffic on the street. But when he turned around to see what Sahara was doing, he immediately reached for his gun.

"Sahara, don't move!"

She saw the gun in his hand and froze, terrified.

He fired.

The bullet went past her ear, through the ceramic pot and into the wall behind them.

Water exploded everywhere, soaking her hair and clothes. Flowers were in her lap and on her shoulders when he yanked her to her feet and into his arms. The moment he had her against his chest, he fired once more.

Sahara threw her arms around his waist.

Lucy came running into the room with Billie not far behind her.

"What the hell happened?" Lucy cried.

Billie saw it first and made the sign of the cross and then met McQueen's gaze.

"She is okay? It did not bite her?"

"No, it didn't bite her," Brendan said.

Sahara pushed out of his arms and turned around.

"What are you talking about?"

Billie pointed at what was left of the snake on the back of the sofa.

"Cottonmouth. Where in God's name did it come from?" she cried.

"Out of those flowers," Brendan said.

Sahara grabbed his wrist as her knees started to buckle.

"I've got you," he said, and put an arm around her waist to steady her. "Lucy! Who delivered those flowers?"

Lucy was already a crying mess. "I don't know! The doorbell rang. The flowers were on the threshold and the van was already driving away. It was a gray van. Maybe it'll be on the security footage?"

"Good call. It should be," Brendan said. "Bring me the card that came with these. Wait! No. Get a plastic bag first and carefully slide it inside. No more finger-prints than necessary."

"Yes, yes, I'll be right back," Lucy said, and rushed out of the room.

Billie was pulling flower petals from Sahara's hair.

"Brendan, she needs a warm shower and dry clothes."

"Don't move anything in here," he said. "The cops are going to need to see it."

Billie glanced at Sahara again.

"Do you need me?" she asked Brendan.

"No, ma'am. I'll help her."

"Then I'm going down to check the flowers still on the tea carts again. We don't need any more surprises."

"The police are coming?" Sahara asked, as her mother hurried away.

"Yes. You just survived another attempt on your life, and they need to know about it."

"Need to know about it," she echoed.

He put his hand in the middle of her back. She was clearly in shock.

"Can you walk?"

She nodded but wouldn't turn loose of him as he walked her into the bathroom. He was already calling the New Orleans PD when she sat down on the closed lid of the toilet and started taking off her shoes.

The call went through and began to ring.

"New Orleans PD. How may I direct your call?"

"Homicide."

"One moment, please."

"Homicide, Detective Wells."

"This is Brendan McQueen. There's been another attempt on Sahara Travis's life at her family home. Notify Detective Julian or Detective Fisher. They're investigating her mother's recent murder."

When he turned around, Sahara was standing in her underwear, shaking from head to toe.

"Will a warm shower hurt your foot?" he asked.

She shook her head, so he turned on the shower and adjusted the water. When he turned around again, she was naked, and the look on her face was so broken he was almost afraid to touch her.

"Easy does it," he said, and held her hand as she stepped into the shower. "There's shampoo on the bench," he said. "Are you going to be all right?"

"Yes. Thank you."

"I'll be outside. Call if you need me," he said, and walked out.

Nine

The room was empty, but it wouldn't be empty long. This was going beyond bodyguard duty, but she would need to be dressed before she came out of the bathroom. He gathered up underwear and a bra from her dresser, then headed for the closet, where he picked out a pair of slacks and a blouse, then took all of it into the bathroom. He hung the clothes on the rod on the back of the door and put the underwear on the counter.

The shower glass was fogged over now. All he could see were faint glimpses of an arm, the tender curve of her lower back and the slope of a shoulder. But she was upright and washing her hair, and that was a good sign.

He stepped back out and took a stance outside the bathroom door. He was still there when Lucy returned with the card from the flowers in a plastic bag.

"It doesn't have a business name on it," she said. "I should have noticed that. It's my fault."

Brendan shook his head. "I'm the one who carried

the damn pot up the stairs and somehow missed a snake hiding in it. It's more my fault than yours."

He turned the bag over to read the message.

Our sympathies,
The class of 2002

"That's the year she graduated high school," Lucy said.

"That leaves a lot of suspects to wade through. The police are on the way. They're going to ask you the same stuff I did. Tell them everything you remember. Even the tiniest of details."

"Yes, yes, I will," she said. "Where should I wait?"

"Front door. Billie's still going to need help. They can come get you when they want to talk. As for accepting any more flowers into the house, that's not going to happen. Tell the florists if more come, to take them back and hold them for delivery to a funeral home."

"Yes, okay," Lucy said, and hurried out.

He could still hear the water running.

He peeked back inside and saw her sitting on the bench, unmoving.

"Sahara."

She jumped.

"Are you finished?"

"Yes."

"Then turn off the water and get dressed. Police are going to be here soon, and they'll want to talk to you."

"Yes, okay," she said.

He waited until the water went off before he closed the door. After that he heard drawers opening and closing, a hair dryer, then a few quiet moments and guessed she was dressing.

She came out dressed, face devoid of makeup, hair down and barefoot.

"There's glass all over the floor. Wait while I get your house shoes," he said, and ran back to the closet, grabbing a pair of cloth slippers.

She stepped into them and then stepped back behind him, leaning against the bathroom door for stability.

"You can sit down on the bed," he said.

She looked at the bed. Her voice started to shake.

"What if there's another snake? What if it crawled out under the bed?"

"There wasn't time," Brendan said. "I set the flowers down, turned my back on you for less than ten seconds and then turned back around, and the one wasn't all the way out of the water, even then."

Her dark eyes widened, thinking about that moment when he'd told her not to move. She had obeyed without question because she trusted him, and if he said there wasn't another, then she needed to trust that, too.

"You're sure?"

He slid his hand beneath her hair and cupped the back of her neck.

"I'm sure."

She took a deep breath, crawled up into the middle of the bed and crossed her legs.

"I was in shock. I'm sorry I stripped in front of you."

"I'm not," he said.

She blinked, then glanced up.

"A work of art is meant to be appreciated…in the most innocent of ways, of course," he said.

A flush spread up her neck onto her cheeks.

"You are so full of shit, Brendan McQueen."

"There is always that possibility," he said, smirking.

And then the police walked in.

Detective Julian took one look at the mess.

"What in the name of—"

Brendan pointed to the headless black snake lying among the shattered spears of purple gladiola.

"Cottonmouth. Came out of the water the flowers were in. I shot it just before it reached her shoulder. The flowers were brought here in a gray van. No name on the vehicle. Here's the card. Billie can show you security footage." He handed the plastic bag to Detective Julian. "Lucy Benton's fingerprints will be on it because she was the one pulling cards as the arrangements came into the house. I had her put the card in this bag. I doubt there will be other prints, but we could get lucky."

"What makes you think this was intentional?" Detective Fisher asked. "Snakes are pretty common around here."

"Obviously, so are killers," Sahara snapped.

Fisher had the grace to look embarrassed.

"I just meant—"

Sahara swung her legs off the bed and stood up.

"He doesn't need to talk to me. I'm going down to the kitchen with Billie."

"Then that's where I go, too," Brendan said. "If you want a statement, you know where to find us," he said, scooping Sahara up in his arms and carrying her over the broken glass before putting her down at the doorway and leaving the police to do as they pleased.

They walked without talking. The last thing she expected was her word to be doubted again. How had her world gone so wrong, so fast?

When the echo of the doorbell rang again, she stopped in a hallway, her hands doubled into fists, her eyes blurry with unshed tears.

"Damn it! Why is this happening? How many times can I cheat death and get away with it? I don't want to die!"

He saw the tears and her hands doubled up into fists, and took her by the shoulders.

"As many times as it takes. I already told you I won't let anything happen to you, and I meant it."

She covered her face.

He put his arms around her.

"You have what it takes, lady. Don't quit on yourself now."

Sahara could have stayed in his arms for the rest of her life and never moved again, but he was right. Quitting was not a choice.

"Sorry. Momentary weakness."

She turned him loose and walked away.

He was shocked at how empty his arms felt without her and lengthened his stride to catch up. They entered the kitchen in tandem.

Billie was at the sink, but the kitchen was overflowing with flowers…on the floor, on the counters, even on the floor of the adjoining utility room.

"The flowers are going to keep coming unless someone stops them," she said.

Sahara paused. "We already told Lucy to refuse any more deliveries, but I can do better than that," she said. "Do you still have a phone book around?"

"Of course I do. I don't hold with all that computer business replacing what already works," Billie said. "Last drawer on the left beneath the phone."

Sahara found the phone book and took it and the portable phone to the kitchen table. She went straight to the Yellow Pages to search for local television stations and then called the first one. As soon as the call was answered, she identified herself and asked to speak to the station manager.

Once he answered, she began explaining about what had happened with the flower delivery and that it was linked to the attacks on her life.

"My dear Miss Travis, that is appalling, but exactly why are you calling?"

"Yes, sir, it was horrifying. The reason I'm calling is to ask if you would please help me notify the community that, due to the recent attacks on my life, the Travis family can no longer accept visitors or flowers at the home, and donations made to their favorite charity in Katarina Travis's memory would be appreciated instead."

"We can certainly do that and gladly. What would be even better, though, was if we had a film clip from you stating the urgency. It would come across so much better. Would you be willing to let us come there and film that?"

"Yes, send the crew. I'll do the piece. You can air it first, and then if you'll share it with the other local stations, that would be so helpful."

"Certainly. We can do that."

"Wonderful."

She disconnected and then looked up. "Done. A film crew will be here within the hour."

Billie was a little impressed by how easy she'd made that happen.

"How did you do that?"

Sahara shrugged. "This is when being a famous movie star pays off."

Brendan tugged at a stray curl against her cheek.

"I don't suppose you went to school with any of the film crew, too?"

She threw a pot holder at him.

The film crew was all but strip-searched before they were allowed to enter, then led into the library, where they set up to film the announcement. Sahara said what she needed to say, and the crew began wrapping up when Lucy left the room to get dressed for dinner.

However, Sahara was still in character as the bereaved daughter.

"I can't thank you enough for helping me get the word out during such a difficult time," she said.

The journalist was all smiles, imagining the scoop this was going to be.

"Of course, Miss Travis. We're happy to help, even in this small way. I can't imagine the stress of what you've been going through, then your mother, and now this. I fear the world is becoming an ugly place."

"Indeed," Sahara said, and then walked all the way to the door with them before stepping aside to let Brendan see them out.

He shut the door, turned around and gave her a thumbs-up.

She shuddered. The smile she'd worn just seconds ago was gone.

"I need a drink."

"Yes, ma'am," Brendan said, and followed her back into the library.

This time she skipped the mini-fridge with soft drinks and poured herself a whiskey, neat.

"Want one?" she asked.

"I don't drink on the job," he said.

She looked at him through tears and then laughed and poured herself another shot.

"Right. I keep forgetting *I am* the job," she retorted, and downed the shot as fast as she had the first one. "That's better. My dinner guest should be arriving soon. Where's Lucy?"

"Getting dressed, remember?"

Sahara glanced in a mirror long enough to straighten the neckline of her little black dress, then eyed Brendan, who was standing behind her.

"You're looking nice tonight. I like the blue shirt. It's a good look against your tan."

"Not a tan, and thank you."

Her eyes widened as she slowly turned around to face him.

"You're that color all over? Not even a spray tan?"

"Not even."

"Italian? Spanish?"

"My grandmother is Lakota, from North Dakota."

"Ah…that would explain it, and lucky you. I can't tan. Just this freakishly white skin. The kids used to call me white bread."

"Did it upset you?"

She shrugged. "I had so much crap going on at home that school was an escape. Even when it was a drag, it was better."

"Do you have any good memories from this place?" he asked.

"Just Billie. Let's go see if we can sneak a taste of something. I'm starving."

He watched her wipe away tears as casually as she pushed the hair from her eyes. He couldn't help but stare at the lithe perfection of her body beneath that bit of black fabric as she turned away. He'd already seen her without a stitch of clothing. So far, she had yet to wear anything that came close to the beauty of that sight.

They watched the six o'clock news, saw Sahara's piece being aired, then talked about the flowers all over the kitchen and decided there was nothing to do but set them out in the garden and let them die a natural death.

* * *

Bubba heard the news anchor talking about a failed attack on Sahara Travis's life on the six o'clock news. To add insult to injury, there was a clip of her announcing an end to accepting flower deliveries. He roared in frustration and threw a full glass of sweet iced tea against the wall.

"Son of a bitch, this is getting ridiculous! Does she have a straight line to God Almighty keeping her alive? To hell with subtlety. What the fuck did I do with that hunting rifle?" Then he pivoted sharply, slapping the sides of his legs with his fists. "Well, shit. I think I pawned it. It's just as well. I'm a terrible shot."

He eyed the tea soaking into the area rug and headed for the utility room to get a mop. He was still cleaning when he thought of Harley Fish. Harley hunted gators for a living and claimed he would kill anything or anyone if the money was right.

Maybe it was time to give him a call…

Marcus arrived promptly at 7:00 p.m. and was buzzed into the property. When he rang the doorbell, Billie let him in.

"Good evening, Marcus," Billie said, eyeing the pristine cut of his gray slacks and crisp cotton, butter-colored shirt.

"Good evening, Miss Billie," he replied, and handed her a bottle of white wine. "It's a California label, but one I discovered a year or so ago. I've become a fan. Hope you enjoy."

Sharon Sala

"Thank you," Billie said. "The others are in the formal dining room. Follow me."

Marcus rubbed his hands together in anticipation of fine food and a good evening as he followed the elder woman down the hall. He'd been here a time or two delivering flowers for one of Katarina's famous parties. He'd seen the grand ballroom at the opposite end of the mansion, but never the family living quarters. Even though the mansion was from the early 1800s, after all this time, the elegance of it was still a bit overwhelming.

He heard voices and then the lilt of Sahara's laughter and smoothed a hand over his hair just before entering. It was a damn shame the bodyguard wasn't his type. It would have made the night that much more interesting.

Billie stopped at the doorway to the library.

"Sahara, your guest has arrived and came bearing a gift." She held up the bottle of white wine. "It will go well with the pecan-encrusted bass."

"Wonderful," Sahara said, as she walked toward Marcus with outstretched hands. "I'm so glad you could join us. Lucy has a perfect little aperitif that you have to try."

He gave her a brief kiss on each cheek.

"Ooh, fun drinks," he said, and followed her to the bar, took an appetizer off the tray and then picked up his drink. He took a sip. "Mmm, what is this?" he asked.

"Sahara calls it Hollywood After Dark," Lucy said. "She taught me how to make it."

Marcus laughed and then popped the appetizer in his mouth, enjoying the earthiness of the mushroom and the sweet meat of the Cajun-flavored crabmeat baked inside it.

"The drink is delicious and so was that tasty little bite. Crab-stuffed mushrooms are one of my favorites."

He'd purposefully been waiting to make eye contact with Brendan because he liked to savor his pleasures, and looking at that man was definitely a pleasure. After another sip of the drink, he glanced toward the window.

"Ah, Mr. McQueen. Good evening."

"Good evening, sir," Brendan said.

Marcus shook a finger. "No, no, no, not sir. Just call me Marcus, please."

Brendan nodded once and then glanced at Sahara. She was enjoying Marcus's flirting with him far too much.

"Another appetizer, Marcus?" Lucy asked, as she carried the tray around the room.

"Please. They're wonderful. One of Billie's concoctions, I presume?"

"Who else?" Sahara said, and took the tray out of Lucy's hands and carried it to Brendan.

"Windows!" he said.

"Then get away from them. I'm bringing you food."

"Yes, ma'am," he said, and took an appetizer from the tray and put it in his mouth.

"Seriously? Just one?" Sahara asked.

He took two more, one for each hand.

"That's better," she said, and set the tray back on the bar.

When she turned around, Lucy was refilling Marcus's drink and laughing at something he said.

Sahara watched, thinking it was good to see Lucy enjoying herself. She didn't smile nearly enough.

"So, what do you think?" she asked.

Brendan swallowed, his eyes narrowing as he tried not to notice the length of her legs and the lack of skirt on that dress.

"About what?" he asked.

"The stuffed mushrooms," she said.

"Oh. Good."

She poked him lightly on the arm.

"That's it? That's all? Good? He who has constant words of admonition for me has suddenly run dry?"

"I don't get nearly as excited about food as I do other things," he said.

She started to comment, and then the look in his eyes made her shiver. At any other time she would have been ready to challenge him, but today had been harrowing, and somehow the energy had changed between them.

"You need a stiff drink," she muttered.

"I rarely indulge…in alcohol," he added.

Her eyes narrowed. "Are you messing with me?"

"Yes."

"Well, stop it before you start something I won't let go," she snapped.

"See to your guest, Miss Travis. I'm just the help, remember?"

She reeled as if he'd just punched her, and turned away before he saw her tears, leaving him alone by the windows.

Brendan sighed. That had hurt him more than it

did her. He was trying damn hard not to fall for "the job," but it was getting harder to ignore his feelings every day.

For Sahara, it was the longest fifteen minutes ever before Billie came to the doorway.

"Dinner is served."

Sahara set her empty glass on the bar. "It smells wonderful. Shall we go, my friends?"

Brendan offered his arm.

They led the way into the formal dining room, where Brendan seated her at the head of the table, then took the seat at her right.

Marcus took the seat at her left.

Lucy the seat next to him, and the meal began.

Billie surprised them with a soup course, serving small bowls of French onion soup, accompanied by crusty chunks of rustic bread bites to sop up the savory brown soup beneath the thick stringy cheese.

"This is amazing," Sahara said.

"Wonderful," Marcus echoed.

Billie beamed and began preparing to serve the next course.

"Fish," Lucy said when she saw her plate. "I went fishing once. I cried when Mama put the worm on the hook, because I was afraid we'd killed it. I vowed to never fish again."

Sahara laughed. "But it hasn't ruined your taste for eating it, because we've had it too many times together to make me believe that," she said.

"True," Lucy said.

Marcus shuddered. "I'm a carnivore—I eat meat and love it, but I want no part of harvest or butchering."

Sahara was debating with herself about drawing Brendan into the conversation or leaving him there in brood mode, but she couldn't resist hearing another one of his tales.

"Brendan, what about you? I'm guessing you have thrown a few hooks in the water in your lifetime."

"Yes, ma'am. That I have," he said.

"Brendan is the oldest of four boys," Sahara added.

"There are more like you? Be still my heart," Marcus said, and pretended to fan himself.

Brendan shook his head. "I'm thinking you've used that line a time or two before."

Marcus smirked. "Possibly!"

As soon as Billie served the entrée, they opened the white wine Marcus brought and poured it as they began to eat. But while everyone else was eating and talking, Brendan was focused on a noise he kept hearing outside the windows. It almost sounded like someone was pecking on the glass, but since he was unfamiliar with the exterior of the house, he guessed it could just be some bushes tapping at the window.

When Billie came in to clear the table before bringing dessert, Brendan quietly excused himself, heading straight to the windows and carefully lifting one side of the curtains to peer out into the night.

The motion detector lights that Will had installed with the security system were on, but there was no one in sight. He frowned and sat back down.

Sahara had stopped talking and was watching every

move he made. When he sat down, she exhaled slowly. If he was calm, then she could be, as well.

"It's okay," he said quietly. "No one there."

Nervous that something serious might be going on, Marcus stopped talking midsentence and focused on Sahara.

"What's happening? Is everything okay?"

She nodded and tried to smile. "Just a little jumpy after today," she admitted.

Marcus stared around the table. "I'm sorry. I don't know what that means. Something happened today? What did I miss?"

"You must be the only person left in New Orleans who doesn't know," Lucy said. "One of the flower arrangements delivered to the house had a poisonous snake in it! It was on a table behind the love seat in Sahara's bedroom, and it was about to crawl onto her shoulder when Brendan saw and shot it."

Marcus gasped. "Sweet baby Jesus, please tell me that did not come from my shop!"

"No, it was dropped off by an unmarked van after you'd left," Brendan said. "But it was probably from someone you know. The card said it was from your class. The class of 2002."

"There were hundreds of us," Sahara said. "Take your pick."

Marcus looked properly horrified. "I am beside myself. I just cannot fathom someone doing this to you. Why? I don't understand. Why is this happening?"

"Nobody knows. The police are investigating, but I

have no personal faith in any of them, not in LA, and not here in New Orleans."

Marcus reached for her hand. "My dear, I am sincerely sorry this is happening to you."

"Thank you, Marcus. And thank you for coming to dinner. It feels good to reconnect with old friends."

"Maybe you won't be such a stranger now," he said.

"Maybe," she said, and was grateful when Billie entered with a tray of desserts and changed the conversation.

"Lord, but that looks amazing, Miss Billie," Marcus said.

Billie looked pleased as she continued to distribute the strawberry shortcakes with Chantilly cream.

Even Lucy voiced her appreciation. "Oh my God, this is the best strawberry shortcake I've ever had. I officially like sweet biscuits as shortcake better than actual cake," she said, and sprinkled a tiny bit more sugar over her dessert before she took another bite.

Ten

The evening ended with amber brandy and a toast to old friends as Sahara's film clip aired on the other local channels.

She bid Marcus a good-night in the hallway and then left with Brendan at her side as Billie let him out of the house.

Billie glanced once out into the darkness, then to the streetlights beyond the gates before closing the door and locking it. She set the security alarm and then locked down the front gate as she passed through the kitchen, taking no small pleasure in knowing that, for the time being, her precious daughter would be safe.

Billie retired to her little apartment while Sahara and Brendan took the stairs up to their room.

Sahara was as tired as if she'd been on set all day. She felt used up. She'd gone from one end of the emotional scale to the other, but this wasn't acting. The gun Brendan used wasn't loaded with blanks. The snake was not a harmless one with its handler nearby waiting to retrieve it. She didn't have to pretend to panic. She had nearly lost her mind.

She wasn't pretending Brendan McQueen had saved her life again. And when he walked in behind her and closed the door, the sensation of being safe was overwhelming. He was all that was keeping her alive.

She kicked off her heels and then pulled the length of her hair across one shoulder.

"Lucy zipped me into this. I need a little help getting out."

She thought she heard a sharp intake of breath and then decided it was just his boots scooting across the floor as he came toward her. One second the zipper was up. The next it was down.

"Thanks," she said, and headed for the bathroom as he went to the closet.

The minute she closed the door between them, Brendan took off his dress clothes, put on a pair of sweats and a T-shirt, and then walked barefoot across the floor to check the windows and the hall. He could hear the television in Lucy's room, and when he glanced at the security panel in the upstairs hall, he noticed Billie had already armed it.

Perfect.

He took a deep breath and walked back into the room, and this time he didn't just close the door, he locked it. It took him a few moments to come to terms with the fact that he had just locked himself in with the one person who could bring him to his knees. Then he remembered something his commander used to say just before they'd go out on a mission. They used to rib the captain for using a naval term, but they believed that it brought them good luck.

"Steady as she goes, McQueen. Steady as she goes," he muttered, and hoped it worked the same for him as it had the captain.

He glanced toward the bathroom door, then picked up the remote and turned on the TV. It didn't matter what he watched, as long as it gave him something to do besides think about taking Sahara Travis to bed.

As soon as he found a show, he stretched out on the bed, lowered the volume and began to check his phone. He had a half-dozen requests for his services, but they wanted him now. He sent back texts telling them he was unavailable and then set his phone aside. He heard the water shut off and braced himself, and none too soon.

Sahara came out within moments, still damp and with the T-shirt she slept in clinging to her body in intriguing places. Her hair was piled up on top of her head, but it was the tiny tendrils brushing the back of her neck that made him ache to touch her. Instead, he upped the volume.

Between the fear and frustration of this day, Sahara felt helpless. She didn't like not being in control of her life. It was an ugly reminder of what life had been like living here. She needed to get Katarina's funeral service over with and get out of here.

And the sight of Brendan stretched out on that bed didn't help the frustration factor. How could he lie there so calmly when her world was coming apart? Didn't he care about anything beyond the job? Didn't he care about her…even a little?

"Brendan?"

"What?" he asked, without taking his eyes from the TV.

She glared at him, then strode across the room until she was standing directly in front of his line of sight.

"I'm talking to you."

He hit Mute and got out of bed. "Yes, ma'am?"

Her eyes narrowed angrily. "Don't do that. Don't placate me. I'm about to lose it and you stand there all calm, like nothing has happened today."

"I'm sorry, Sahara. I didn't mean to be insensitive."

"I'm stressed beyond words," she muttered.

"What helps you relieve stress?" he asked.

"I like to run, but I can't because someone would shoot me out of my running shoes."

"What else?" he asked.

"Sex usually works."

He froze. "I do a lot of things for money, but that's not one of them," he snapped.

Her eyes narrowed angrily. "I didn't ask you for sex. I answered your damn question. I wouldn't have sex with you if you were begging for it," she cried, and then burst into tears.

"Oh hell, don't cry," Brendan said.

"I'll cry if I want to," she said, then yanked the covers back from her bed, got in and pulled them back up over her head.

He could still hear the quiet little sobs, and he felt like a heel. He sat down on the side of his bed and stared at the lump she formed beneath her covers.

"I'm sorry. I didn't mean to make you cry."

She yanked the covers a little farther over her head and rolled up into a tiny ball.

"Whatever," he muttered, then got back in bed, turned off the TV, then turned out the lights.

Sahara cried herself to sleep, and it took everything Brendan had not to pull her out of that bed and give her a dose of what she'd asked for. It didn't have to mean anything. Except for him, it would and so that was that.

By morning the new attempt on Sahara Travis's life had become national news. It ran through the Hollywood crowd faster than a scandal, giving them something new to talk about.

Harold Warner was in shock. Another attempt had been made on Sahara's life, and she hadn't called to let him know, which reminded him that she'd asked him to get her phone and purse from the penthouse and overnight them to her.

He made a call to The Magnolia.

"Good morning. This is Adam."

"Adam, Harold Warner here. I have a favor to ask of you. It's for Sahara."

"I'll do anything for Miss Travis. What does she need?" he asked.

"Are they already working on the elevator?"

"Yes."

"Would you have access to the penthouse yet?"

"Maybe. What does she want?"

"Her phone and purse. She says she dropped them in the hallway between the elevator and the penthouse when the bomb went off. They may have been ruined, but we need to find out because she wants them back."

"If I can find them, where should I send them?" Adam asked.

"Do you have pen and paper?"

"Yes, sir."

"Then write down this address. That's where she is for the time being," Harold said, and then gave him the street address.

"Okay, got it," Adam said, then added, "I just heard on the news this morning that there was another attempt on her life. Is this true? Is she okay?"

"I heard the same thing. I haven't heard from her yet, but I'm sure it's true," Harold said.

"This is awful. I hope you have a good bodyguard on her."

"Brendan McQueen."

Adam whistled softly. "Isn't he the bodyguard who was in the mountains on a ski trip with that Swedish movie star and her husband when someone tried to kidnap their kids?"

"Yes, that's him. He comes highly recommended," Harold said.

"He should," Adam said. "He took out the trio of kidnappers before they could get out of the house with the kids."

"I know. So, about the phone and purse," Harold prompted.

"Oh. Yes, sir. I'll get right on that. I'll let you know if I can find them."

"Thank you. Much appreciated," Harold said, and

hung up, but he couldn't quit worrying about the latest news.

Did this mean the killer followed her to New Orleans, or did the killer originally come from New Orleans to Hollywood? But if Sahara's mother had been killed on the same day that someone had tried to take out Sahara, then… Like McQueen, he did the math and realized there had to be more than one person involved to have done all that damage in one morning in two states hundreds of miles apart.

Detective Shaw of the LAPD learned about the latest attempt on Sahara Travis's life while getting ready for work. He had the television on in his bedroom while he was shaving when the news flash aired. He came out of the bathroom wiping shaving cream off his face to watch. She was back in her hometown of New Orleans to bury a parent who'd been murdered, but was still dealing with a killer who had made another attempt on her life. This fit in with what he already believed. There had to be more than one guy behind this, or else he was hiring out the hits.

This kind of desperate attack could only be motivated by one of two things: greed or revenge. Who stood to inherit from the Travis family if they were all gone? Or who hated the family enough that they wanted all of them dead? The answer to one of these questions would lead him to the killer.

He needed to contact the New Orleans PD. Maybe if they pooled what they knew, they could figure out who was doing this and why.

He picked up his cell phone and saw he'd missed a text from Miss Travis's manager, Harold Warner, while he was shaving. Harold wanted him to email security footage from the airport to Sahara's bodyguard so Sahara could see if she recognized the bomber. Shaw kicked himself—he should have thought of this earlier. It was a good idea, and as soon as he got to the precinct, he would send over what they had.

Sahara was dreaming that she was running through the mansion, trying to get away from the killers, but there was a different killer in every room. She kept screaming for help, but she'd done exactly what Brendan had told her not to do. She had gone somewhere without telling him, and now he couldn't find her. She was caught in a hallway with nowhere to run when she suddenly woke up.

"Oh my God," she muttered, rubbing her eyes and trying to shake the awful feeling the dream had left her with. She looked to Brendan's bed for comfort but saw that it was empty.

She got up and heard the water running in the bathroom. Well, that would give her a moment to collect herself. There was something that she had to do before she could begin this day. She needed to apologize for last night. Damn it.

She sat down on the bed and waited, practicing what she should say. Maybe something about having had too much wine at dinner? No, that wasn't sincere. She could claim it was the bad vibes in this house, but that felt like a poor excuse, too. She sighed. Something would come to her. It always did.

The bathroom door opened abruptly and Brendan came striding out, bare-chested with tiny beads of water sparkling on his skin. He was barefoot and wearing blue jeans.

Sweet bird of youth!

She grabbed the covers to give her hands something to do besides feel him up.

"I'm sorry about last night. Very sorry. It won't happen again," she said.

He took in the distraught expression on her face and tried not to grin.

"If I, in any way, added to your unhappiness, I am sincerely sorry, too," he said.

"Well, then, we are a sorry lot," she said.

And once again, her good humor surprised him.

"I won't be long," she said, as she got up.

She had to pass him to get to the bathroom, and just the scent of shampoo and soap from his body gave her a buzz.

As for Brendan, when she came toward him, he was forced to look away. He didn't want to see that sexy backside this early in the morning. Instead, he turned on the television as he finished dressing, then sat listening to the news while he waited, and like everyone else, he quickly discovered Sahara Travis was big news all over the world.

Lucy was used to busy days with Sahara, and this inactivity at the family home was making her nuts. She got up early and saw she had a text from Wiley telling her to call no matter what time.

It sounded like he was in trouble, and her heart was pounding as she made the call.

"Please don't let anything be wrong," she said to herself, as the phone began to ring.

Wiley answered almost instantly. "I miss you so much," he said, completely skipping a hello.

"Wiley! Honey! Is everything okay?"

"Yeah, it's fine. I was just wondering when you're coming home."

"I don't know. You heard about the snake, right?"

"I saw it on TV last night. A poisonous snake? Damn, that's reaching for rainbows. How would he know who the snake would bite, or if it would even be found? A lot of assumption going on."

Lucy sighed. " It was too random. It made no sense."

"So you don't have any idea when it might be?" he asked.

"Not really, but hopefully all of this will soon come to an end," she said.

"Well…at least dream of me and don't forget that I love you madly?"

"I love you, too," she said.

Lucy hung up and went to get dressed. If Billie was up, maybe she could help her in some way. Anything was better than standing around.

When she got to the kitchen, Billie was carrying out pots and vases of flowers onto the patio.

"Good morning, Billie. Need some help?"

"Good morning to you, too, Miss Lucy. I would love

some help. I need to get all this out of my kitchen. I can't stand the mess another day."

"Where do we put them?" Lucy asked.

"I'm setting the potted plants out in the flower beds so that the next time Sutton Davidson and his crew come over they can replant them. And I'm putting the cut flower arrangements outside on the flagstones against the house."

As soon as the last of the flowers were carried out, Billie took a broom to the floors to sweep up the loose leaves and petals. Her kitchen was back in order.

"Thank you for helping me," Billie said.

"Sure thing," Lucy said.

"Now to breakfast. I wonder if Sahara and Brendan are up," Billie said.

Lucy glanced at the clock. "It's almost eight thirty. I'd say yes. Brendan doesn't appear to sleep in."

"Then I'd better hustle," Billie said. "Coffee is already made. Turn on the TV if you want, and sit and rest yourself."

Lucy poured herself some coffee and opted to skip TV. Instead, she pulled out her phone and began reading the news.

Sahara came out of the bathroom in a robe and headed for the closet to finish dressing.

Brendan glanced up and then back to his phone. His gut was telling him whoever was behind the attacks was getting desperate. The attempts were getting closer together, and the snake incident was so random it felt like panic.

He'd just sent an email to his brother Carson asking him to do some research for him. Carson was as good on a computer as Brendan was with a gun, and if there was anything wonky going on with the Travis family, he would find it. He couldn't prove it, but instinct told him these attacks were all about money. Leopold and Katarina Travis were well-heeled, and the mansion was a showpiece. And then there was Sahara—worth millions.

When she came out of the closet, dressed now all but for the shoes she was carrying, he lost his train of thought.

"How's your foot?" he asked.

She glanced down. "Not bad. That new skin is tender, but it's healing and these shoes won't aggravate it."

"Good. Can I ask you something?"

She looked up. "Yes."

"Do you have a will?"

She sat down, the shoes still in her hands as her heart began to pound.

"No."

"And you're sure you and your parents don't have any extended family set to inherit if you were...?"

"None that I know of," she said. "Why? What are you thinking?"

He took a slow breath, considering how to reply.

"I think I remember you saying something to the effect that your father was a womanizer? Is that right?"

She nodded. "I overheard plenty of stuff I wasn't supposed to hear when I was a kid. I'll never forget when I heard Katarina crying one night, begging him to stop what he'd been doing…telling him he'd promised he wouldn't do this again and that he was breaking her heart."

"What did he say to that?" Brendan asked.

"He apologized profusely, begged her not to cry, bought her another expensive piece of jewelry and then did it all over again the next time the opportunity presented itself."

"So he got Billie pregnant. But…what if she wasn't the only one?"

Sahara's lips parted. "Oh my God. I don't know why I'd never considered that… I mean, it makes sense. But if there are others, where are they?"

"You said Katarina wanted to pass you off as hers, but I'd say she wasn't in the mood to adopt a litter. She may have just ignored the idea of any other children. Or maybe she just never knew."

"How can we find out?" she asked.

"I'm already on that," he said. "Sometimes Carson researches stuff for me. I have him checking into personal info on Leopold."

"Leopold used to have an office here in the mansion that was off-limits to everyone. If it's still there, I'll show you after breakfast if you're interested."

"Yes, I'm interested," he said. "I'm also hungry and I smell coffee."

Sahara slipped on her sandals. "So, let's get this day started," she said.

Brendan got up to open the door, then paused with his hand on the knob.

"You are a beautiful woman, Sahara, but you're also

a survivor. Don't ever forget your strength lies in your wits, not your looks."

Sahara hadn't seen that coming. "Uh...thank you."

The door swung inward as he stepped back for her to lead the way.

They could smell bacon cooking as they were coming down the stairs, and then all of a sudden Sahara stopped, staring down into the vast foyer below as a memory from the past began to unfold.

Brendan grabbed her, thinking she was going to fall. "What's wrong? Are you okay?"

She wiped a shaky hand across her face.

"Coming down these stairs, I suddenly remembered something...something from when I was young. Katarina had sent for me to come upstairs to fix my hair a certain way because she was taking me to some event with her that day. I was coming back down when I heard crying and loud voices. I paused on the stairs and then hunkered down, wishing I could hide, because I knew something was wrong and it scared me."

"What did you see?" Brendan asked.

Sahara pointed toward the doorway at the front of the house.

"There was a woman standing in the doorway crying, and Leopold was yelling at her, cursing her, telling her to never come here again."

"Did you recognize her?"

"No, but when she turned to walk away, I saw her belly. She was very pregnant."

"Bingo," Brendan said softly. "Way to go."

She shivered, still locked into the memory.

"Leopold was so mad, and I was so scared. I knew that was something I shouldn't have seen."

"After the woman left, did he see you on the stairs?" Brendan asked.

She didn't answer.

He reached for her hands.

"Sahara…look at me." He saw the horror on her face as she raised her head. "He did see you, didn't he? What did he say to you?"

She was reeling from how he'd said her name—*Sahara*—all soft and coaxing.

"Uh…he said… He said that he would hurt Mama if I told anyone. I had nightmares for weeks that something would happen to her, and then gradually I forgot about it. I think it was you talking about other children that made me remember it."

He cupped the back of her neck and then pulled her toward him.

Sahara leaned her forehead against his chest, taking comfort in the warmth of his hand.

"I hate this place," she muttered, and then put her hands on his chest and pushed out of his grasp. "I'm not going to freak out on you. I'm okay."

They walked the rest of the way down in silence, and nothing more was said until they reached the kitchen. By then it was obvious to Brendan that she'd slipped into an act.

"Morning, Mama. Morning, Lucy! Something sure smells good in here."

Billie smiled. "Good morning, darling. I hope you brought your appetite."

Sahara laughed. "I brought someone *with* an appetite. Brendan already told me he's hungry, and I could be convinced to eat, as well."

"Sit, both of you," Billie said. "Fried eggs, cheese grits and bacon."

"And a stack of hot buttered toast to go with," Lucy added.

"All this great cooking could get addictive," Brendan said, and then seated Sahara before sitting at the end of the table nearest her.

Moments later Billie brought plates to the table while Lucy brought the coffeepot to fill the cups.

"Something's different around here," Brendan said. "Oh…the flowers are gone!"

"They're all outside," Billie said. "I wanted them out of my kitchen. Lucy helped."

"Good," Sahara said, and shuddered again, thinking of the snake.

They were all seated and eating while listening to Billie outline her day. Even though one of her employers was dead and the other missing, until someone told her differently, she had her chores to attend.

"I'll be shopping for groceries, stopping by a bakery for croissants and stopping at Sam Wing's to pick up the dry cleaning. If there's anything you need, just let me know before I leave," she said.

"Sahara, if you don't need me for anything specific, I'd be happy to go along and help Billie," Lucy offered.

"That's a great idea," Sahara said.

Billie smiled at Lucy. "I always appreciate a second set of hands. That's so kind of you."

Brendan got up to refill his coffee cup. "Anyone else want a refill?" he asked.

"No, thanks," Sahara said, as the other two women shook their heads.

He poured the coffee, and then instead of returning to the table, he leaned against the counter, his arms folded across his chest.

"Billie, I need to ask you something."

She turned around.

"Ask away."

"Did you ever hear gossip about any of Leopold's other women being pregnant?"

"There was no gossip about Leopold one way or the other," Billie said. "I know there were other women, but I'm sure after whatever transpired between them, he paid them to disappear. He protected Katarina at all costs. Why?"

"We don't know where Leopold is, his wife is dead, and someone wants Sahara gone, too. There's a decent inheritance at stake in this."

He took a sip of his coffee as his gaze slid to Sahara. She was watching him with an intensity that was slightly unnerving. And then he noticed Lucy was watching Sahara just as intently.

He took his coffee to the kitchen windows to look out. The sun was bright, the sky filled with towering clouds that appeared to be building.

"Yesterday it looked like rain, and then it didn't happen, but I think it's going to hit today," he said.

Billie jumped up and ran to the window.

"Oh, I think you're right. I'd better get this kitchen

cleaned up so we can go run the errands before the storm arrives."

"I'll help," Lucy said.

Sahara didn't say anything as she began stacking plates and taking condiments to the refrigerator. When she finished, she walked up behind Billie and hugged her.

"I love you, Mama. I still can't believe you're here, but I am so happy you are."

Billie dried her hands and patted Sahara's cheek. "We'll get this all sorted out soon enough. Until then, rest assured you will never be without me again."

Sahara's joy surged. To know she was no longer alone in the world was huge.

"Hurry home before the rains," she said.

"Don't worry. With Lucy along to help, it won't take nearly as long."

Sahara kissed Billie on the cheek and then turned around to look for Brendan. He was waiting for her to make a move.

"Are you ready to check out that office?" she asked.

He nodded.

"Then let's do this."

Eleven

Sahara led the way through the winding hallways of the ground floor to a small room tucked away between a ballroom and a utility closet.

"This is it," she said, as she opened the door, but Brendan stopped her on the threshold.

"Wait," he said. "Don't turn on the lights."

"Why not? Is something wrong?"

"I thought I saw something. I want to see this in natural light first," he said, pointing toward the mullioned windows and the sunshine coming through the leaded panes. Then he squatted at the doorway and began scanning the floor.

Curious, she dropped to her knees beside him and rocked back on her heels.

"What are you looking at?" she whispered.

He put an arm around her shoulders and pulled her toward him, then pointed down.

"What do you see?" he asked.

She was so distracted by his arm around her shoulders that she couldn't think what he meant.

"I see the floor and a little dust, which would freak Billie out. They used to hire weekly cleaners. Maybe the cleaners aren't being watched as carefully as before," she said.

"Look again, Sahara…at the wood."

And then she noticed what he meant. She crawled into the room a few feet to touch the flooring where he pointed.

"It looks like a path worn on the floor, and it even feels different."

"There's another that goes straight to the bookcase. It's the first thing I saw when you opened the door. Leopold Travis walked these two paths so many times that he's worn off enough of the finish that it's visible."

He stood up and offered her a hand. She took it without thinking, curious as to where this was going.

"Now we go in…with lights."

She flipped on the switch and glanced toward the desk, imagining Leopold sitting behind it, glaring at them for intruding into his private lair.

"Yes, well, we're here because you're not, so save it," Sahara muttered.

Brendan turned. "Were you talking to me?"

"No, sorry. Just thinking out loud," she said, then realized Brendan was already following the first path all the way past the desk to the corner of the room.

"This is strange," he said. "There's nothing here. No table, no liquor cabinet. No reason to wear a path to this spot. What used to be here?"

"Nothing that I can remember. But I wasn't allowed in here, so I only ever caught stolen glimpses inside."

He stood there a moment and then took a couple of steps back and looked down. There was a shorter piece of hardwood that finished out the corner. He squatted again, and when he pushed down against the plank, he felt it give.

"This piece is loose," he said, pulling a Swiss army knife from his pocket. He opened the blade and within seconds pried up the plank.

"Oh my God," Sahara said. "There's a hole. Is anything in it?"

"Not anymore," he said, and slid the plank back in place, then stood up and looked back across the room while Sahara moved to the desk and started going through drawers.

She went through all of them without finding anything of note and was about to quit when she thought to check the underside of the drawers, and started over.

It wasn't until she got to the second drawer on the left side of the desk that she felt what she thought was a leather-bound book.

"There's something underneath this drawer," she said.

Brendan quickly helped her pull it out, then removed what looked like a journal that was taped to the bottom. The leather covering was old and cracked. The lined pages were yellowed with age, and each line had a single notation. The notations were similar. Each consisted of a letter of the alphabet, a date and then numbers.

"This is weird," she said, leaning closer to read over his arm as he gave the pages a quick glance.

"It's in code. There needs to be another book somewhere with names that correspond with the alphabet letter."

"What would they mean?" she asked.

"Who knows…but it's something he didn't want to advertise or he wouldn't have gone to these lengths to hide it."

Sahara frowned. "Why does anyone keep a record of something they didn't want known?"

"Oddly enough, for the same reason that serial killers often take a souvenir from each victim. Looking at them, handling them, gives these people a high, like reliving the murder all over again. In this instance, if this had to do with Leopold's indiscretions, it could be one way to relive his conquests…or possible reminders of payoffs he gave them to make them go away."

She sighed. "What about the other path on the floor? The one that leads toward the bookcase?"

"We just need to look at what's there," he said. "So, since they go all the way to the ceiling and I am an ungainly six foot five, how about I search the top five shelves and you do the bottom five. Maybe we'll get lucky again."

"You're not ungainly," Sahara said, eyeing his very fine physique.

He grinned. "That's what Mom used to say about me when I was a teenager. I just kept getting taller and taller. It kept my younger brothers in clothes for years, wearing my hand-me-downs because I outgrew the stuff before I wore it out."

"Is your dad tall?" Sahara asked.

"We all are," he said, then eyed her. "You're tall. Is Leopold tall?"

She nodded, then added, "So were Billie's parents. Her mother was from Jamaica. Her father was a merchant marine."

Brendan sat down on the side of the desk and let her talk. They had all day to search, but talking was good medicine for her. Everyone needed to be reminded of their roots from time to time.

"I suspect there's a story in that love affair."

She nodded, then pushed a pen set and a day calendar aside and scooted up onto the desk beside him.

"Oh yes. They were utterly devoted to each other and died together in a car wreck when Billie was seventeen."

Brendan frowned. "Which helps explain how Leopold managed to seduce her. Grieving young girl alone in the world, and probably wooed her with gifts until she gave in. It's not until conquests become a burden that they get dumped."

"I was the burden, and you cannot know how many times I wished we *had* been dumped."

Brendan gave her a quick hug.

"Look at it this way, honey. In the end, your success is the best revenge."

Sahara glanced up at him with a smile on her face, only to realize there were only inches between his mouth and hers. Breath caught in the back of her throat.

She saw his nostrils flare slightly and knew he was feeling something, but what?

Brendan saw her eyes widen. Her lips parted. He wanted to kiss her. It would be a mistake, but he wanted it just the same.

It was his cell phone ringing that finally broke the tension. He looked away as he answered.

"McQueen."

"This is Harold Warner. I wonder if I might speak to Sahara."

"Sure. Just a minute," Brendan said, and put the phone in her hands. "It's Harold."

She grimaced. "I should have called," she whispered, then answered. "Hello."

"You didn't call me," he said.

"I was in shock?"

Harold sighed. "Are you trying out excuses, or are you not sure why you neglected to tell me what's happening over there?"

"A snake crawled out of a vase of flowers and was aiming for my neck when Brendan shot it. It was terrifying, and I pretty much lost my mind. I will not apologize for that. Where's my phone? If I had my phone, I might think more about using it."

Harold was horrified. "Oh my God. I didn't know details. I'm sorry, honey. I'm so sorry. As for your phone, I put Adam in charge. I haven't heard yet whether he found it or not."

"Okay. Sorry I snapped at you."

"It doesn't matter. As long as you're safe…that's all that matters. Are you satisfied with Brendan?"

She shivered. "Yes."

"Good, good. I sent a text to Detective Shaw suggesting he send the video to McQueen's email, so tell him to be looking for it. Is there anything I can do for you?"

"No, I don't need anything more than I already have. I'll try to do better about staying in touch, even if I don't have my phone, okay?"

He chuckled. "That would be appreciated. Goodbye, dear. Take care."

"I will. Bye, Harold."

She handed the phone back to Brendan. "He said to tell you he sent a text to Detective Shaw about sending the security footage, so you need to be watching for it."

Brendan nodded.

She got up and headed to the bookcase, then stood there a moment, thinking of Leopold and where he would most likely hide the key to decoding the ledger.

"I'm going to start on the bottom shelf. You start on the top one. The Leopold I remember would never have put anything secret within arm's reach."

Brendan regretted that their moment was over, but got up without comment to do as she suggested. Soon the books were being pulled out of order and every page was searched.

After a while, a rumble of distant thunder sounded. It was finally going to rain.

Adam had just come on duty when the workers repairing the elevator entered The Magnolia. He knew the crew boss by name and hailed him as they came toward him.

"Hey, Russell, we had a request from Miss Travis to see if we could recover her purse and cell phone. She says she lost them in the hallway between the elevator and the penthouse right after the bomb went off. Everything became so dusty and smoky she couldn't find anything, and then, as you know, she was rescued from the roof with no chance to take anything with her. Will you be anywhere in that area today that you could look for it?"

The crew boss nodded. "She's sure having a rough time now, isn't she? I'd be happy to check that out for her," he said.

"Thanks. If you do find them, bring them to me. I have orders to mail them straight to her."

"I'll go there first thing," Russell said. "It'll take me a bit to climb the ladder inside the shaft, but if the items are there, I'll bring them right back."

"Much appreciated," Adam said.

It was just after 9:00 a.m. as Bubba headed out of New Orleans. It looked like rain later today, and he wanted this trip over with and to be back in the city before that happened. He had an address and directions to where Harley Fish lived. They knew each other only because they'd gone to school together, but he could never claim they'd been friends, and he was nervous about how Harley would receive him. With the wad of cash he had in his pocket, he was hoping the reception would at least be cordial.

It wasn't until he left the main highway and began following directions that took him deeper and deeper into bayou country that he began to feel anxious. These roads were narrow as hell. One wrong turn and he'd be nose down in water with the gators.

Just when he thought he'd gotten himself lost, he saw a green mailbox with the name Fish on the side and took the turn up a narrow one-lane road.

Harley Fish was at the back of his cabin gutting a big-mouth bass when he heard the sound of a car coming toward his house. Harley didn't entertain visitors, so he dropped the knife, grabbed his rifle and slipped into the trees surrounding the clearing, wiping his bloody hands on his pants as he ran until he found a good hiding spot. He had a perfect line of sight to his front porch when the car pulled up to his cabin and parked.

The first sense of relief was that it wasn't the law, and then his relief was replaced by surprise.

"What de hell dat man be wantin' wit me?" he muttered.

Then the man honked his horn as he got out.

Harley walked out of the trees.

Bubba saw movement from the corner of his eye and turned to see Harley coming toward him. The fact that he was carrying a rifle loosely across his belly made him shiver, guessing that same rifle had probably been aimed at him from the woods.

Harley had not aged well. His long, stringy hair was totally gray, and his squat little body had done nothing but get wider and his legs more bowed.

Still, he was the one who'd come into Harley's world, so judgment was not needed. He lifted his hand in a greeting and smiled.

Harley neither waved back nor changed his expression, and he didn't stop walking until he was within spitting distance.

"What you be doin' on my place?" Harley asked.

Bubba had a job to do and wasted no time in lip service. He just pulled out the wad of cash.

"I have a job that needs to be done, and two thousand dollars for the man who'll do it for me."

Harley's eyes narrowed. "What kinda job?"

"I need someone killed."

Harley swung his rifle, pointing it straight at the other man's head.

"Why you think I would do such a ting?"

Bubba shrugged. "I just heard that you were a good shot and that you didn't mind getting your hands dirty."

Harley scowled. "Murder and mud be two different tings. Prove to me you not wired up by de cops tryin' to pin someting on me."

Bubba shivered in spite of his intention to stay calm. "Prove it? How?" he asked.

Harley waved the rifle again.

"Strip where you stand. If dere be no wire, den we talk."

"Take off my clothes? Hells fire," he muttered, but started stripping where he stood.

Harley watched with interest but said nothing, and when all of the man's clothes were on the ground, Harley went through them, checking for bugs.

"Okay...no wires. Now I listen."

"Can I get dressed?" Bubba asked.

Harley waved the rifle again. "You. Take de clothes and follow. We talk in back."

Bubba put on his underwear and picked up everything else off the ground and ran to catch up. Harley was already back at the butchering table, slinging fish guts into the trees.

He dressed quickly as he watched Harley cleaning the fish, and then took the money roll out of his pocket again as a reminder of what was at stake.

"So, who do you want to die?" Harley asked.

Bubba was trying to focus on Harley's words and not what he was doing, but the grossness of the flies, the heat and the bloody table was getting to him.

"A woman in New Orleans. I'll show you a picture. I'll give you the address of the house. You kill her, and another thousand dollars like this is yours."

"Why you want dis woman dead?"

"That doesn't matter," Bubba snapped. "Will you do it or not?"

"You cheat me, I gut you like dis fish."

"Deal," he said.

"Show me," Harley said, and then watched the man pull up a picture on his cell phone.

"This is the woman I want dead."

Harley frowned. "The movie star?"

"Yes, and she's in New Orleans right now. You'll have to do it at her house because she's staying out of sight. There are security cameras everywhere and she has a bodyguard, so make sure you stay in the shadows.

Use a hunting scope on your rifle if you have one. If you do it at night, know that there are motion detector lights all over. Look for the rooms with lights, and then make it happen."

"Give me the address. Give me de money you bring. You come tomorrow morning with rest or I come after you."

Bubba held out a thousand dollars.

Harley motioned for him to lay it on the table.

His nose curled as he tried to find a spot not covered in blood and guts.

Harley stabbed his fish knife through the bills, pinning them to the table to keep them from blowing away, while the man wrote down an address on a scrap of paper he'd pulled from his pocket, and slipped it between the stack of hundred-dollar bills.

"You go now," Harley said.

Bubba didn't have to be told twice, but he had to make himself walk calmly. It wasn't until he knew he was out of sight that he ran the rest of the way to his car and drove away.

Harley slipped the address and the money into his pants pocket, gathered up the fish and went inside. He hadn't had breakfast, and it was nearing noon. This bass would fry up just fine.

But while Harley was heating up a skillet, Bubba was getting uneasy. He'd started a fire that he couldn't put out. Harley Fish was a wild card. Either this could be the denouement he'd been trying for, or it could go to hell in a handbasket. The biggest fear he had was that Harley would fail and get caught. He didn't trust the man to keep his mouth shut, but he'd already started this ball rolling, and he was a thousand dollars into the deal. He just had to trust that it would play out in his favor. After all the mishaps so far, he was due for a win.

Brendan and Sahara's search of the bookcase wasn't any more successful than finding that empty hole in the floor. Whatever Leopold had done with the key to the journal, it wasn't going to be found easily. By the time they'd handled every book in the case, they were covered in dust, especially Sahara.

"That's all of them," she said, as she got up from the floor.

There was dust on her shoes, all over the top of her hair and on her clothes because every book Brendan pulled off the shelf above her had shed a little of the dust down onto her.

He grinned. "You look like you're raising a litter of dust bunnies. There's not a clean spot on you."

She laughed. "No thanks to you."

"Not my fault you were sitting at my feet."

"Whatever," she said, brushing uselessly at her shoulders and the seat of her shorts.

He picked a bit of fuzz from the crown of her head and then dropped it on the floor.

She didn't care about dirt. She wanted answers, but their search wasn't yielding what they needed. In frustration, she threw up her hands and then shoved them through her hair.

"Where is that key? What did he do with it? What if it's not even in here? This old mansion is huge. We could look for years and still never find it. I should have known this would be futile."

Brendan shook his head.

"Just calm down," he said. "Leopold would keep the journal and the key to it close to each other. Whenever he wanted to go through them, he wouldn't be running all over this museum of a house trying to gather them up."

"I guess," she said.

"Let's think of this from another angle. What if the key wasn't written in any kind of book?"

"I can't think like this. I feel gross," she said, and pulled up the tail of her shirt to wipe the dust off her face, baring her belly and most of the bra cupping her very shapely breasts.

Brendan grunted beneath his breath and turned his back, but far too late. What the hell was it with her? She was the least modest woman he'd ever known, and it was driving him crazy.

"Okay, I'm thinking now," she said.

He took a deep breath. "Let me know when you get an idea."

Sahara began to pace the room from one end to the other, then back again, kicking at chairs, rattling cupboards filled with dusty little figurines and poking behind furniture.

"You could help," she muttered.

"I wouldn't know what's out of place," he said.

"Well, hell, McQueen. Neither would I. It's been fifteen years since I set foot in this godforsaken house. And I wasn't allowed in here."

"Then tell me what's familiar. Start with furniture."

She pivoted, pointing things out one by one.

"The desk. The bookcase. The mantel over the fireplace. The——" Her lips parted as she stared at the fireplace. "It's brick. It used to be stone."

"Good work," he said, and headed for the fireplace again, only this time he began looking from a different perspective.

The brick had been laid in a herringbone pattern, and this time he started at the floor and began working his way up. About halfway up on the right side, he saw a slight gap between the brick and the grout and pushed. A picture hanging above the fireplace swung forward like the page of a book, revealing a wall safe hidden behind it.

"Shoot. Now we don't have the key or the combination," Sahara said.

Brendan stood there a minute, thinking, then asked, "What was Katarina's birthday?"

"Uh…January 2, 1947."

He turned back to the safe, spun the dial to clear it, then made the first turn to right 1, left 2, then right 4, left 7. The click was loud and distinct as the door opened.

"Bingo," Brendan said, and thrust his hand inside. "And that's why they always say to never use obvious dates or names as your password." He pulled out a small black notebook, opened it and then looked at Sahara and grinned. "This is it! Grab that journal from the desk and let's go back to our room. You can clean yourself up while I see what I can make of all this."

Sahara threw her arms in the air and did another little pirouette.

Brendan sighed. She danced when she was happy. That might have just sealed the deal with him. He wanted her and was getting tired of fighting the truth.

"Lead the way," he said.

He shut and locked the safe, replaced the picture and then closed the door to the little room behind them as they left.

A half hour later Sahara was in the shower and he was sitting at the writing desk with both books open, scanning back and forth from book to key and back again when his phone rang. He glanced down, saw it was his brother Carson and answered.

"Hey, Carson."

"Brendan, I heard about the attempt on Sahara's life. Is everything okay?"

"Yes, we're good. How's the research going? Do you have anything for me?"

"I hacked Leopold's bank records as far back as they had them in the system, but not sure it was far enough back to help."

"Did you see any kind of payoff patterns? Anything suspicious to show he was handing out money on a regular basis?"

"He loaned thirty thousand dollars to a man named Sutton Davidson a number of years ago, but the man paid him back in full."

"Yes, that was a housekeeper's son. Sahara said the woman worked here for a while. Sounds like he was helping him start out a business."

"Got it. Okay, here's another one. About thirty years ago he made a large onetime payment of twenty-five thousand dollars to a woman named Julia Bennett, then twenty-eight years ago another large onetime payment to a woman named Barbara Lovett, and three more payments like that in subsequent years to other women."

"Sounds like he was paying off his playmates," Brendan said.

"Maybe," Carson said. "I'll look into the Travis family charitable donations tomorrow. Both kids are sick and so is my honey. I'm on doctor duty until further notice."

"Oh man, I'm sorry to hear that," Brendan said. "Hug the babies from Uncle Bren, and tell Shelly I'm sorry she's sick and to get well soon."

"Will do. When I have more news, I'll let you know."

"Just don't get yourself in trouble on my account," Brendan said.

"It's all good," Carson said, and disconnected.

Thunder rumbled again, this time a little closer. When Brendan got up and pushed back the curtains to look out, he could see that the wind was rising.

Sahara came out of the bathroom wrapped in a bath towel.

"Keep your back turned, McQueen."

He continued to look out the window, but his heart rate picked up with the knowledge that she was naked behind him.

"Carson called," he said.

"Did he find anything?"

"A few things but nothing definitive. The wind is rising. That rain will be here soon."

"Billie and Lucy should be home by now," she said, as she hurried into the large closet and pulled the door partly closed.

She quickly stepped into underwear and a clean pair of shorts, then pulled a sports bra over her head and a T-shirt after that and pushed the door aside. "I'm decent. You can turn around."

He turned.

Her long legs were bare and so were her feet, and even though her hair was up, it was still damp and leaving little wet spots on her shirt where the tendrils were hanging.

"Shiny as a new penny," he said.

"It feels good to be clean," she said, and started toward him, then remembered the windows and stopped.

At that moment, the security alarm chimed, indicating that a door had been opened.

"Billie's back with groceries. We should help," Brendan said. He folded up the two books he'd been reading and slipped them into his suitcase and shut it.

"Then let's go," Sahara said, moving past him to the door with Brendan bringing up the rear.

Twelve

Billie set a sack of groceries on the kitchen counter and was on her way out to get the rest when Sahara and Brendan walked in.

"I'll grab the rest," Brendan said. "Where's Lucy?"

"She got a call. I left her outside in the car for a little privacy."

Brendan took off out the door to carry in the rest of the groceries and passed Lucy as she was coming into the kitchen carrying the dry cleaning.

"Where should I put this?" Lucy asked.

"Just drape the bags over the back of a kitchen chair," Billie replied. "I'll take it all back where it belongs later."

Lucy did as she was told and then glanced at Sahara.

"Your hair is wet. Is everything okay?"

"Oh, I'm fine," Sahara said. "Brendan and I were just digging through old stuff and got dirty."

Billie frowned. "What's dirty in this house?" she asked.

Sahara laughed. "I told Brendan the dust in Leopold's office would make you mad."

"Are you serious? It was that bad?"

"Yes, ma'am. Quite a bit of dust."

"Strange. I would have thought Leopold would complain. He was always so picky about the housework around here. No matter. I'll have a word with that cleaning crew, for sure."

Brendan came back in with the rest of the groceries and set them on the counter.

"It didn't look like he'd been in his office in a long time," Sahara told Billie.

Billie's frown deepened. "What were you looking for?"

Before Sahara could comment, Brendan quickly spoke up.

"Oh, just going through his schedule, stuff like that, trying to figure out if he'd had any meetings scheduled on a planner. I thought it might give us some clues as to who he saw last, if they had any problems…that kind of thing."

"Oh, that's smart," Billie said, then began putting up groceries.

Lucy lost interest in the conversation, and after a quick word to Sahara that she was going up to change, she left the room.

Billie picked up a jug of laundry soap and a package of paper towels and headed for the utility room.

Sahara moved closer to Brendan and then whispered, "Why didn't you mention what we found?"

"Because right now we don't know for sure what we found, and the fewer people who know it exists, the better."

She shrugged. "Okay, but we're talking about Lucy and my mother. They're hardly dangerous."

He didn't argue the point. "Knowing too much could possibly put *them* in danger, so I still want it kept between us," he said.

"Are you going to give the journal to the police?"

"As soon as I figure out what it says. Otherwise, it's too likely to just lie on some detective's desk in wait for him to get time to look at it."

Billie came back in, noticed the two with their heads together and smiled.

At least they'd quit fussing.

She glanced up at the clock. It was already after four. Not a lot of time to get dinner together.

The wind was rising now, rattling shrubbery around the outside of the house. Something was banging around outdoors. She went to the kitchen door and looked out.

"That darn door to the shed is unlatched and blowing about," she said, glancing at McQueen. "Have you been in the shed today?"

He was instantly on guard. That would be a good place to hide until dark. He pulled his gun.

"No. You two stay inside, and keep away from doors and windows."

Now Sahara was nervous all over again. "Is it trouble?" she asked.

"I don't know, but I'm going to take a look."

"Be careful," she said, but he was already out the door.

Just in case someone was in the shed, Brendan exited the house, turned left and walked off into the garden out of the line of sight. He took a quick right and came up behind the shed. The droplets of rain were still intermittent, but it was just a matter of time before it really began to pour. There was a window on the back side of the shed. He saw nothing inside, and when he tried the window, it was unlocked.

He jogged back around to the front, and after another quick reconnoiter, he stepped in with his gun drawn and flipped on the lights.

The shelves were lined with gardening equipment and products. There were old muddy footprints on the wooden flooring that had dried long ago, but nothing he could pinpoint as recent. He walked the length of the shed to lock the window, only to realize the lock was broken.

Well, that explained why it was open, which alleviated some of his concerns that someone could have gone out the window as he was coming out of the house. He looked through the window to the grounds beyond and then frowned. The extent of tropical plants and shrubbery afforded many places for a person to hide. The longer he stood there staring into the greenery, the more tense he became until soon the hair was standing up on the back of his neck.

Something was wrong. He could feel it.

He exited the shed, making sure the door latch caught as he closed it, and ran back through the garden and into the house just as it began to pour. The wind was blowing the rain against the windows in hard, splattering sounds, and thrashing through the landscaping. There would be a mess to clean up once the storm had passed.

When he returned to the kitchen, Sahara was too pale and quiet within her mother's arms. He wanted to reassure her and take away that look of fear, but he needed to be certain things were really safe.

"No one inside, but I'm going to check the grounds."

"You told me to never leave your sight. You said it was the only way you could keep me safe."

The distress in her voice was real. He hated what was coming, but it had to be done.

"And to do that, I have to make sure your environment is also safe at all times, and right now I can't say that with total certainty. The shed is empty, but the grounds are large and the shrubbery is impenetrable in some places. I have to make sure no one is hiding there before it gets dark, understand?"

She pushed out of her mother's arms and came toward him.

"You told me to stay with you," she said, and wrapped her arms around his waist.

He cradled the back of her head as she laid her cheek against his chest. He wanted nothing more than to stay, but he also wanted her alive and well, and needed her mother to help him with her.

"Billie, I'm going upstairs to get some things. When

I come back down, you follow me to the front door and let me out, then set the security alarm. If you hear trouble, just call the police. If everything is okay, I'll be back at the front door, knocking to be let in."

"Yes, okay," she said.

He wouldn't look at Sahara as he moved out of her grasp and left the room.

Sahara stood where he left her, listening to his footsteps running through the hall and then up the stairs, overwhelmed with, yet again, a pending sense of doom.

Harley Fish reached the bushes at the back of the property only seconds before the wind began to rise. When the shed door began to bang, he grimaced. That was on him, and he didn't like making mistakes.

He had opened it slightly to eye the line of sight to the house from the shed and then closed it, but it must not have latched properly.

He was already hiding when he saw a big man come running out of the house with a gun in his hand, and he was not surprised.

The bodyguard, he supposed.

He hunkered down as far as he could go, knowing he could not be seen from his hiding spot, but hoping that big bastard didn't decide to search the grounds. He would have to kill him first, which would alert those inside, and then his window of opportunity would be severely limited. He still wasn't sure how he would get to the woman, but he wasn't a man accustomed to failing and trusted the opening would come.

When it began to rain in earnest, he grabbed a black,

lightweight slicker from his backpack and pulled it over his head, then yanked the hood down over his forehead. All he could do was wait, so he sat down with his back against the wall to wait for sundown. As heavy as the storm clouds looked, dark would come early, which suited him just fine.

Billie looked at her daughter but didn't touch her. Sahara was obviously trying to hold it together, and too much sympathy might be the trigger to a break-down they didn't need.

Within minutes they heard Brendan coming down the stairs, and when he ran toward the front entrance, it was just to motion for them to follow.

To Sahara, it looked like he was going to war. All he needed was a backpack, a helmet and a rifle. There were ammo clips in the pockets of the green army jacket he was wearing, a knife in a scabbard at his waist, and the automatic normally in his holster was in his hand.

"Let's go," he said.

A sharp clap of thunder sounded overhead as they ran. The thunderstorm was worsening.

He reached the door, opened it quickly and then paused in the doorway to look back.

Sahara's gaze was fixed on him. She'd become so reliant on him to stay alive that any separation now probably felt like a personal threat. He didn't say any-thing because he couldn't make the promise he wanted to make, and so he turned and ran out into the rain.

Billie quickly shut the door behind him and locked it, then ran to the security panel and set the alarm.

"I have to see if he's okay," Sahara said.

Billie grabbed her arm. "No, child. He told you to stay away from windows, and that's what you have to do."

"There's a window in the attic that looks directly over the back grounds. I'll stay in the shadows. If anyone is out there, they won't be looking up at a darkened attic window. They'll be waiting for dark and looking where there are lights."

She pulled out of Billie's grasp and started running.

She was halfway up the stairs when Lucy appeared at the top.

"Hey, what's going on?" she asked.

Sahara ran right past her without answering.

"Just come with us. I'll explain later," Billie said.

Lucy followed, quiet but anxious.

Access to the attic was the single door at the end of the second-floor hallway, next to a narrow set of stairs that came up from the kitchen.

Sahara paused only long enough to yank it open, then went up the wooden steps two at a time.

She had expected a dusty room full of junk and was surprised to find it was basically clean, organized and obviously in constant use. Christmas decorations were packed and labeled, as were Thanksgiving, Easter and Fourth of July boxes. But the party hostess was on a slab in the morgue, so it was doubtful this elaborate regalia would ever be used again.

Sahara headed for the window, aware of the footsteps behind her, then stopped in the shadows just short of the window and flattened herself against the wall. Now she could see out, but no one would see her.

"What's going on?" Lucy asked again, and while Billie was explaining, Sahara was scanning the green growth surrounding the elaborately landscaped yard, desperate for a glimpse of the man who'd become her world.

"Where are you, Brendan McQueen?"

Unaware she'd said it aloud, she kept staring into the downpour, despite the fact that it was blurring her sight of the space between them. When she finally caught a glimpse of him moving between some palmettos, she breathed a sigh of relief.

"Did you see him?" Billie asked.

"Yes."

"Then we will pray the worst thing that happens is he gets very wet," Billie said.

Lucy felt obligated to stay focused but was distracted by the size of the attic and the opulence that had been relegated to storage. She couldn't wrap her head around the paintings and the china—they even kept sculptures up here. It was like being in a secret museum.

"I don't see him anymore," Sahara said.

"He's trying not to be seen, child. Stop worrying," Billie said.

"Right, yes, you're right," Sahara whispered. "Stay safe. Stay safe."

The wind was changing. Now the rain was being blown against this window. She frowned.

"Oh my God… Billie, we didn't check the weather. What if there's a tornado warning?"

Billie fumbled to get her cell phone out of her pants pocket.

"I'll check it for you," Lucy said, and began scanning her phone for a local weather station.

Seconds later, the rapid-fire sound of gunshots sent all three of them running to the window. They could see one man running through the bushes, then Brendan following, and then heard more shots.

The man turned toward Brendan. Multiple shots rang out into the night, then the man turned and disappeared, and there was no sign of Brendan.

"Oh my God, oh my God!" Sahara cried. "Where is he? I don't see him anymore."

"And now we can't see the shooter," Lucy said. "What if he got away? What if Brendan is hurt? Should we go out there? What should we do?"

Billie went for her phone again, but this time she was focused. She did exactly what Brendan told her to do and called 911.

Brendan entered the green growth at the front gates and started working his way toward the back of the property. But, between the downpour and azalea bushes as tall as trees, the wild growth of wisteria vines, the bougainvillea and palmettos, it was slow going. The live oaks interspersed around the grounds were heavily laden with sodden clumps of hanging moss, and while they were also a deterrent, they added more cover. The rain helped muffle the sound of Brendan's presence, but it didn't change the tingle at the back of his neck.

A loud crash of thunder overhead made his heart skip, but he kept moving forward in a slow, steady crouch until he was less than twenty feet from the corner of the property where the green growth was the heaviest.

Someone was in there. Brendan could feel it.

He moved another yard forward before he caught a glimpse of a man in a black slicker with his back against the wall. He couldn't see his face for the hood pulled over his head, but he saw the rifle with the hunting scope behind him. It was all he needed to see.

One minute Harley was cursing the fact that he was sitting in water, and then his instincts for survival sensed he was no longer alone. He caught a glimpse of movement, saw the outline of a man's shoulder and leaped to his feet. He grabbed the rifle and fired three shots in rapid succession, then ran for it.

When Brendan saw him go for the rifle, he fired off a shot himself and then hit the ground belly-first beneath a live oak as the shots went flying over his head. He returned fire, grunting softly as the man dropped facedown in the mud and didn't move.

Sheltered from the downpour, he rolled over on his back and pulled out his cell phone to call 911. He was talking to Dispatch when he heard sirens approaching and realized Billie had come through for him, after all.

* * *

Sahara was in shock, her hands pressed to the window as if trying to part the rain for a better view. When police began swarming the grounds and a trio of EMTs followed and she still couldn't see McQueen, she turned away from the window and ran.

Billie caught her on the landing. "You don't go out there! You don't know what's happening, and you could make matters worse! Do you understand me?"

Sahara sank down on the top step and covered her face, too afraid if she cried she would never be able to stop.

Lucy came trailing last, out of breath as she slid onto the stair beside her boss without comment.

Billie hurried the rest of the way down the stairs to release the security alarm.

Sirens were screaming as more police cars arrived. The wind was still slamming rain against the windows, and another clap of thunder rolled across the sky above them as the doorbell rang.

Billie moved to answer it, and Sahara stood up on the step to see who it was.

The door opened, and a trio of uniformed officers in rain slickers walked into the foyer.

She moved down the stairs in measured steps, her gaze fixed on the police, who were talking quietly to Billie and pointing outside. She went down three more steps and saw Billie put a hand to her mouth. By then, Sahara was bordering on panic.

The police were still there when Sahara reached the

ground floor. When they saw her, they said something to Billie that made her turn around.

Sahara was trying to read the emotions on her mother's face when another man walked up behind the officers, then walked between them and came inside. They stopped him at the door.

Sahara gasped. It was Brendan, walking and talking like nothing was wrong. She ran toward him.

"Brendan!"

He looked up and saw her coming, sobbing with every step.

"I'm okay," he called out.

She just shook her head and kept running.

He moved toward her, his arms already opening to gather her to him as she fell into his embrace.

"I thought you were dead," she sobbed.

"The other guy's dead. I don't know who the hell he is, but he's dead," he said.

She just shook her head and held on.

The police left to go back to the scene, and Billie shut and locked the door behind them.

"Billie, I'm making a mess on your floor," Brendan said.

"You never mind. You just go get yourself warm and dry. It will all clean up."

He looked down at Sahara. She wouldn't turn him loose, so he picked her up, carrying her past Lucy, who was standing in the hallway in tears, and took her up the stairs to their room.

He sat her down on the side of the bed, stroked the side of her cheek with his finger, then stepped into the bathroom and started stripping. He was wet clear to the skin.

Sahara could hear him taking off his clothes. As much as she wanted to be in there, she hadn't been invited.

"Will all this be over now?" she asked from where she sat.

Brendan walked back to the doorway. He was nude but for the towel wrapped around his waist.

"Honestly? I don't think so. I think he's a hired gun."

Her shoulders slumped. "Do the cops know who he is?"

"Some local named Fish, they said."

"I don't know him," she said.

"Finally, someone you didn't go to school with," Brendan said, and was pleased when he made her grin. "Hey, I'm gonna jump in the shower, but I'll leave the door ajar. And you need to change your T-shirt. I got you wet and muddy."

She rubbed a hand over the stains. "I guess," she said, and got up to get a clean shirt.

She heard the water come on as she pulled the dirty shirt over her head to put on a clean one. At this rate, she was going to have to do laundry tomorrow. She hadn't come with that many clothes.

She sat down on the side of the bed and then reached for Brendan's phone and entered Harold's number. She didn't want him fussing at her again for not calling about the latest attack.

He didn't answer, so she left him a message and

then rolled over on her side and closed her eyes. The last thing she remembered was the sound of the rain lulling her to sleep.

Breaking news of a second botched attack on Sahara Travis was all over the local media, and within hours spreading all over the nation. Learning the attacker was dead left many believing the danger to her was finally over, but Brendan didn't believe it, and after the New Orleans police identified the man Brendan had shot, they didn't believe it, either.

Harley Fish was a local, had no ties whatsoever to the Travis family, but had a rep as a man for hire. And when they found a thousand dollars and Sahara's address written on the back of a scrap of paper on him, it was obvious to them that what they had was a dead hit man and a killer still on the loose.

It also affirmed the fact that the man they were after was likely hiring out the hits regardless of location.

For Bubba, the fact that his latest plan to take Sahara down had failed again was less concerning to him than the relief he felt in knowing Harley Fish was dead. There would be no way to pin him to Fish now. No way to pin him to what was going on with Sahara Travis.

It would have saved time and money just to get his own rifle from the pawnshop to begin with, but he had to face his own weaknesses. He just hadn't wanted to be the one to pull the trigger. Now he had been given no other choice.

He went to the pawnshop and was relieved to see the rifle was still there, complete with the telescopic sight. He got it out of hock, bought ammunition and took it home. That same night he readjusted the sight, cleaned the rifle and then broke it down and put in it in a case for easier transport. Now he was ready to move it.

He glanced out the window at the storm. He had one other plan in mind but needed to do a little reconnoitering to make sure that it would work. Hardly anyone would be out in a storm like this, which would safeguard what he was about to do.

He changed into dark clothing and left with the rifle. It took a little less than fifteen minutes to get where he wanted to go, and he parked a few doors down along the street. He grabbed the gun case and backtracked in the rain to a grand old mansion with a For Sale sign in the yard.

After a quick check of the perimeter, he found an unlocked window at the back of the property and climbed in, then lowered the window. With the only light being intermittent flashes of lightning, he carried the gun case in one hand and a flashlight in the other as he made his way to the second floor. Once there, he had to search to find the door leading to the attic.

It was summer, and the rain should have made the closed-up empty house feel like a sauna, but it was chilly, and in some places downright cold. He'd always heard that if a ghost was present, there would be a cold spot in the room. What creeped him out was that the whole place felt cold. By the time he finally found access to the third floor, he was looking over his shoulder with every step.

The third floor was more attic than living quarters, although he suspected at one time, like every other old mansion in the city, these would have been servants' quarters.

He moved quickly toward the dormers.

There were four of them, but he was interested in the two in the middle. They were both too dirty to see through, and one was jammed and wouldn't open. However, the second one he tried came loose. Even as he was pushing it up, he knew it was going to work because, even through the rain, he could clearly see the front gates of the Travis mansion across the street highlighted by the streetlights.

Rain was blowing in his face as he lifted the rifle and scanned the scene through the scope. The security lighting on the Travis property gave him a clear sight to the front door, which was exactly what he needed.

Now all he had to do was put the rest of this new plan into motion. He closed the window, replaced the rifle inside the case and left it below the window, then rushed out of the attic and back down the stairs. The closer he got to the window he'd entered through, the more anxious he became. It felt like he was being chased. He reached the window, shoved it open and climbed outside in haste.

Lightning flashed as he closed the window behind him and once more circled the house to get back to the street. Just as he walked out from behind the house, lightning flashed again, spotlighting him to the world before encompassing him in darkness and rain.

He reached his car in record time and drove away. By the time he got home, he'd calmed down, telling himself there were no such things as ghosts.

Thirteen

It was a loud clap of thunder that woke Sahara. She immediately rolled over looking for Brendan and saw him sitting at the writing table, shirtless and in a pair of jeans with Leopold's journals open and the laptop lit up like a beacon in the dark room.

Was it wrong to call a man beautiful?

He glanced up at her over the laptop as she swung her legs off the bed and sat up.

"Do you feel better?"

"I guess. I didn't mean to fall asleep."

She combed her fingers through her hair and then stretched as she got up, went into the bathroom and closed the door.

Brendan's eyes narrowed as he watched her. So she was pretending her emotional breakdown never happened. He sighed. It was just as well. He went back to his research.

"Why are you sitting in the dark?" she asked when she came back into the room.

"Because you were asleep," he said.

"Want lights?"

"Yes, please," he said.

She flipped a switch that bathed the room in light, then walked over to where he was sitting and leaned against his back as she read over his shoulder.

He was trying to ignore the feel of her breasts against his skin when she thrust her arm across his shoulder to the names he had written down on his notepad.

"Who are those people?"

"Women who received onetime payoffs of twenty-five thousand dollars from Leopold."

"Wow. There are five of them."

"So far," he said.

"And those dates indicate when the payoffs were made?"

He nodded.

"Do you think this has anything to do with what's been happening, or is it just an unrelated part of Leopold's life coming to light?"

"Right now, I honestly can't say, but my instincts tell me there is some kind of connection."

The house phone rang, and she turned away to answer it.

"Hello?"

"Dinner will be ready in about fifteen minutes," Billie said.

"Okay, and I'm sorry I didn't come help. I fell asleep and just woke up a few minutes ago."

"It's all good, baby. You needed the rest. It's been a stressful day. Come on down soon, but wear shoes.

All this rain will wash the scorpions and centipedes out of their hidey-holes."

"Ick. Yes. I'd almost forgotten that little aspect of Louisiana. We'll be right there. Did you tell Lucy?"

"She's already here with me."

"Okay," Sahara said, and hung up.

"Dinner is ready," she said, and headed for the closet.

"Are you changing clothes?" Brendan asked, eyeing her shirt and shorts.

"No, but I'm putting on shoes. Mama reminded me that the rain will bring out scorpions and centipedes."

Brendan closed the books, shut down his computer and put all of it back in his bags.

Sahara frowned. It wasn't the first time she'd seen him do that, but she didn't say anything. She guessed in his line of work, it was best to trust no one.

Brendan followed her into the closet to get a shirt and shoes as well, and all of a sudden the huge walk-in closet felt tiny and enclosed.

She watched the play of muscles on his body as he reached up to get a shirt, and that was when she saw a long, thin scar that ran from the middle of his back, around his side and then disappeared into the waistband of his jeans.

Without thinking, she reached out and touched it.

"This scar. How did you get it?" she asked.

"While I was in the Rangers."

"I didn't ask you when, I asked you how."

"Machete. In a jungle. Special ops."

She stared, trying to imagine something that brutal happening to him and him surviving it.

"That's a pretty short version of the story. Is it one of those 'I'd have to kill you if I told you about it' stories?"

"No, but after today, I don't think you need any more gory bedtime stories," he replied, then pulled the blue knit shirt over his head and reached for his socks and boots.

She stepped into her shoes and then went into the bathroom to wash her face and brush her hair. The rain was making it frizzy, so she put it up in a ponytail on top of her head, letting the curly strands fall down around her face and the back of her neck, then led the way out of the room.

Brendan watched the gentle sway of her hips and the long stride of bare legs just long enough to remind him how naturally she moved within her sexuality. She was sexy as hell, but she didn't flaunt it. Some jobs were harder than others, and this one just might be his Waterloo.

Dinner that night was a far cry from the elaborate meal Billie made for them when Marcus had been their dinner guest, but it was just as delicious.

Tonight they had steaming bowls of beans and rice, crusty fillets of fried catfish with a spicy tartar sauce and endless pitchers of sweet iced tea to cool the fire in the food.

"This is so good," Brendan said.

Billie beamed. "Thank you."

Sahara glanced at him and then looked away. There

was a wall between them that he had erected the moment they met, and she wanted it down. She just didn't know how to make that happen, because always he kept her at arm's length.

"Cream puffs for dessert," Lucy said. "I know because I put the pudding inside them."

"French vanilla custard to be exact," Billie said.

"I would love one," Sahara said.

"I would love some," Brendan said, which made them all laugh.

Billie served dessert while Sahara got up to fill her iced tea glass.

"Anyone else want a refill?" she asked.

The phone rang, startling them. It was the dinner hour. People knew better than to call at this time.

Billie frowned, but Brendan spoke up.

"I'm not a local. How about I get it for you and save you the trouble of being pissed off that they interrupted your meal?"

Billie giggled. "I would be pleased," she said.

Brendan grabbed one little cream puff and poked it in his mouth as he got up to answer. He chewed and swallowed on the way to get it, licking custard from his thumb as he spoke.

"Brendan McQueen speaking."

"Hello, McQueen, this is Detective Fisher. Is Miss Travis there?"

"Yes."

"I have some news regarding her father. I can tell her, or I can tell you, and you can relay it."

"Go ahead," Brendan said.

"Leopold Travis's body was found in an empty house in the Ninth Ward around noon today. It was too decomposed for an immediate identification, but dental records gave us the ID. The medical examiner says he was likely killed the same morning that Katarina was killed."

"Was that house the murder scene?" Brendan asked.

Fisher hesitated, then finally answered. "Yes."

"I'll give her the message," he said, hung up and turned around.

Sahara stood up. "What?"

"They located your father."

"I heard what you asked. He's dead, isn't he?"

Billie reached for Sahara's hand, but she pulled away.

"For God's sake, McQueen! Talk."

"He's dead."

"Good," Sahara said, and walked out of the kitchen.

Lucy gasped.

Billie stood up. "Where did they find him?" she asked.

"In an empty house in the Ninth Ward."

Billie shuddered, then dropped back down in her chair and covered her face.

Brendan pivoted quickly and took off after Sahara, then realized she was just outside the door.

"What are you doing?" he asked.

"Waiting for you. I'm the last one now, aren't I? The last Travis, I mean. Who hates us this much… and why?"

"I don't know, but I'm trying to find out."

She stared at him a few moments, meeting his steady gaze and noticing the muscle jerking in his jaw.

"I don't think we'll do it in time," she said.

"Do what?" he asked.

"Find out who did this. I think I'm going to die soon. I'm going to die without ever knowing what it's like to make love with you."

If she'd slapped him, he couldn't have been more shocked.

"I won't let anyone hurt you, Sahara," he said.

She laughed, but it ended on a sob, because he'd ignored the obvious point she was trying to make.

"What are you going to do, Brendan McQueen? Move in with me for life? Put me in your pocket like a traffic ticket you keep meaning to pay? This can't go on forever. I'm just a job, remember?"

When she doubled up her fists and turned away, he felt her pain.

He put his hands on her shoulders. "We've done this all wrong. I would give a year of my life to have met you as a woman and not a client. And as much as I wish it wasn't true, whatever it is you think you feel about me…it's just because I keep you safe. If these were normal circumstances, you might not be attracted to me at all."

She shrugged out of his grasp and pushed him away.

"You don't know what I think. You don't know what I feel."

The anger in her voice shattered him.

"And you don't know how I feel," he said. "This started out as a job, but you've evolved into this burr under my skin. Now you're a woman whose beauty and sense of humor and gentle spirit breaks my heart, a woman I've come to love…and you're also the woman who is going to break it again when you realize it wasn't love you felt, it was fear overriding everything else. I've come to represent your safe haven, which you've mistaken for real romantic feelings…but you win, Sahara. I'm done fighting this."

She froze. *Is this happening?*

He lowered his head until his mouth was only inches away from her lips. *Oh dear Lord, it is going to happen.*

And then he kissed her.

The grim-lipped, hard-jawed bodyguard put his arms around her, and all of a sudden her feet were dangling against his legs as his mouth slid off her lips and then down her neck before he swept her up into his arms, moving in long measured strides through the house and up the grand staircase to their bedroom.

It was dark in the room and sheltered from the ominous sounds of the storm. It became the refuge they both needed.

He laid her on his bed, locked the door and then had her out of the shirt and shorts so fast she didn't have time to think. He unhooked her bra with one hand and pulled off her underwear with the other, then took a slow, deep breath and stripped himself.

Sahara's eyes widened at the size of him. She got wet just thinking about him inside her.

Lightning lit the stage, and thunder orchestrated the music of what came next. She turned to him as he stretched out on the bed beside her.

Her heart was pounding.

It hurt to breathe.

The ache in her lower belly was nothing but pure want.

And his skin…like silk over steel.

She ran her fingers along the scar all the way to the juncture of his thighs and circled her fingers around his erection, feeling the pulse of his lifeblood and the shaft of muscled velvet that she wanted inside her, and when he thrust his knee between her legs, she parted them to let him in.

He groaned against her ear as she wrapped her legs around his waist, pulling him deeper into her warm, wet heat.

No foreplay.

No sweet talking.

No time.

Sahara moaned. They were a perfect fit.

When he began to move within her, she closed her eyes and pulled him closer, deeper. She'd been waiting for this moment—this man—all her life, and he was never going to believe her.

Rain blew against the window, running down the glass like tears as he kept moving, lost in the woman beneath him.

She matched him move for move, her breath coming in short, desperate gasps as the climax built within her. Just when she thought it would go on forever, it hit like a fist to the gut. She cried out, stunned by the power and the waves of pleasure washing through her, and still he moved, unwilling to let go of the woman in his arms until he was aching from his own need and had to let go.

They fell asleep in each other's arms as the storm moved on, leaving trees and yards in shambles, but clean, rain-washed streets.

At the morgue, Katarina and Leopold had finally been reunited. On the far side of town, Bubba lay staring up at the ceiling.

Brendan woke up before daylight with Sahara wrapped in his arms, her head pillowed on his shoulder. He wanted her again but didn't act on it. He closed his eyes, memorizing the silken feel of her hair against his cheek, the curve of her backside pressed against his belly and the weight of her breasts lying on his arms. She'd done something no other woman had ever done. He'd let her get too close, and she'd stolen his heart. The fact that he was going to leave her when this was over seemed impossible to consider, but he wasn't the kind for Hollywood affairs.

She sighed in her sleep and he pulled her closer. Come sunrise he would have to give her up, but for now Sahara Travis was his—only his.

Sahara thought she was dreaming about making love until she woke up to the fact that McQueen's hands were between her legs and she was coming too fast to think. Instead, she rode out the climax with his breath against her neck and his name on her lips.

When she could breathe and talk at the same time, she rolled over to face him and cupped his face.

"I loved last night. I loved making love with you. I love everything about you, Brendan McQueen. Last night was the most perfect night of my life."

"It was pretty damn special for me, too," he said softly. "But...it can't happen again."

She stiffened. "Why not?"

"I can't be distracted. It could get you killed, and you mean too damn much to me to let that happen."

She didn't know whether to be elated that he admitted she mattered, or hurt that he'd just set her aside like yesterday's clothing, but she wasn't going to let him know how much it hurt.

"You already mentioned that. I mistakenly thought you saw differently now," she said, and pushed out of his arms. "I'll take the shower first." She got up and walked into the bathroom.

Brendan closed his eyes and then scrubbed his hands across his face as an ache spread within him. He got up, put on a pair of shorts and got out his laptop and the journals again, and started working. He was going to email everything he had to the detective heading up her case in LA, and another email with the same information to Detectives Fisher and Julian here in New Orleans. It was past time to let them in on what he'd found. Maybe they'd find a connection he wasn't seeing. He was, after all, just a bodyguard. Solving crimes wasn't his thing.

He heard the water come on and swallowed past the lump in his throat.

God in heaven, help me get through this to keep her safe.

Then he sorted his info into a file and sent one copy to the LAPD and another to the NOPD along with a brief cover letter. Hopefully something positive would come from this.

Sahara walked into the bathroom, blindsided by what just occurred. She had not expected this. Not after last night. Not after the way they'd given themselves to each other. Not after he'd cradled her in his arms as she fell asleep. She'd never felt that loved.

Growing up, she had always known Billie loved her, but Billie also let Leopold and Katarina have the first say in her life, and so she'd been forced to divide her life into two portions to keep the craziness at bay, pretending to love two people who didn't matter, and having to pretend she didn't love the one who did.

And then last night happened, and for the first time ever, a man had made love to her because she mattered to him. Not because she was beautiful, or because she was famous, but because he loved her. But he wouldn't let her love him back. That wasn't fair.

She turned on the shower and then stood staring at herself in the mirror, wondering what was wrong with her that kept making people push her away.

Tears came without warning as she stepped into the shower, and when she moved beneath the spray, she cried freely, knowing that the water would be washing them away.

Brendan heard her sobs, which only added to the burden he already carried. He knew better than to get personal with a client, and he'd done it anyway.

"Son of a bitch," he muttered, and turned on the TV to drown out the sound of heartbreak.

A short while later the bathroom door flew open, and Sahara came out wrapped up in a big bath towel and with a foamy toothbrush in her hand. Her eyes were red from crying, and her hair was still wet and dripping all over the floor.

"You don't get to tell me who I can love, McQueen. I will love you if I want to, and you can stuff that up your ass. Since we've already seen each other naked numerous times, and we were all over each other last night, you may as well get in here and take your shower. I won't jump your bones, and I'm almost through brushing my teeth. And while you're at it, hurry up. I need a cup of coffee."

Then she spun around and went back to the sink, muttering to herself and spitting and rinsing erratically.

He closed the laptop, put everything away and did as she asked. She sailed out of the bathroom past him as he entered, flashing him an angry glare, and headed for the closet to get some clothes.

Brendan closed the door behind him and then stood there for a moment, trying to absorb what had just happened. He wasn't sure, but he might have just unleashed more woman than he could handle. She clearly had no intention of abiding by his rules of war. He'd just have to see how this played out.

While he was showering, Sahara called Harold. This time he answered immediately.

"Sahara, darling! I'm so glad to hear your voice. Thank you for calling earlier. You won't believe what happened to me today! I slipped in the shower this morning and actually had to go to the ER to get stitches in my head."

"Oh no! I'm so sorry."

"So am I. Hurts like hell, but I'm fine. No need to worry. It'll leave a scar, though..." he grumbled. "It mars the perfection of my countenance."

She laughed. "Oh, Harold. You are good for what ails me," she said.

"You're okay?"

"Thanks to Brendan I'm still alive, so that's good for something."

"That's good to hear. Clearly he's worth every penny! I'm so glad you finally came to your senses about hiring him," he said. "Please be careful, though, okay? You are dear to me, Sahara. I don't know what I'd do if anything happened to you."

She sighed. "Thank you, Harold. I really needed to hear this today. Now I'm going to change the subject. The penthouse. What's happening there?"

"Nothing yet, but I don't think it will be long. The elevator repair crew has been working long days. I got a text from Adam this morning that they should have the elevator up and running by sometime tomorrow. If so, I'll get the cleaning crew in there ASAP."

"Okay, sounds good. Actually, there's something else you can help me with. It was brought to my attention the other day that I don't have a will, and that may be a lure for a killer who might show up later to lay claim on my inheritance after I'm dead."

"Good Lord, I already told you to see to that. I

should have known you would put it off," Harold said. "So they think these attacks are about inheriting your parents' money?"

"Nothing's been confirmed, but it seems like the best motive at this point. It turns out Leopold wasn't as devoted to Katarina as he seemed..."

"Wait—you think he has other children? Oh, Sahara, this must be so difficult for you to deal with right now."

Sahara shrugged. "Honestly, I couldn't care less about what he'd been getting up to behind Katarina's back. And since this person is out to kill me, I'm pretty sure I don't have a happy sibling reunion to look forward to."

Harold sighed. "How can I help? What do you want me to do?"

"Just to expedite the matter, get a standard form and tell my lawyer that in the event of my death, I want everything I have to go to a woman named Billie Munroe."

"I haven't heard that name before. Who is she?"

"My biological mother—and don't ask," she added when she heard him exclaim in surprise. "It's a long story, and I don't want it bandied about."

"I'm in shock! Then Katarina isn't... How long have you known about this?"

"Always. I said, it's a long story. Also, please make sure it's noted that if anything happens to Billie before I die, then everything goes to Brendan McQueen, and in the event of his passing as well, it all goes to

The Lillian Booth Home for Aging Actors of The Actors Fund."

He gasped. "Brendan? You're naming him in your will out of gratitude?"

"No, that's not why. But it's none of your business, Harold. Just do what I've said and fax everything to me so I can sign it and fax it back. I'll bring the originals back to you, but the copy will be a safeguard until it arrives. If there's someone who thinks they have a claim to the Travis family money and is killing us off to get to it, they're going to be sadly disappointed. Leopold and Katarina's estate has been left to me, and if I'm gone, it will lump in with my holdings, so Billie or Brendan will get it all. There is no law that says children automatically get family holdings, unless they are named in a will, and since they aren't named, they don't stand to inherit anything, regardless of whether they succeed in killing us all. There's a fax in the office here. Do you have a notepad to take down the number?"

"Yes, go ahead."

She gave him the number.

"I'll get right on this and text you when your lawyer is ready to fax it so you can be ready," Harold said.

"Okay, but tell him to expedite. My existence can change at a moment's notice, and I do not want to die without this in writing."

"Absolutely. Consider it done."

"Thanks, Harold. And I'm so sorry about your fall. Be well."

"You, too," Harold said, and disconnected.

She sat there a few moments, listening to the water

shut off and bracing herself to see Brendan's gorgeous body again. He would be coming out any minute, and she needed clothes and her game face on, so she jumped up and headed for the closet, chose a pair of lightweight slacks, a sleeveless blouse and shoes.

Brendan came out of the shower with a towel wrapped around his waist and headed for the closet just as she walked out. He gave her a look as she passed, but she wouldn't meet his gaze.

Brendan sighed.

So much for another confrontation. Just as well. She wants coffee. Maybe later.

She was leaning against the door waiting when he came out fully dressed. No matter what he wore, he turned clothes into a sexual come-on. She would have blamed it on his body, but it was the attitude that sold it. She waited as he buckled on his gun and holster and pocketed his cell phone. As soon as he looked at her, she unlocked the door and walked out, well aware he would be right behind her.

As usual, Lucy was already in the kitchen when they arrived. She was definitely the early riser of the bunch. The table was set and food was warming. Billie turned around, smiled when she saw Sahara and opened her arms for a good-morning kiss, which she promptly got.

"What a night of storms! Did you two manage to get any rest?"

"Not a lot," Sahara said.

Billie patted her daughter's cheek. "Too much drama yesterday. Hopefully today will be calmer. Hope you're hungry. French toast and sausage links."

"Sounds wonderful," she said.

Billie smiled at Brendan. "I hope you brought your appetite."

"And then some," he said. "Can I help you in any way?"

"No, but thank you for asking," Billie said.

"My mama would box my ears for not at least offering," he said.

"A good mother raises good sons," Billie said. "Sit, everyone. Breakfast is served. Lucy, please put that trivet in the middle of the table. I'm going to set the platter of toast on it."

"Yes, ma'am," Lucy said, and took it from the sideboard to the table just ahead of the hot platter Billie was carrying.

Sahara turned around to sit down and Brendan was standing at her chair, waiting to seat her. She sighed. He was determined to maintain the professional relationship despite her declaration, but it didn't change her determination. It remained to be seen which one of them would prevail.

He pushed her chair closer as she sat, then took his own seat. Within minutes they were all eating and so the day began.

Fourteen

With the two-hour time difference in California, Brendan's email to Detective Shaw arrived while he was still at home and in the shower. It was the first thing he noticed when he logged on to his computer, and then it reminded him that he still hadn't sent that security footage, and he did so right then before he opened the new attached file.

He was unprepared for what Sahara and Brendan had found, but it did, however, explain why all of this was happening. What if there *was* another heir? One with a grudge of massive proportions? He printed off a hard copy for their working file and then saved it to the efile before he got up to refill his coffee cup. He took it and another Danish back to his desk as he settled in to study the new info in depth. Once he had this straight in his head, he was calling the New Orleans police.

Detectives Fisher and Julian received the email within moments of Brendan hitting Send. Fisher read the letter, then opened up the attachment. It was with no small amount of shock that he learned what a predator Leopold Travis had been. Knowing this and remembering how distant Sahara Travis had been about her relationship with her parents was now beginning to make a little sense. He could only imagine the turmoil that had gone on behind their privileged life.

"Hey, Julian!"

His partner looked up from his desk.

"Did you get an email from Brendan McQueen?"

"Yes, I'm reading it now. Don't know what to think about all this. It's sure not how the New Orleans elite thought of Leopold."

Once they were both finished reading, Fisher pulled the case file on Travis and found the address where his body had been found.

"I'm gonna run with a hunch," he said.

"What kind of hunch?" Julian asked.

"I didn't think the house where Leopold was murdered was a random choice, and neither did you. So what do you think the odds are of one of these women's names showing up as a prior owner?"

Julian grinned. "So maybe Travis paid off a pregnant woman, and not just another affair gone cold? The killer chose this house for a reason. What if it was where he grew up?"

"Why not? It happens," Fisher said.

Julian nodded. "Then let's get busy. You take half the names, I'll take the others. Let's run background checks and see what comes up."

A couple of hours later Fisher got a call from Detective Shaw in LA and put him on speaker so Julian could hear.

"I'm calling about the email from Brendan Mc-Queen. I would like to hear that you've got a handle on a viable suspect," Shaw said.

"And we'd like to tell you we do, but we don't. However, the info Brendan sent might be the break we were waiting for."

"I started background checks on the names," Shaw said. "But what's going on in your city is out of my jurisdiction."

"Before the email, we had what we thought was a random crime scene where Leopold Travis's body was discovered, but after reading through all of what Brendan sent, we're checking to see if any of the women on this list ever owned that house. The killer had to have chosen it for a reason."

"Where was the house?" Shaw asked.

"When Hurricane Katrina struck, the Ninth Ward was the hardest hit part of the city. It's building up again, but very slowly, and there are a lot of empty houses that are still in the same shape they were when the water went down. It was in one of those."

"Wow. How did you ever find the body?"

"Some kids messing around where they didn't belong. They found it and their parents called it in."

Shaw made a few notes as he spoke. "I have a couple of leads, but so far they're not going anywhere. The killer either hired out the hits or there's more than one person behind all this."

Detective Julian broke in then, wanting to follow up on their earlier conversation.

"Last time we spoke you were talking to a woman at The Magnolia who claimed she might have seen the man who planted the bomb where Sahara Travis lived. Did anything come of that?"

"Grainy security footage. He was posing as an elevator repairman. Pretty sure he was wearing a wig and a fake mustache. He had a stolen ID and toolbox, and we found out later that the van he drove was a rental. There were fingerprints all over it, but nothing we could find in the system. I'm inclined to think this guy was just hired on to do the job. If he was a pro, he'd most likely have a criminal record."

"What about the bomb that was supposedly on Miss Travis's private jet?" Julian asked. "How did you come to find that?"

"Her bodyguard called us, told us they were flying commercial to be safe and asked if we would have someone check her plane for sabotage. But by the time we got out to check it, Homicide was already there working a murder. The mechanic had been killed and tossed in a Dumpster. That intensified our search, and yes, we found a bomb, so he was definitely trying to cover all the bases. However, once she left LA, our whole case here went cold, which led us to believe he followed her."

"And obviously you were right," Fisher said. "However, this last attempt was most certainly a hired hit. The bodyguard took him out before he got a chance to launch any kind of attack, but the dead guy had payoff money on him, along with the address of the Travis residence written on a piece of paper. And he was a local with a known reputation to do most anything if the price was right."

"Which still leaves us both in the cold as to who's responsible," Shaw said. "At any rate, stay in touch. I'd like to tie this up as soon as possible."

"As would we," Fisher said, and the call ended. He looked at Julian, and then glanced at the clock. "Let's get some lunch before we get back to this."

Before Julian could answer, the phone rang, and Sahara Travis's stalker was put on the back burner for a drive-by shooting that left a mother dead and her teenage son, a known drug dealer, wounded. When you lived life in the fast lane, some things never changed.

It was nearing noon when Brendan checked his email and found the security footage they'd been waiting for. He and Sahara had been sitting quietly in the library all morning, browsing through the books and mostly keeping out of each other's way.

"Sahara, pull up a chair," he said.

She was reading the very last pages of *The Velveteen Rabbit* with tears in her eyes—it was a childhood favorite of hers—when Brendan called her. She laid it aside and dragged a chair to the table where he was working and tried not to think about how she felt.

"What's up?"

"The security footage came. It's not very good quality. Let me know if he even looks familiar."

"Okay."

He hit Play and then turned the laptop toward her.

She watched intently, eyeing the man walking into the service entrance, talking to a woman behind a desk and then walking out sometime later. Then she watched footage of him captured at the airport where her plane was kept. She gasped when she saw the body being dumped.

"Oh my God," she said, and pressed her fingers to her mouth to keep from screaming.

She was sick to her stomach when it ended.

"I don't know who that is, and he didn't look at all familiar. Not even the way he walked. I'm sorry."

"No. Don't be sorry. It was just something that needed to be run by you. I'll let them know you couldn't identify him."

She nodded and was getting up from the chair when the house phone rang. When she turned to answer, Brendan caught her by the wrist.

"Aren't you going to let Billie answer?"

"She went to the store. Don't worry, it will be fine." Then she picked up the receiver.

"Hello?"

"It's me, honey."

"It's Harold," she said, eyeing the satisfied nod from McQueen, then turned her attention to the call. "What's up?"

"Your lawyer is faxing over the will. He says to tell you it's a basic boilerplate, but it would stand up in court should the need arise. When you get back, come in and he'll itemize it all to specify your holdings."

"Okay. Many thanks for this," she said.

"You're welcome. Stay safe."

"That's all up to Brendan, and he's doing a rather spectacular job. All I can say is, so far, so good."

Harold sighed. "Just so you know, I hate that you have to live like this."

"I don't like it, either, Harold, but right now we have no other choice."

"I know, but I had to say it."

"Thank you, and you stay safe, too. No more falls in the shower, okay?"

He groaned. "Deal."

"Oh! Please give Adam a hello from me next time you talk to him."

"Sure thing."

She replaced the receiver.

Brendan listened to the whole one-sided conversation and thought nothing of it until her last comment.

"Who's Adam?" he asked, without looking up from the computer screen.

She glanced over her shoulder and thought about making something up to see if he cared and then thought, what the hell. Playing games wasn't her style and she wasn't starting now.

"The security guard at The Magnolia," she answered honestly.

"Oh," Brendan said, and for the first time in hours, he met her gaze.

Sahara looked back, then put her hands on her hips and lifted her chin.

"Were you jealous?" she asked, and then walked out of the library.

"Damn it," he muttered, shut down the laptop and followed.

"Where are you going?" he asked, as he caught up.

"To the fax machine in Leopold's office. I have some papers coming that I need to sign."

"Oh, okay."

She entered the room without hesitation. Whatever ghosts had been there before were off her radar. She went straight to the fax and began gathering up the pages and the cover letter that came with instructions.

She stood there long enough to scan the pages, then picked up a pen from the desk, signed the papers, then turned around and faxed them back.

"That didn't take long," he said.

She shrugged. "I already knew what was coming."

As soon as the last page ran through, she gathered them up, found an empty file folder and slipped them inside.

"I'm through. I guess lunch will be ready soon, but I don't want to eat. I want to go for a walk. I want to go to the French Quarter and get a box of pralines. I want to hear the music on Beale Street. I want to go down to the river and watch the riverboats. Did you know the streets on the riverfront are paved with ballast stones? You know what ballast stones are?"

Brendan heard in her voice a longing to revisit her childhood, and frustration at being cooped up in a house she hated because showing her face could get her killed.

"Tell me," he said. "Tell me about the ballast stones."

She sat down on the edge of the desk, her long legs dangling almost to the floor.

"Back in the late 1700s and early 1800s, plantations ruled, cotton was king, and slaves were bought and sold like products rather than people. If a ship would sail into the harbor to pick up goods, like bales of cotton or whatever else was being shipped out of New Orleans, they usually came laden with goods to trade, which were unloaded on the docks. But if they set sail without goods, coming only to pick up the huge bales of cotton, they still couldn't sail empty, because they needed weight in the hold to keep from tipping over and sinking in storms. So they loaded up stones for ballast, big heavy stones that were put down in the hold. Then when they got here, the slaves had to bring the stones up and dump them in the river to make room for the goods. As the city grew, someone got the fine idea that the riverfront needed to be paved and that same someone thought those ballast stones would be perfect for pavers, and they were free. So they made the same slaves who dumped them in the river dive down and bring them up."

She paused a minute, biting her lip, as if trying to control emotion, and when she looked at him, there were tears in her eyes. She sighed. "Hundreds of slaves died trying to get those damn ballast stones off the bottom of the river, but eventually they hauled up enough to pave the river walk. When I was young, I used to say a prayer for the ghosts I felt there. It's a haunting place at night, but a beautiful place, too. I wish I could show it to you. I think you'd like it."

Without giving him a chance to answer, she slid off the desk and brushed off the seat of her slacks.

"So, want to walk me down to the kitchen instead and see what Miss Billie is making for lunch?"

He nodded.

She tossed her hair back and laughed, but it was as false as the smile on her face, and he knew it. She leaned against the office wall.

"You know the routine. Follow me, McQueen, lest I am beset upon by nefarious men and meet my doom somewhere between here and the kitchen."

When he crooked an eyebrow at her, she added, "Those were lines from a movie I was in. My character was a flighty, ridiculous woman from the Victorian era. I was glad when that movie was over."

"Then I should probably lead the way," he said, moving toward her. "Just in case."

He slid a hand beneath her hair and stroked the side of her face with his thumb.

She looked up at him, clutched the wall a little tighter and then stepped away.

"After you," she said.

He strode out of the office, then waited until she was right beside him before taking another step. The fact that he'd been the cause of her latest grief and heartache was killing him. He didn't know how this would end, but he was suddenly willing to risk another heartbreak to find out.

"How about we take this trip together and see what happens?" he said, and then held out his hand.

"Are you going to throw me away again when the mood strikes?" she asked.

It was the tremble in her voice that told him he'd made the right decision.

"No. I won't ever do that again."

She took his hand. Daring to trust one more time, she tightened her grip, as if that would somehow make the decision stick.

He led the way out of the office, and when they got to their bedroom, she paused.

"I want to leave the papers here."

She slipped into the room, leaving him in the doorway as she dropped the papers in the drawer by her bedside table. She came back to him with a slight bounce in her step.

He thought it was because they had just made a truce of sorts, when in fact it was from the relief of knowing that even if she died, there wouldn't be an estate for anyone to contest. What was hers was hers to do with as she chose, and she'd chosen. This mysterious killer wasn't the only one with secrets, and she'd just decided to beat him at his own game.

When they got downstairs, Billie had already returned from her errand.

"Where's Lucy?" Sahara asked, noticing she wasn't helping Billie out with the meal as she usually did.

Billie pointed. "She's helping out in the garden. I sent her out to tell Sutton I want all of those peace lilies planted among the hostas before I left. They'll do better in a little shade than in full sun."

Brendan moved toward the window. Lucy was

standing beneath a shade tree talking to Sutton. He watched her for a few moments.

"Looks like Lucy made a conquest," he said. "I've never seen her so animated."

Sahara frowned. "I think she has a boyfriend back in LA, but she doesn't talk about him much. She doesn't have a lot of free time, which is my fault, I suppose. If I'm on the move, then so is she."

Brendan watched Lucy throw her head back and laugh, then looked at the tall, skinny man she was flirting with. He wasn't doing much talking, and he kept looking toward the house. Maybe he was concerned that she was keeping him from his work.

He turned back to find Sahara and her mother head to head, talking. It wasn't like they were sharing secrets, but it was touching to see. And then Sahara moved to the cabinets to set the table.

"Prepare yourself, McQueen. Crab salad, fresh croissants and bourbon-flavored ice cream. I will require a nap later, I think."

He patted his stomach. "I'm going to start packing on the pounds if we're here much longer," he said.

Billie eyed his flat belly and well-muscled body and rolled her eyes.

"You are not packing anything but muscle, Brendan McQueen, and you know it. Would you please let Lucy know we're going to eat?"

"Yes, ma'am," he said, and opened the door. "Hey, Lucy. Billie says lunch is ready."

Lucy jumped as if she'd been punched, but when she started back to the house, Sutton came with her.

She ran into the house, her face flushed.

Sutton paused on the threshold and smiled at Sahara.

"Well, hey...long time, no see," he drawled.

"Hi, Sutton. It's really good to see you! Congratulations on the business. I hear you're doing great."

"I can't complain," he said, then glanced at Billie. "Miss Billie, I can't plant the peace lilies in the hosta bed around the live oaks like you wanted. There are too many tree roots. I suggest a bed for them on the east side of the shed. They would get early light and then shade by midday and after."

"Oh. I didn't think of that, but it's a good idea," Billie said.

"Okay, then, I'll get back to work. Lucy, nice to meet you," he said.

"Nice to meet you, too," Lucy said.

Sutton closed the door.

Billie smiled. "That man. He's still as friendly as he was when he was a child."

Sahara sat silent among the chatter without really listening. Her mind was on getting Leopold and Katarina interred.

"Mama, we have a problem," she said.

Billie frowned. "What kind of problem?"

"Something just occurred to me regarding Katarina and Leopold's memorial service. Traditionally, I would be attending it in church, and we would host snacks and drinks for the closest friends afterward."

"Yes, that's true," Billie said.

"But that's not going to happen," Brendan said.

Sahara nodded. "Exactly. Without knowing the

enemy's face, I cannot expose myself to hundreds of people and expect Brendan to be able to keep me safe."

Lucy spoke up without being asked. "Why don't you just inter them and announce in the paper there will be a memorial service held at a later date?"

"That's a good idea," Brendan said.

"Yes," Sahara agreed. "That would work. Thank you, Lucy. Thank you again for helping my messed-up life run smoother. That's absolutely the perfect thing to do."

Lucy smiled. "Happy to help. Besides, it's why you pay me."

"Okay, then. I'm going to call a funeral home and tell them to retrieve the bodies after the police release them, and inter them in the family mausoleum. I can have a notice put in the paper stating a later date will be set for a memorial service, which will satisfy everyone else," Sahara said.

"Lunch will be ready in five minutes," Billie said.

"Okay. I'll wait and do it after lunch," she said.

Billie relayed a funny story she'd seen as she was coming out of the bakery today. A toddler who was obviously potty training pulled down his pants and was peeing on a sidewalk, embarrassing the mother to no end as she grabbed him up and ran, unaware he was still peeing down the leg of her pants.

It was the perfect story to lighten the mood, and the joy that came with the telling was the only dessert Sahara wanted.

Then she told the group about her plans to clean up the penthouse and sell it.

"Really?" Lucy said. "Were they able to get the elevator fixed?"

"According to Harold, it should be fixed within a day or two."

Lucy sat for a moment, as if considering her words. "If you want, I could go back and see if there's actual damage visible after the cleaning crew went through it. Maybe do a little staging to sell, and pack up your clothes for you," she said.

"You would be willing to do that?" Sahara asked. She had a feeling Lucy's offer might have more to do with her wanting to get home to her boyfriend than it did with helping out Sahara, but after seeing her get perhaps a little too friendly with Sutton, she figured it would probably be a good idea.

"Yes, of course," Lucy said.

"Then I'll see where they are with the elevator repair and let you know when you'll have full access again. I'll check with Harold about arranging the trip and let you know."

Lucy smiled, pleased her idea had been well received.

Brendan's phone signaled a text. He glanced at it briefly. It was from his brother Carson.

I have news. Call when you get a chance.

He dropped the phone back in his pocket and finished eating while keeping an eye on the workers just outside the door. They were on the patio now, cleaning up the scattered pots and mangled flowers from the storm.

They finished the meal, helped Billie clean up and then went their separate ways. Lucy took Billie's car to run errands for herself. Sahara watched her drive away from her bedroom upstairs and wished she had the freedom to just jump in the car and go anywhere at will. Instead, she was in jail—a luxurious one, but nevertheless, a jail.

But she had tasks to do.

"McQueen, I need to call Leopold's lawyer."

Once again, he handed her his phone.

She Googled Chapman Farraday, Esquire, then called.

The secretary answered. "Chapman Farraday's office."

"This is Sahara Travis. I need to speak to Mr. Farraday."

"Yes, Miss Travis. One moment please."

Seconds later she heard a click.

"Miss Travis, this is Chapman. My sincere sympathies on the deaths of your parents."

"Thank you. The reason I called is to ask if my parents had prior plans made for burial."

Farraday cleared his throat. "Why, yes, they did. I was reminded as I was rereading the papers regarding their estate. You are their sole heir and—"

"That is of no consequence to me," she said. "I need to know where to bury them. I was never privy to the information regarding their family mausoleum."

"Really?"

"Yes, really," she said. "What cemetery?"

"Umm, that would be Lafayette Number 1. The family mausoleum is Greek Revival architecture…in the Travis name, of course."

"Of course," Sahara said. "Did he have any kind of prepaid funeral plan or a funeral home preference?"

"None mentioned," Farraday said.

"Can you recommend a decent one? I would hate to pick something socially unacceptable."

Farraday hadn't seen Sahara since she was a girl, and it sounded as if she'd grown into a very aggressive woman—like Leopold, he supposed.

"Schoen Funeral Home would be a good choice."

"Thank you," she said. "And just so you know, their bodies will be interred without ceremony once they're released from the morgue. I'll hold a memorial service at a more dignified time…when I'm no longer the target of a killer. I'm requesting that you publish that notice, worded without mention of my current situation, of course, in all of the proper papers."

Farraday was just slightly less than horrified.

"Oh dear, yes…of course."

"Thank you for your help," she said, and disconnected, then handed the phone to McQueen.

He was leaning against the desk with his arms crossed across his chest, watching her.

"What?" she said.

"Nice performance," he said.

She frowned. "I must be losing my mojo if that came across fake."

"Only to someone who knows you are everything *but* an ice queen."

She sighed. "Whatever. By any chance do you know the number to the New Orleans PD?"

"Detective Fisher's number is in my contacts."

Her hands were starting to shake. "Would you do something for me?" she asked. "Would you call him and tell him that when they release the bodies, the authorities are to contact the Schoen Funeral Home, who will pick them up?"

He took the phone from her fingers and brushed a thumb across her lower lip.

"Yes, Sahara, I will do that for you."

Exhausted, she threw herself belly-first onto her bed, legs sprawled, her cheek against a pillow, and closed her eyes. The last thing she remembered was hearing the low rumble of McQueen's voice, and then she was dreaming.

Fifteen

"Sahara! Sahara! Where are you?"

Sahara curled up into the tiniest ball beneath the bed and closed her eyes, thinking if she couldn't see Katarina, then Katarina could not see her. Then she heard a slap, and her mama's high-pitched voice.

"I don't know where she is, ma'am. I swear I don't," Billie said.

Katarina's voice was strident and angry. "You find her now, or I'll punish her myself and neither one of you will like that. The Garden Club ladies will be here in just over an hour, and we still need to do the child's hair and change her clothes."

"Yes, ma'am. I know, ma'am. I'll find her, I promise," Billie said.

Sahara was sad now, wishing she hadn't hidden. She'd gotten Mama into trouble.

Billie sat down on the side of the bed, wiped her eyes and took a tissue from her pocket and blew her nose.

"You can come out now," Billie said.

Sahara crawled out from under the bed, her eyes welling with tears.

"I'm sorry, Mama. I didn't mean to get you in trouble."

Billie lifted Sahara into her lap and gave her a brief hug.

"You go tell Katarina that you were outside in the garden and didn't hear her calling. Tell her you're sorry."

"Yes, ma'am," Sahara said, and left their bedroom with her steps dragging.

But she was soon running, her little footsteps echoing throughout the house.

Katarina heard her and came out of her bedroom with an angry look on her face.

"I'm sorry, Katarina! I didn't hear you calling. I was in the garden."

Katarina sighed. Children were such a burden sometimes.

"It's okay, child. I thought you were hiding."

"Oh no, ma'am. I would never do that," Sahara said, and then smiled.

Katarina looked down into the beautiful little face before her and imagined she saw herself in those perfect features.

"Well, then," she said. "We need to hurry. You're going to sit beside me during Garden Club as a reminder to the members to vote you in as Little Miss Rosebud. Come Mardi Gras, you will be riding with me in the Garden Club float. Isn't that exciting?"

"Yes, ma'am, exciting," Sahara said.

* * *

Bubba was running out of ways to get rid of Sahara without revealing his identity. If he managed to get inside the house, he would have to deal with the bodyguard, which was out of the question. And while he had been using bombs earlier, he had no intention of blowing up the mansion. Poison hadn't worked. Deadly snakes didn't work. Hiring a hit man was a bust. Every time he changed his modus operandi and failed, it was a cautionary warning to them of impending dangers.

He was walking past a mirror in his house when he paused, intently eyeing his reflection. He didn't look like a murderer. He didn't feel like one, either. What he felt was cheated. He hadn't started out intending to hurt others to get what he wanted, but in war, collateral damage was inevitable.

He leaned closer. He had his mother's eyes and coloring, and he'd also inherited from her an ingrained hate for the Travis family as a whole, which was why he had no problem ending their time on earth. They'd lived in opulence long enough. It was his turn to share in the wealth, and there was only one more person standing in his way.

He made a quick trip to the supermarket and was back home in less than an hour, carrying the sacks up to his third-floor apartment.

When he reached the third-floor landing, he stomped loudly, certain that the lady who lived across the hall from him would open her door to see who was making noise in the hall.

And just as he expected, she did.

"What's going on out here?" she cried.

"Oh, I'm sorry, Mrs. Lively. I didn't mean to disturb you," he said.

The old woman frowned. "Well, since it's you, it's fine. For a minute I thought it might be some kind of burglar, kicking in the doors to rob good folks like us."

"No, ma'am, just me. I'm really sorry. Oh, by the way! Did you hear the news about Sahara Travis?" he asked.

She frowned. "Hear what? That they found her daddy dead? Yes, everyone heard that."

"No, not that. I just heard on the news as I was driving home that she had been killed. She was the last of that family—now they're all gone. Sure is a shame."

"Oh my Lord!" the woman cried. "I hadn't heard. What a tragedy. So beautiful and so young," she said, and shut the door in his face.

He grinned. Mrs. Lively was the building's gossip, and she had a reputation for spreading even a hint of a rumor the second she heard one. She loved being the center of a good story, and so Bubba knew she was on her way to share this tidbit with anyone who would listen. She would have it on Facebook to all of her family all over the United States, and he knew that because he saw her posts to them regularly. If he was lucky, she'd also text her daughter who had a big following on social media as a stylist to the rich and famous on the East Coast, and the rest would take care of itself. The story would blow up before anyone thought to verify it because that was how social media worked these days. If he was lucky, Sahara would come out of hiding just to prove she was still alive, and he would get one clear shot at her and change the rumor to a truth.

He put the groceries away, took time to eat some lunch and send a couple of texts to make sure all was going as planned, then changed into old jeans and a lightweight T-shirt, tennis shoes in case he had to run, and headed out the door, this time taking care to be quiet.

He drove back to the street where the old house was located, then drove another half block and parked. He got out and began walking, as if out for a stroll, and when he got to the old three-story house, he stopped to stare at it, as if he was a prospective buyer casually walking around the house. He slipped back into the unlocked window when the coast was clear, and this time ran all the way up to the attic.

The fact that the house was hot as hell now was not lost upon him. So the ghosts didn't hang out here in the daytime, or if they did, they were lying low. He got down on his knees and quickly reassembled the rifle, loaded it, checked the scope and then stood up to look out the dormer.

As he'd hoped, locals were already beginning to gather at the front gates to the Travis estate because the old gossip would have told her local friends first. They were taking pictures on their phones and likely posting them back to Facebook, Instagram and Twitter, innocently furthering the lie that he'd told. There were a couple of empty wooden boxes in a corner that he hadn't seen from the time before, so he pulled one of them up to the window and sat down to wait.

Soon, sweat was pouring out of his hairline and down his face. His clothes were stuck to his body, and he wished another thunderstorm would come through and cool off the city. But he refocused his thoughts on the task at hand.

The longer he waited, the larger the crowd grew, and the more pleased he became. When the cops showed up and then left without dispersing the crowd, he laughed.

"By God, this just might work."

While Brendan was confident the police would be pursuing the info he'd sent them, he wasn't going to quit now. Carson had given him some very interesting information, and it would either play out in their favor or not.

The good news was that Shelly and the kids were getting well, and Carson hadn't caught whatever it was they'd all had. Concerned that Carson would get caught hacking into something that would get him in trouble, Brendan ended his brother's participation with a thank-you, the promise of a steak dinner and a bottle of his favorite wine next time he saw him.

He glanced up from the desk to check on Sahara. She was still sleeping. At least it was helping pass the time, but as he watched, she whimpered, then rolled off her belly and curled up onto her side, her knees drawn up as far as they would go.

Frowning, he got up and pulled the afghan off the end of his bed and covered her with it. He didn't think she was cold, but the weight of covers could be a reassuring feeling to someone who was afraid. He wished so much for the freedom to just lie down beside her and wrap her up in his arms, but they needed to find a killer worse than she needed the end to a bad dream. He leaned down, brushed a kiss across her forehead and went back to work.

Carson had given him the address of where Leopold Travis's body was found—an abandoned house in the middle of the Ninth Ward. There were many buildings like it that were rotting and in disrepair because of Hurricane Katrina, but he had a strong suspicion that the building of the murder scene was special for some reason. In no way was he going to buy someone kidnapping Leopold from his own home, taking him to what amounted to an abandoned house in the middle of a dead zone and then randomly killing him there.

So he logged in to a site he often used and began to research the owners of that particular property through county records. What he hadn't figured on was the actual age of New Orleans and how many records were attached to a single property. But he could contain his search to within a certain span of years. After he found the names, he began researching census records to see if those owners had heirs with birthdays that would fall within the timeline of the payoffs they'd found.

It was a tedious task. He got up a couple of times to go to the bathroom and to stretch his legs, and like Sahara, he felt confined because his job was to stick with her and she wasn't going anywhere.

When he heard a soft knock at the door, he got up.

It was Billie. She saw Sahara asleep and motioned for him to come out in the hall so they could talk.

"What's up?" he asked.

"There's a crowd of people gathering outside the gate."

He scowled. "Again? What the hell for? Is the media there, too?"

"I can't tell. I didn't even know they were there until one of them buzzed to be let in, and I didn't recognize the name. I looked out to see if he was still there after I'd refused, and that's when I saw them all. I'd guess there's at least fifty or more."

"Damn it," Brendan said. "Call the police."

She took off down the hall.

Brendan went back into the bedroom and then looked out the window in disgust.

"Hell's fire," he muttered. "What now?"

He watched until he heard sirens, and then saw a half-dozen cruisers pull up and police getting out to disperse the crowd. He watched the cops moving toward the gates, then walking aimlessly through the crowd for a few minutes before a couple went back to their cruisers.

Within minutes, the house phone rang. He picked up. "Hello?"

"Brendan, it's me. The police just called. The crowd is putting up some kind of memorial. There are flowers and candles and stuffed toys all along the fence," Billie said.

"For Katarina and Leopold? Why now?"

"No," Billie corrected him. "They think Sahara was killed today."

"Well, hell, why would they think—" And then it hit him. "I continue to marvel at the depths to which this person will go."

"What do you mean?" Billie asked.

"How much do you want to bet that our killer started this rumor, knowing it would escalate to this? The national news will report it. The crowd outside will grow larger, and the makeshift memorial larger and a bigger freaking mess…unless Sahara, herself, shows up to prove she's alive. And when she does, there'll be a sniper somewhere waiting for a kill shot. One shot is all it takes if he's good."

Billie gasped and then started to cry. "Why won't this madness end? What are we going to do?"

"Don't worry, Billie. This guy thinks he's smart, but he's clearly desperate and hasn't thought this through. In a world where social media reigns, why would anyone ever need to go outside? Hell, she could probably do a live Skype call and that would be all it takes to squash this rumor. But we'll go a step further just to prove it's legit. I'm going to wake up our Sleeping Beauty and have her make another call to her friends at the local television stations. A live, on-the-spot interview inside the mansion will do it and added verification from the media who saw her."

"Oh, Brendan, that's brilliant! Yes, that should work," she said. "If I need to do anything, just let me know."

"Will do, and thanks," he said, and hung up.

Sahara was sitting on the side of the bed when he turned around.

"So Sleeping Beauty woke up and without the kiss from her prince. What's going on?" she asked.

"I can fix that," he said, then sat down beside her and took her into his arms. The kiss he gave her was soft and searching and ended far too soon.

She groaned softly when he pulled away.

"I'm sorry, baby, but you heard what I said. There is a large crowd gathering at the gates, and the beginnings of a makeshift memorial. Flowers, candles, teddy bears…you know the drill. If this catches on, it's going to take the physical sight of you to end it. But if you go outside, you'll become a sitting duck."

She stood abruptly, anger in every feature on her face.

"Oh my God! This is never going to end! So this is why you mentioned the television station to Billie."

"What do you think?" he asked.

"I think if they've heard the rumor, too, they'll be all over getting the scoop directly from the source. Yes, I'll call, but I don't remember the freaking number. I have to go back downstairs to—"

"Wait," Brendan said, and handed her his phone. "Google it."

"Oh. Right," she said. Within minutes she was, once again, speaking to the station manager who was in shock that he was hearing her voice.

"I can't believe I'm speaking to you. We just heard this a few minutes ago and have been trying to get verification from the police department, but no one's called back," he said.

"If you'll send your crew over here again and put me on the air live, you'll have yourself another scoop and hopefully end this before it gets too far."

"Oh…it's already ridiculous. That's why we've heard about it. Someone came into the station talking about an unsubstantiated story spreading all over social media that the killer finally took you out. Since no one has seen sight of you since the day you arrived in New Orleans, the viewing public bought it."

Sahara groaned. This was the nightmare that kept on giving.

"So when can you come?"

"As soon as we can round up the crew."

"You better ask for a police presence or you won't get through the crowd," she said.

"Yes, yes, we'll be there soon."

She handed the phone back to McQueen and then ran into the bathroom to look at herself.

"I have bed hair, no makeup on, and look at what I'm wearing! And I have to be on air in less than an hour."

"I like that sleepy-eyed bedroom look myself," he said, and then grinned when she glared at him. "Want me to go get Lucy?"

"If I went on air looking like this, they wouldn't believe it was me, so yes, please. I'll need all the help I can get to be ready before the film crew arrives."

She heard Brendan cross the hall and knock, then a murmur of voices. She grabbed a hairbrush from the bathroom and walked back into the room, trying to tame the curls, as Lucy came hurrying into the bedroom with purpose in every step.

"Sahara! I don't like this. The only strangers who have been in this house so far are the TV crew. What if the killer is one of them? He'd have seen the whole setup of the house once. What if he's the one who started this lie, knowing it would give him the chance to come back in again? What if this might be the time he makes his move?"

Sahara's heart skipped as she looked at McQueen, suddenly doubting their decision.

Brendan was staring at Lucy. This was the most he'd heard her say since they'd been introduced. It was also the first time he'd heard her express concern for Sahara's welfare since that day in the hospital when she'd arrived bloody and in tatters. Still…she had made a good point.

Then he heard the tremble in Sahara's voice.

"Brendan, what do you think? Should I not let them in? We could do just a brief word at the door, couldn't we?"

He shook his head. "I don't like that idea. That leaves you open the moment you show your face."

She looked at Lucy, and then at Brendan, back and forth, back and forth.

He could tell she was wavering, and then she took a quick breath and blurted her decision.

"We're doing this inside as Brendan suggested. He's in charge of keeping me safe."

Brendan exhaled slowly. "And I still will," he said.

Lucy shrugged. "That's fine. I just felt I had to say

my piece. You do your makeup while I take care of your hair. I think we should put it up, don't you? It'll save having to style it too much. And you can wear one of the dresses we brought. Anything but black, though. That's too reminiscent of a funeral, which is the opposite message we're trying to achieve here."

And just like that the tense moment had passed and Sahara appeared to pull herself together, going willingly into the bathroom with Lucy.

Brendan wanted to hug her. He wanted to tell her that he would not let her down. That he would die before he'd let anyone touch her. Instead, he pointed to the table where he'd been working.

"I'll just be over here," he said to no one in particular, and sat down because his legs were suddenly shaking. All he could think was *Please, God, help me keep her safe*.

A long hour passed as the crowd grew larger and larger. When Bubba saw a van from a local television station coming up the street, he frowned. Here was where it got tricky. If she came to the door for a few words, he was gold. But if they went inside to get a full interview, once again this was wasted effort.

The van passed through the crowd toward the gates, and two police cruisers stopped and got out for crowd control to let the van pass through.

When the van drove up to the house, he saw the crew get out and head toward the door.

He opened the window and stood all the way up.

He recognized the reporter—an anchorman who

did the six o'clock news on that station. If he had to, he would shoot through him to get to Sahara Travis.

He took aim. Now the front door was in the cross-hairs. Perfect.

The door began to open.

"Hold it, hold it, hold it," he muttered, then to his horror, the door swung all the way inward with only a fleeting glimpse of the housekeeper as the whole crew filed inside.

A wave of disappointment swept through him, followed by growing frustration. He'd known it would be a long shot, but it could have worked.

"Just fuck it," he said, then dropped back into the shadows and closed the window.

He sat down and quietly disassembled the rifle, repacked it in the case and made his way out of the house, then back to his car while frustration slowly turned to rage.

The air-conditioning in the car was on high as he drove through the city, then headed out into the coun-tryside, wondering what his life might be like if he just turned his back on all of this now and kept driv-ing. Right now, they didn't even know where to look. They couldn't prove anything. They couldn't pin any-thing on him.

He drove all the way to Baton Rouge, stopping at a little restaurant he used to go to with his mother. It was barely the dinner hour, but close enough.

He ordered a bowl of gumbo and, for an entrée, blackened shrimp and grits. The food was tasteless, but it didn't matter. It was the ritual of remembering his past that he'd come for.

He stayed only long enough to finish, then left a dollar tip when he paid, like his mama always had. Not because she was cheap, but because they never had enough. He left before he could see the angry look on the waiter's face.

He started driving around the city, remembering when he'd lived here, the school he'd gone to, the park he'd played in. Remembering everything.

Billie was upset and trying to hide it as she welcomed the film crew back into the mansion.

"Good afternoon, gentlemen. Miss Travis is in the formal living room. This way, please." She led them back to the white room, where, days earlier, Sahara had received Katarina's friends.

She saw Sahara sitting in icy silence with McQueen only feet away and then left them to it.

"Stop there," Brendan said, as the news crew froze. "One at a time, please," he said shortly, and again patted down every member of the crew, including the anchorman, searching duffel bags with sound equipment and any place a weapon could be stored, before letting them into the room.

For the crew, it was their second time to be searched here, and it brought home the seriousness of Sahara's situation in an unexpected way.

Sahara sat without speaking, letting Brendan do his job and making no apologies for the reason.

Last time she'd worn white to match the room, but

this time she was wearing a navy blue minidress with three-quarter-length sleeves and a plunging neckline. Her dark hair appeared to have been carelessly yet perfectly piled up on top of her head, leaving tantalizing wisps dangling around her face and neck. She was limited on dress shoes, but in deference to the tender skin on her foot, she had chosen the same sandals she'd worn before.

Lucy was absent at her employer's request. Sahara was adamant that the fewer people the killer could connect to her, the safer they would be. Since she wasn't needed, Lucy escaped to the kitchen to stay with Billie.

Buzz Jordan was the six o'clock news anchor and would be the one with the lead-in. Despite the heat, he was wearing a pale gray summer-weight suit, a pink shirt and a maroon-colored necktie. He was a confident thirtysomething man who knew he was good-looking but managed to carry it off without seeming cocky.

"Okay, Miss Travis, we're just about ready. I'll do the voice-over, the camera will cut to the date on my cell phone to verify this isn't a prerecorded clip, and then the camera will cut to you. You will say what you need to say, and then I'll thank you, do a wrap-up, and we'll be out of here."

She glanced at McQueen. He had the curtains drawn, the crew thoroughly vetted, and stood just out of the shot with his hand on his gun. The quick nod he gave her was the cue she was waiting for, and she gave the anchorman a thumbs-up.

He had his earpiece on. The voice in his ear began the countdown.

"In five, four, three, two and...you're live!"

Buzz Jordan turned to the camera. "We are here with breaking news to quell a rumor that has gone viral on both local and national news, thanks to social media. The rumor involves Hollywood megastar Sahara Travis's death, and the claim made that she was murdered today. Efforts to stop the rumor have been unsuccessful, partly because she has been forced to stay in hiding, since her life is still in danger. To prove this is not a stunt, or a prerecorded clip, I'm showing you the current date and time on my cell phone."

The camera did a close-up as Buzz Jordan kept talking.

"Miss Travis is here with us now to make a statement that will end these foolish rumors once and for all, and stop the memorials gathering all over the country. Miss Travis, what would you like to say to the millions of viewers who are watching this live?"

The camera cut to Sahara as she looked straight into the lens.

"I think I was as shocked as you all were to hear that I was dead. As you can see, that is anything but the truth. I was so touched to see the crowds outside my family home, and to learn of the mementos being left at the gates. My fans mean the world to me. I take pride in my work and would never want to let you down. It is touching to know that you really care.

"So, as you can see, I am alive and well, and putting this rumor to rest for good."

Then her expression changed. Brendan saw a muscle jerk at the side of her jaw, and when her hands doubled up into fists, his heart skipped a beat. What the hell was she about to do?

"Now I have another message," she said, and slowly stood. "It's for the gutless coward who murdered my parents...the same asshole who's been trying to kill me."

The whole crew gasped, as did McQueen.

She stared straight into the camera. "Look at me, you slimy little weasel. If you want me dead, you're going to have to come into my world to do it. Every attack you've made has been behind my back, or in the dark. You've killed two elderly people, an innocent young woman, an airport mechanic, and got your own hired gun killed—all because you're afraid to face me. That says coward to me, and I'm not afraid of cowards. If you want me, you know where I am. Come and get me."

Brendan strode over to where Buzz was standing. "Cut the feed now," he snapped.

Buzz nodded at the cameraman, and the live feed ended.

Brendan turned around and stared at Sahara as if she was a stranger. He had not seen that coming, and now it was too late to take it back.

"What the hell did you just do?" he asked.

She lifted her chin and wouldn't answer in front of the crew.

Brendan hustled them out of the house, then ran back to where she was waiting.

She was standing in the doorway.

"Why?" he asked, then took her in his arms and held her.

"Because I'm sick of this, and I want it over. I set the trap. Now it's your job to figure out a way to make him think I will be unprotected."

"Damn it, Travis," he said, then tilted her chin up and kissed her.

Sixteen

Bubba drove around the city until it was full-on dark, rented a room in a motel with a clerk who wouldn't ask questions, then called an escort service. He was numb, and he needed to feel something.

When the prostitute showed up, he handed over the money and sat down on the side of the bed for the blow job he'd just paid for. He watched what was happening from a detached state of being. His body was reacting to the prostitute's wet mouth and long tongue, knowing that the blood rush moving from his heart to his groin was going to explode inside him in a sensuous rush. And when it did, he grabbed the prostitute's head, pushing it down upon his erection as he came.

With the ripples of the climax still rolling through him, and the prostitute flailing her arms in wild abandon as she struggled to breathe, he grabbed her head and pulled it back until they were staring face-to-face.

"Get out!" he said.

The prostitute scrambled up and left on the run.

He got up to clean himself, and then ashamed of what he'd done, he began wiping down everything he had touched in the room. He felt that if he left no trace of himself behind, then he could pretend it had never happened.

He drove back to New Orleans in the slow lane, with the rest of the travelers on the highway whizzing by.

It never occurred to him that he was losing it. That the decision to kill had split his psyche straight in two. The fact that he could obey traffic laws while blindly disregarding other laws in his hunt for revenge didn't seem strange at all.

It was late when he got to his apartment, and he was careful to walk quietly down the hall. He locked the door behind him and put the rifle case in the top of his closet, stripped naked and took a shower before crawling into bed.

Sahara picked at dinner. Her appetite was a joke, but so was her life.

She glanced up at Billie. She seemed bothered, too. The smile was gone from her eyes, and she was far less vocal than normal.

Finally, Billie said what had been on her mind ever since she heard it.

"Why did you challenge a killer?"

Sahara reached for her mother's hand. "To end this. I don't like being a sitting duck waiting for the hunter to reload."

Billie's chin trembled. She was struggling very hard not to cry.

"I just got you back in my life. I would not live through losing you again."

"You aren't going to lose me. Brendan won't let that happen."

Billie shook her head. "You laid a terrible burden on his back, child. How can he protect you from the unknown?"

Brendan interrupted. "It won't be hard, Billie. At any time, only three other people besides myself are supposed to be in this house, and they're all sitting here at this table. Anyone else comes in here, and I shoot first and ask questions later."

"I don't get out of his sight, Mama. I'm not stupid," Sahara said.

Billie wiped a shaky hand over her face and then stood. "I made an Italian cream cake for dessert. You picked at your food. Technically you should not get a piece."

Sahara smiled ruefully. "I remember that rule, but the day I passed thirty I earned the right to skip the entrée and go straight to dessert every now and then."

Billie sighed. "And you always outtalked me, too."

Lucy was quiet, watching the back and forth between mother and daughter, and wondering how much of Sahara Travis came from her father rather than Billie. She wondered how Billie had coped with giving up her claim to her daughter just to give her a better life. This whole scenario was foreign to her, but it did explain a lot about her boss. She'd always felt like Sahara was a woman with secrets, but she would never have imagined all this.

McQueen's phone began to vibrate across the table as Billie got up to cut the cake. He glanced at it, saw it was from Harold and just handed it to Sahara.

"It's Harold. You may as well answer," he said.

Sahara frowned. "All he's going to do is read me the riot act. Excuse me, people. I'll step out into the hall to take this so you won't have to hear me grovel."

"If you go to the hall, I go to the hall," Brendan said. "Just sit. When someone continues trying to kill you, then you know manners have gone all to hell."

Billie giggled. "Answer it and don't worry about me," she said.

Lucy nodded. "Answer it or he'll have a stroke."

Sahara sighed and answered the call. "Hello, Harold."

He didn't bother to say hello. He just started shouting.

"Have you lost your ever-loving mind? What the hell was Brendan thinking letting you do that?"

"Stop shouting at me. He didn't know I was going to do it, so don't play the blame game. This was my decision, and I'd do it again. I'm sick of living like this. You're not the sitting duck, I am. I want this over, so I've set a trap. The end."

"I may never sleep again," he muttered.

"Go have a drink. Eat some pie. Chill, Harold. We've got this."

She heard him sigh, then clear his throat.

"I've been meaning to tell you this for ages, and now is as good a time as any. You mean the world to me. I love you like a daughter. I had hopes of a son-in-law and grandchildren one day. Don't get all brave on me and screw this up!"

The call ended with her eyes swimming in tears.

"He hung up on me," she said, and gave the phone back to McQueen.

"You're crying. What the hell did he say to you?" Brendan asked.

"It was a sweet thing, not a bad thing. I'm crying because it touched me."

"What did he say?" Lucy asked.

"That he loved me like a daughter. He's expecting grandchildren and me not to screw this up."

Lucy giggled. "Harold is never subtle."

Billie was a little jealous that a man she didn't know had fifteen years of a relationship with Sahara that had made them close like family. It was only two years less she'd had with her daughter, but it was so long ago and filled with too many ugly secrets they'd had to keep. If she had it to do over again, she would never have given up her baby to others. But hindsight was a whole other thing, and she was going to have to live with guilt for the rest of her life.

Sahara wouldn't look at McQueen, but she didn't have to. The words had already rattled him. Sahara, love and babies in one sentence was enough to make his head spin. Instead of commenting, he got up and began refilling coffee cups to go with the dessert.

A short while later the meal finally ended.

The day had been stressful for everyone, and by the time the kitchen was clean, Billie retired to her rooms.

The rest of them went to the library for an after-dinner drink. When the conversation hit a lull, Sahara glanced up at Lucy.

"Remember the other day when you offered to go back to LA to see to the cleanup of the penthouse? Well, I want you to go. Tomorrow."

Lucy's eyes widened. "Okay, but why so sudden?"

"Because I have invited a killer into this house, and I do not want you in the line of fire. You've done so much for me, and I refuse to put you in any more harm."

Lucy stared until her chin began to tremble. "Yes, of course. I'll pack tonight. Do you think I'll be able to get a flight for tomorrow this last minute?"

"I'll find one for you," Brendan said. "Don't worry."

Sahara's hands were shaking. This was the first move in acknowledging the reality of the killer who would be coming after her. She cleared her throat.

"Of course I don't have a key card to the penthouse anymore, but I'll make sure Adam has one for you. If there's smoke damage, then call an interior decorator and have it staged to sell after it's cleaned as you suggested."

"I will," Lucy said. "If there's no damage, I'll get your clothes packed up and stored."

Sahara thought of the day she'd moved into the penthouse and how safe she'd felt in her aerie high above the streets. To think it had become a trap that nearly killed her had ruined the magic. She didn't ever want to set foot in it again.

"Yes, all right," Sahara said. "And have someone pack up my kitchen. I want my pots and pans and cookbooks."

"What about all the china and crystal?"

"Yes, that, too," she said. "And the awards. I spent fifteen years earning them. I won't throw that away."

"Don't worry. I'll get it done," Lucy said.

"I'm paying you extra for this. Your annual salary for the year in a lump sum, over and above your monthly salary."

Lucy gasped. "I can't! That's…that's so generous of you, Sahara."

"You'll take it, Lucy. I insist. You're worth it," Sahara said.

Lucy ducked her head. "Thank you. I'm going to my room to pack. I'll see you tomorrow."

"Give me your cell number and I'll send the plane ticket and boarding passes to your phone," Brendan said, then entered the number in his contacts.

She waved a quick goodbye and left.

Sahara set her wine aside. "We may as well go up so you can work on her reservations."

Brendan slid an arm around her shoulders and gave her a quick hug.

"Did anyone ever tell you that you rock?" he said.

"Not and mean it," she said, and slid her arm around his waist.

"Then follow me," he said.

"To the ends of the earth," she said.

He wanted so much to believe this was true as he leaned down and kissed her.

She groaned as the kiss deepened, and then Brendan stopped.

"Hold this for later and don't forget where we were."

"It will be my pleasure," Sahara said.

They left the library arm in arm.

He set the security alarm in the upstairs hall and then walked her into the bedroom and locked the door.

"Why don't you soak in the tub for a while. It'll help you relax. I'm going to get Lucy's ticket out of the way."

She wasn't going to argue and began undressing as she walked away.

Brendan got his laptop. A short while later he was on a ticket search for a one-way ticket to LA.

Across the hall, Lucy was packing, but with a tumble of emotions. She wanted to be back in LA with Wiley, but it would be different this time. She would be the one in charge. She'd be giving orders and making decisions. She tossed another blouse into the suitcase and then smiled. This might turn into a cool gig, after all.

Brendan sent the ticket info to Lucy's phone and got a quick thank-you as a response. He grimaced. She wouldn't be thanking him tomorrow when she had to get up at 5:00 a.m. to make the flight. To make it up to her, he'd also hired a car and driver to pick her up here at the house. It was the best they could do on short notice.

He paused to listen, but there was total silence coming from the bathroom. Soaking was in progress, so he opened the file on Leopold Travis and read through his last notes, then picked up where he'd left off.

He had pared the list of past owners of the house where Leopold was killed down to a woman who fit Leopold's timeline of payoffs. Now he had to run a background check on her, see if she married, if she had children, and, if she did, match birth dates to the date of the payoff.

But before he could begin, Sahara opened the door, turned out the light behind her and walked into the bedroom. She pulled back the covers and stretched out on the sheets—naked as the day she'd been born.

Brendan shut down the laptop, taking off clothes as he turned out the bedroom lights, and was in her bed within seconds.

Sahara turned on her side to face him, then closed her eyes and began tracing the shape of his face with her fingers.

"What are you doing?" he asked.

"Memorizing you."

His heart sank. "So you'll remember what I look like after I'm gone?"

Her hands stilled on his face as she opened her eyes. "I don't want you to leave me."

He sighed. "Just take this on a day-by-day basis. I'm here now. You already know if it happens it won't be me quitting you."

When she started to argue, he rose up on one elbow, slid his hand beneath her neck and kissed her. Her hair was silk against his skin. Then his mouth was on her breast and his hand on her belly as his search moved lower, then lower still. When his hand reached the juncture of her thighs, she parted her legs and arched against the heel of his hand as he began to stroke.

Over and over, slow and steady, then faster in a pounding rhythm that mimicked her heartbeat. At that point, Sahara lost focus on everything but the waves of pleasure that slowly turned into a climax on the verge of exploding.

Brendan felt her fingernails digging into his arms and knew she was close, so close to coming. He kept stroking, making that tiny nub harder and hotter until she gasped.

Sahara was blind to everything but the blood rush bursting through her body in one overwhelming rush. The sensation of free fall was so real that she grabbed him to keep from crashing to the ground. When she could breathe without screaming, she pulled him down to her.

"Ah, Brendan...how I love you," she whispered, as he raised up his hips and slid inside her, and like before, her body adjusted to make room to let him in.

The deep tenor of his voice was raspy-rough with emotion.

"I will love you until the day I die, and for however long this lasts between us, and I will ruin you to ever loving another man."

Then he began to move.

One stroke, then another, and another until the joining was a hammer of flesh against flesh, spiraling into a need so maddening that nothing else mattered. Seconds turned to minutes as the sweat grew on their bodies.

Sahara kept pace with every stroke as he drove deeper and deeper. That burn in her belly was turning into a fire again as she wrapped her legs around his waist. And then she moaned when he went deeper.

The sound sent him into another level of need, moving faster, stroking harder. She heard his breath catch, and then he groaned, rocking against her as he came, sowing his seed in the warm fertile bed of her body.

It was McQueen's undoing that tipped Sahara over the edge. She came again as his body was still rocking. She kept kissing his face, and then his lips over and over.

"Love you...so much," she kept saying.

"Love you more," he whispered, then gathered her close as they fell asleep in each other's arms.

Brendan had set the alarm on his phone to wake him before Lucy had to leave, and when it went off, Sahara woke up with him.

"What's going on?"

"Lucy's car will be here in a little less than an hour. I need to carry her bags down the stairs."

Sahara brushed a quick kiss across his mouth. "You are the best, Brendan McQueen, and I should tell her goodbye."

She got out of bed and ran into the bathroom, only to come out a couple of minutes later with her hair and teeth brushed. She ran into the closet to get clothes and met Brendan coming out already dressed. When they passed in the doorway, he gave her a quick pat on her bare backside.

"That's a good look on you," he said, and winked.

She was still smiling as he went into the bathroom, and within minutes they were out of the room and knocking on the door across the hall.

Lucy looked worried when she opened the door. "What's wrong? What's happened?"

"Nothing's wrong," Sahara said. "Brendan is carrying your bags down the stairs, and I came to tell you goodbye."

Lucy smiled. "Really? Thank you so much. I'm already packed. All I need is to get my purse and phone, and I'm ready to go."

"Then we'll get your stuff downstairs by the front door and go see if we can rustle up some coffee and maybe a sweet roll," Sahara said.

Lucy was beaming. "This is awesome. I really appreciate it," she said, and pointed to two bags. "Both of those go with me."

Brendan picked them up as if they weighed nothing. "After you, ladies," he said.

They headed downstairs, talking as they went. He set the bags by the door, released the security alarm and then went to the kitchen with them. Since they were up, he could do with a cup of coffee.

To their surprise, Billie was already at the stove.

"Just in time," she said. "I made French toast. Not good to travel on an empty stomach." She gave Lucy a quick hug. "I'm going to miss having you around. You were so sweet to help through all of this."

A little uncomfortable with all of the attention, Lucy shrugged it off. "I was happy to do it, and it helped pass the time."

Billie gave Lucy the first plate and pushed her toward the table.

"Eat up."

She reached for the syrup to pour on her toast without waiting for the others to join her. This morning it was all about her and her need for haste.

Time passed too soon. The driver was at the gates buzzing the gate to be let in, and then Sahara was hugging Lucy goodbye in the foyer before moving back to hide in the shadows as the driver rang the doorbell.

Brendan opened the door, gave Lucy a pat on the back as the driver took her bags to the car, and then they were gone.

He turned. Sahara was in the shadows, watching his every move. And just like that, the fear was back.

It was still dark outside when Bubba's alarm went off. After a quick shower and shave, he dressed and went to the kitchen to make breakfast.

He had no thoughts one way or the other about what he'd done last night, focusing only on what had to be done today. It was his habit to eat while watching the early-morning news, and so the television was on for company as well as information.

He was pouring cereal into a bowl when the news anchor began talking about Sahara Travis. He poured milk onto his cereal and carried it to the table to eat, curious as to what she'd said about the rumor.

His eyes narrowed when she appeared on screen. He appreciated beauty and she had it, but she was in his way. He spooned up a bite of cereal and began to chew as he listened to her statement, and then got up to pour himself a cup of coffee.

"Okay, fine. You proved your point, bitch," he muttered, then carried his coffee back to the table and sat down, thinking that the clip was over.

Then she stood up. The camera pulled back to get a full view, and when he saw her eyes narrow and her hands curl into fists, the hair crawled on the back of his neck. He'd seen Leopold do the same damn thing when he got mad.

The first words out of her mouth were to him, and for a moment he half expected the cops to come breaking into his room and arrest him, then realized she hadn't called him by name because she had no idea who he was.

He listened, shaking with growing rage.

She called him a coward!

She said it to the world!

She dared him to come into her world, and he knew what that meant. If he wanted her dead, he would have to get into that house to do it. So be it. Maybe she was right. It was time for all this bullshit to end and he didn't intend to fail, even though it was going to take some planning to make this happen without getting caught.

He turned off the television, then took a deep breath and set all of this aside to finish his cereal. He set his cereal bowl in the sink, grabbed his keys and sunglasses, and headed out the door. It was time to get to work.

Seventeen

Beloit Blooms was unusually busy for a weekday, although Marcus was not going to complain. He'd been on the phone almost nonstop for an hour taking orders. The one he was taking now was for a delivery of two dozen roses to be delivered to a woman who worked in the courthouse.

"It's our twenty-fourth wedding anniversary," the caller said. "A rose for every year."

"Congratulations," Marcus said, and meant it.

Making people happy was part of why he was in this business. Even when it involved floral arrangements for funerals, he still felt the need to make them visually perfect. It was his way of showing his sympathy for the family's loss.

"And you can deliver this before three this afternoon?" the man asked.

"Absolutely," Marcus said. "In fact, I'll get this out with the first morning delivery. She should have it by noon. What do you want me to put on the card?"

"To the next twenty-four. Love, George."

"Okay, George, and how do you want to pay?"

The man gave Marcus a credit card number, and then the transaction was finished. He printed out the order and took it back to the workroom to his three floral designers.

"Shawna, get this one out with the morning delivery," he said.

"Yes, sir," she said, and laid it on top of her work orders to do next.

The welcome bell rang over his door as it opened. He looked up as he returned to the front of the shop and then smiled at the silver-haired lady who walked in.

"Welcome to Beloit's."

She smiled, then began to explain what she needed for a dinner party tomorrow night and when she wanted it delivered.

It wasn't until there was a lull in calls that he focused in on the discussion going on in the workroom about Sahara Travis. He walked back to join in.

"Hey, Marcus. You know her, right?" Shawna asked.

"I sure do. We went to school together. She is a doll, and I am just sick about what happened to her parents and what continues to happen to her."

"So, she's really nice?"

"She is, as they say, the real deal. Not one bit stuck up on herself and doesn't forget her friends."

Shawna sighed. "That is so cool that you grew up with someone famous."

Marcus laughed. "But she wasn't famous then. We were just kids in the same class, you know?"

They laughed but continued to be properly impressed about his close connection with such fame.

He got busy again, and it wasn't until he took off for lunch that he thought about calling her. He should have called after the news broke about finding her father's body, but he'd had no idea what to say. He still didn't, but good Southern manners won out. He was still in the parking lot when he turned up the air-conditioner before making the call.

Billie answered. "Hello."

"Hello, Miss Billie. This is Marcus Beloit. I am already terribly late in calling Sahara about her father, but my conscience wouldn't let me slide. Is she available to take a call?"

"She is," Billie said. "Just a moment, please."

Sahara looked up from the paper she was reading and frowned. "Who is it, Mama?" she whispered.

Billie covered the phone. "It's Marcus."

Sahara sighed. Ever since Lucy's early-morning exit she'd been feeling a little down. She didn't feel like talking, but that would have been rude. She took the phone and then upped the tone of her voice.

"Marcus, how are you?"

"I'm the one who should be asking you," he said. "I should have called sooner, but you know me. I'll tell you the truth whether you want to hear it or not. I just didn't know what the hell to say. First your mother and now your father. It's heartbreaking, and I am so sorry that this is happening."

"Thank you. I still can't wrap my head around someone wanting all of us dead, and for what?"

"I know, dear. It is a ridiculous and devastating scenario. Listen, part of the reason I called was to ask if there's anything I can do for you. I know you're housebound, so is there anything that would take a burden from you? It would be my honor."

"Thank you, Marcus, but I don't know what that would be."

"I understand, but if something comes up, please call. I am at your service, and hopefully next time we talk, the subject will be much happier."

"For sure," Sahara said. "Thanks again, and goodbye."

"Goodbye," he echoed, disconnected, then took himself to lunch.

Sahara hung up the phone and then sank into a chair at the table.

"I don't feel very good, Mama. After all the trouble you've gone to making those shrimp po'boy sandwiches, I'm going to pass on lunch."

Brendan was worried. Her eyes were glazed, almost as if she had a fever. He put a hand on her forehead. The skin was cool, almost clammy to the touch.

"Do you hurt anywhere, baby?"

She drew a deep, shaky breath and then pounded her chest with her fist. "Here. I hurt here. I don't know how to feel. I've sent Lucy away so she wouldn't be caught in the crossfire, and now I have to face the possibility that I might not live through this. I don't know whether I need to pray to a God I don't trust, or prepare for the role of dying."

Before Brendan could respond, Billie slapped her hand on the table, rattling the dishes.

"Hush, child! I won't hear such talk! You aren't going to die. You're scared, and so am I. You're exhausted, and so am I."

She got up and went to the pantry, dug around a few moments, then came out with several items in her arms.

"What are you doing, Mama?" Sahara asked.

"I'm making a potion for you. Mr. McQueen, finish your meal. Sahara, this is not a movie, so stop acting like you're on your deathbed. Do you hear me?"

Sahara took a deep breath. "I hear you, Mama."

"No more talk about dying?"

Tears rolled down Sahara's face. "No more talk about dying."

Brendan watched the mother schooling the child and couldn't help but wonder how many times Sahara had needed a mother's love and guidance, but never got it because there were two women playing that role. She must have been so confused. Too many secrets. Too many lies. No wonder she was such a good actress. She'd been acting a part all her life.

But he couldn't stand to see Sahara like this and do nothing. He shoved his plate aside, tugged at her hand until she got up and scooted into his lap. Satisfied, Brendan wrapped his arms around her.

The microwave dinged.

Billie removed the cup that she'd filled with milk, sugar and chocolate, dropped a handful of miniature marshmallows on top of the hot liquid and carried it to the table.

"If you remember, this potion cures sad days, bad grades on tests and tummy aches."

Sahara watched her mother set a steaming mug of hot chocolate with marshmallows in front of her and sighed.

"I remember. Thank you, Mama. I will drink it. I promise."

Billie smiled, pleased with the familiarity between them. At least one good thing had come from all this. They belonged together.

"I'm going to get the mail. I'll be back shortly."

Brendan pulled the cup closer as Billie left the kitchen.

"Do you want some now?"

"After it cools a little," Sahara said. "Mama's potion. I hadn't thought of this in years. No matter the weather, this was the cure-all for things she couldn't fix."

"She loves you very much," Brendan said.

"I know. I love her, too, and am sick at all the years we lost. I thought she left me behind. I shouldn't have believed Katarina and Leopold. I don't know why I did. All I saw was an empty room, and then shock set in. But the irony of all this chaos is that if the killer had not set out on this path, I might never have known she was still here."

Brendan picked up the cup and began blowing on it to cool the surface, then dipped a spoonful into his mouth to test.

"Here you go, honey. It won't burn you now."

She took it and the spoon in her hands, stirring until the last of the marshmallows had melted into a floating froth. She lifted it to her mouth, thinking there wasn't a taste better in this world than warm, sweet chocolate.

"Taste good?" Brendan asked.

"You be the judge," she said, and kissed him.

He could taste the chocolate on her lips.

"Spectacular," he said.

"You need to eat your sandwich," she said, and slid out of his lap as Billie returned, laying the mail on the sideboard, then handed Sahara a large padded envelope with The Magnolia letterhead on it.

"Oh, I think it's my phone and purse," Sahara said, as she tore into the envelope. Her phone and her Yves Saint Laurent Classic handbag slipped out onto the table, along with a new cord to charge the phone. "I sure hope this still works."

She attached the phone charger and then plugged it into an outlet before going back to her hot chocolate. She drank the potion until the cup was empty while Billie and Brendan ate shrimp po'boys slathered with spicy rémoulade sauce and crunchy coleslaw.

"Feel any better?" Billie asked.

"Yes, Mama. I do."

"Good. No more talk about being defeated," Billie said.

"I promise," Sahara said.

Brendan heard the lilt in her voice and saw the smile on her face, but he still wasn't convinced she was okay.

Billie left later to run some errands, and as soon as she was out of the house, Sahara took her things and the charging cord upstairs with her, plugged the phone back in there, set her purse aside and then wound up falling asleep. It left Brendan free to pass on the latest information he'd found regarding the possibility of other heirs to both police stations.

He sent another email with an attachment regarding everything he'd found about Sutton Davidson and his mother, Barbara Lovett, who later married a man named Davidson. It included info about Leopold lending Sutton a large sum of money some years back to start a business, which Sutton had already paid back with interest. There was nothing to point to him being a killer except that he and Sahara Travis were very likely half brother and half sister, and if anything happened to her, he would be blood heir to everything.

As soon as he hit Send, he shut down the computer, locked the bedroom door, then took off his boots and crawled into bed behind her.

Her hair was silk against his cheek as she spooned against him, her breasts soft against the back of his arm. The steady rise and fall of her breathing became the touchstone to his own heartbeat as he drifted off to sleep.

Sometime later, Sahara roused.

The wall of McQueen's body behind her was her bulwark to safety. She lay without moving, wanting to remember what it felt like to be loved like this.

Brendan had only been dozing and felt the change in her breathing when she woke. He wanted to love her the rest of the way awake, but there was something she needed to know.

He kissed the back of her neck.

"Sweetheart…?"

"I'm awake."

"I need to tell you something," he said.

She stilled. "What's wrong?"

"Short of a DNA test to positively prove it, I think I found another heir. You have a half brother. The pay-off money from Leopold to a woman named Barbara Lovett coincides just right with a baby boy born five months later. And she was living in the house where Leopold died when the baby was born. She lived there until he was six."

Sahara rolled over to face him.

"Oh my God! Barbara, that's Sutton's mother! Are you saying Sutton—our *gardener* Sutton—is my brother?"

He sat up, but when he went to reach for her, she pulled away. "No, don't. Just say it."

"Yes."

Her face lost all expression. "Do you think... Is he behind all of this?"

"I honestly can't say. His entire background check was clean. He's a model citizen and is making a good living."

"I don't understand. If Leopold paid them off to get rid of them, then why did he hire Barbara six years later and let Sutton come into the house with her? We went to school together in the morning, came home together after school and played until she got off work at six o'clock."

"I don't know, but consider this. If Katarina didn't know who the other women were, then she would have had no problem with Barbara and her child being in the house after school, because she's just another servant. And maybe Leopold was vain enough to not want to lose contact with a son."

"That sounds plausible," Sahara said.

"Maybe she hit hard times, and Leopold offered her a job with the caveat that Katarina could know nothing about their prior relationship," Brendan said. "However, she married a man named Davidson right after she quit working here, and he adopted the child. That's why Sutton goes by Davidson instead of his mother's maiden name."

She got out of bed, took a few steps and then stopped in the middle of the floor.

He went after her.

"This is the break we've been waiting for. We have a potential suspect."

Her voice was shaking when she replied, "Does he know we're related?"

"Obviously, there's no way for me to know that. If I had to guess, though, I'd say yes. I would imagine he was told after he grew up, if not before."

She threw up her hands in disbelief and then started pacing.

"Why didn't he tell me? We played together. We were friends! I would have liked knowing I had a brother."

"Maybe he didn't know it back then. I can't say anything for certain except that he is now probably the police's number one suspect. The LAPD will compare his photo to the security footage they got of the man who sabotaged the elevator in The Magnolia. Even if he was in disguise, between physical build and facial recognition, they could nail him. But even if he's not a match, it still doesn't clear him. This killer we're after hired Harley Fish, so it's easy to assume he has hired out some of the other attempts, as well."

She shuddered. "The other day when they were here cleaning up after the storm, Sutton stood in the doorway and smiled at me."

Brendan slid a hand beneath her hair and pulled her to him.

"This information gives us an edge. He has no idea that Leopold kept that journal or that we've been looking for heirs."

"This hurts my heart," Sahara whispered. "I feel betrayed all over again by this place and the people who were in it. I hate it. If I live through this, I'm never coming back here again."

McQueen's voice deepened with emotion as he pulled her closer.

"Baby, don't doubt me. I need you to believe I will not let anyone hurt you."

She leaned back, looking at the man he was—a bodyguard, a man who put his life on the line for the job…for her. The fact that they'd fallen in love had caught both of them by surprise.

"I believe you and I believe *in* you, so how are we going to set this trap? As long as you're here, it gives any would-be attacker cause for hesitation."

He looked at her in disbelief. "Well, I'm damn sure not going anywhere."

"But what if people think you did?"

He looked at her intently. "What are you getting at?"

"People have accidents all the time, right? They get sick. They get hurt. So I have to believe that, whoever the killer is, he's watching this house all the time, waiting for an opportunity just like that."

"Oh, he's definitely watching now," Brendan said. "You dared him. You called him a coward in front of the whole world. He needs to show you what a badass is he."

"I'm just pissed off enough now not to care," she muttered.

He grinned. "Okay, tough stuff, I hear you. But I love you too much to let you run with that attitude. However, your idea isn't half-bad. What if we set something up with the police? We could have someone else come into this house posing as your attacker. Sutton would know it wasn't him, and would be suspicious, but he'd also know that I would do whatever I had to do to protect you from anyone. So we convince the world that I killed your attacker, but that I was hurt in the process. We can arrange for an ambulance to take me away…and a medical examiner will haul out a body bag with the fake attacker in it. To the world, the danger to your life is over, which means I'd be okay with leaving your side to get medical attention. If Sutton thinks I'm not on-site, he'd assume this place was completely unguarded and that you're alone. He'd definitely try to make his move."

"Yes! Exactly like that," she said.

"Only… I'll have to figure out a way to get back in the house unseen almost immediately."

Sahara snapped her fingers as an idea came to her. "Oh! I know a way!" she cried, and grabbed his hand. "Come with me. I need to find Billie. Last time I saw this, I was just a kid, but there's more than one kind of secret in this house."

Billie had a pie cooling on the sideboard and was in the laundry folding towels when she heard Sahara calling for her.

"I'm in here!" she shouted, and reached for another bath towel.

Sahara came hurrying into the room. "Mama! Remember the time you showed me that secret passageway to the basement?"

Brendan frowned. "There's an actual basement in this house? But there aren't any windows to allude to that. This is New Orleans. It's below sea level. The place where they bury people aboveground so they don't float up later."

Billie laid the folded towel on the stack. "Basements are ground level in New Orleans because of the water level. It's why the front steps are so high and the veranda so wide. It hides it from the front of the house, and in this case it was always kept secret."

"We need to see that secret exit, to see what shape it's in," Sahara said.

Billie looked nervous. "What are you planning to do?"

Brendan quickly outlined the plan, including the detail about needing a viable entry back into the house without being seen.

"Dear Lord," Billie said. "I can tell there's no way of talking you two out of this, so follow me."

They followed her into the butler's pantry, where she opened an upper cabinet and pushed a panel at the back of the wall. A four-foot-wide section of floor-to-ceiling cabinets swung out, revealing a narrow stairway leading down to the ground floor.

"There is a six-by-nine-foot room at the bottom of the stairs that's always been called the basement, when in fact it is only a room, and with a single door that leads outside into an arbor of wisteria vines. You will see how it's laid out as you go. Follow the tunnel of vines until they end at an ivy-covered wall facing the alley. There is a door hidden somewhere within that ivy. Both sides of the wall are covered in vines, so the door is not visible, and I have no idea how long it's been since anyone used it."

"How did you come to know about this?" Brendan asked.

Billie glanced at her daughter, then back at him. "Because that's how I came into the house when I was young. That little room at the bottom of the stairs used to have a small bed in it. It's where Sahara was conceived."

"Oh, Mama," Sahara said, and just held her.

"Okay, then," Brendan said, patting her back. Then he flipped a switch just inside the opening. A single light at the bottom of the stairs lit the way.

"I'm going down," he said.

When Sahara started to follow, he hesitated.

"You told me not to leave your sight," she said.

He sighed. "Not the first time something I've said

has come back to haunt me," he said, then saw concern on Billie's face. "She'll be okay with me. We won't be long, but I need to see if this will serve the purpose I need, or if we need to figure out something else."

"Okay, but I'm standing right here until you get back," she said.

Brendan stepped down onto the first step. "Sahara, stay a step behind me and hold on to my shoulders as we descend."

"Okay," she said, and down they went with Brendan swiping cobwebs away as they went.

They reached the small room at the bottom of the stairs.

"Would you look at this," Sahara said.

There were shelves on one wall, a small antique-style desk beneath it with a handmade, three-legged stool on which to sit, but no bed. The surfaces had more mold than dust, as did the brick walls.

"There's a padlock on this door," Sahara said.

"Let's look for a key first before I go out to the shed to look for a tool to cut it off."

Sahara turned to the shelves, eyeing the scattered items as Brendan headed for the small desk. She opened boxes, shook old bottles for a rattling sound, but found nothing. She was all the way to the end when she saw an old key hanging on a nail between the shelf and the wall.

"Here it is!"

"Good job!" Brendan said, and gave her a quick kiss. "Now, here's hoping this thing will still turn enough to unlock."

"Billie keeps WD-40 in the utility room," she said.

"Ask her to bring it to you at the top of the stairs."

Sahara started back up the stairs, calling out as she climbed up.

"Mama, we need some WD-40."

Billie disappeared as Sahara paused on the top step to wait. Moments later she was back with the blue-and-yellow can of lightweight oil.

"Here you go," Billie said.

"Thank you, Mama," Sahara said, and hurried back down.

Brendan sprayed the inside of the lock and then the key as well, removing as much dirt and grime as he could see, then set the can on the shelf.

"Here goes nothing," he said, and slipped the key into the old padlock and tried to turn it.

At first, it would go only partway, and then it would stick, so he sprayed it again and tried once more. This time, it turned all the way.

"Bingo," he said, removed the lock and laid it on the shelf with the spray.

The door was as stuck as the padlock had been, but it was no match for Brendan McQueen's strength. He put his shoulder to it and hit it like a linebacker taking out the quarterback. The hinges squeaked as the door popped open, revealing the inside of a tunnel formed entirely of thick verdant vines and dangling clumps of purple wisteria.

Sahara was entranced. "If I had known this was what was at the end of those stairs, this would have been my secret place. Just look how far this arbor goes."

"Hey, honey, grab that can of WD-40 and the key. We might need it to open another lock."

She dropped the key in her pants pocket and took the can as they started through the arbor.

Years of dead leaves and blooms crunched beneath their feet as they started down the concrete path beneath. Sunlight coming through the vines shimmered like tiny rays of gold.

Sahara was so entranced that she was whispering. "*The Secret Garden* was my favorite book when I was a girl. I feel like I've just stepped into one of my own."

Brendan looked back, saw the wonder on her face and reached for his phone.

"Drop the can," he said.

She did.

"Beautiful, so beautiful. I don't ever want to forget this," he said softly, and began taking pictures of her amid the tangled vines and purple blooms. The scent of the wisteria and the tiny rays of sunlight on her face and clothes were images he would never forget. He didn't see the love on her face until he was seeing her through the lens of the camera, and when he did, it brought tears to his eyes.

He put the phone back in his pocket and then kissed her. The words came out of his mouth without warning, but he could no more have stopped them than he could have stopped his own heartbeat.

"I love you, Sahara…so much."

The smile that spread across her mouth matched the joy on her face.

"Oh, Brendan! I love you, too! You are the best thing that ever happened to me."

Brendan brushed his lips across her forehead and made himself stop before this got out of hand.

"This is crazy. I'm trying to find a way to keep you safe, and all I want to do is make love to you. Come on. Let's find the end of this tunnel."

She picked up the spray can and then took his hand, following a step behind him until they came to the end, facing a wall covered in vines.

"Now to find a door," he said, and began pulling at vines.

Eighteen

Within minutes the door was revealed, and as suspected, locked with a similar padlock.

"I just realized something. The last person to come through this tunnel was going *into* the house, because this padlock is inside the wall, just like the other padlock was inside the house."

"Oh, you're right!" Sahara cried. "Let's see if this key works here, too."

He repeated the process, spraying the padlock and then inserting the key. After a few tries, the lock turned. This door opened inward, revealing a wall of more green vines, but as she pushed some aside, she recognized the location of the exit.

"This is perfect. It opens into an alley," Brendan said. "Wait here a second, I'm going to squeeze through. I need to orient myself as to what streets are at both ends and which way I would return. As soon as I'm out, you can watch, but don't come all the way through, okay?"

She nodded, her heart pounding with anticipation as he pulled out a pocketknife and began cutting straight down through the vines, like parting a curtain. It took a few minutes before the opening was large enough for him to slip through.

Sahara pushed the greenery aside to look out, watching him as he ran from one end of the alley to the other end, pausing each time to identify cross streets.

He slipped back into the tunnel, pulled the vines back in place, then shut and padlocked the door. They made their way back through the tunnel, returning to the house and padlocking that door as well before hanging the key back on the nail. He grabbed the can of WD-40.

"Come on, baby. Up the stairs we go. You first. I'm right behind you."

Billie was still waiting for answers.

"It'll work," Brendan said, as they reached the top of the stairs.

Billie sighed. "When is this crazy plan supposed to take place?"

"I have to talk to the detectives and set it up. Hopefully in the next day or so. I need to use the WD-40 again on these hinges. Once all this goes down, I don't want anyone hearing me coming back inside."

Sahara stood out of the way as Brendan began spraying the hinges to the passageway, then opened and closed the doors over and over until they were silent. When they went shut for the last time, he gave the spray back to Billie and winked at Sahara.

"Now we lay the trap."

* * *

Detective Shaw found the email from Brendan late in the afternoon after he got back to the precinct. When he opened the attachment and realized the bodyguard had actually uncovered a probable half brother to Sahara Travis that no one knew about, and that he was someone she'd known all her life, his first thought was to compare the DMV photo Brendan had sent to the security footage they had from The Magnolia.

It took a few minutes to get everything set up. When he notified his lieutenant to update him, Lieutenant Coleman opted to sit in on the viewing.

"Afternoon, Lieutenant. Go ahead and take that chair if you want."

"Now, what is it we're going to be doing here?" Coleman asked.

"I received a DMV photo of Sahara Travis's newly discovered half brother. We're going to compare it to the security footage from The Magnolia and see if there's a match."

Shaw started the playback where it picked up the repairman on security cameras outside The Magnolia, then again inside at the service entrance, then in the elevator going down to the basement.

They could tell the man's approximate height from stationary objects he had passed, and they were assuming the hair and mustache were fake. Then they picked a still shot from the security footage and on a split screen brought up the DMV photo.

"What do you think?" Shaw asked, as they eyed both faces.

"I don't think it's the same guy," Coleman said.

"Neither do I, which is disappointing. Still, to be on the safe side I'm going to put them in facial recognition."

It didn't take long for the program to kick out an answer. No match.

"Well, that's that," Coleman said. "Keep me in the loop. We're getting flack from some Hollywood big-wigs because Sahara Travis is still in danger."

"Yes, sir," Shaw said, and then sat down at his desk and called Detective Fisher in New Orleans.

Fisher was already working on the new information from McQueen's latest email, going through Sutton's bank records to see if he'd made any large cash withdrawals that would coincide with the cash found on Harley Fish's body, and was going through his credit card accounts to see if he had made any recent flights to LA, but so far they'd found nothing.

And then his phone rang.

"New Orleans Homicide. Detective Fisher speaking."

"Detective, this is Detective Shaw in LA. I assume you also received the new email from Brendan Mc-Queen?"

"Yes, sir, we did. We already knew he's a damn fine bodyguard, but he's not half-bad as a detective, either. We're understaffed here, so there's no way of knowing how long it would have taken us to dig all this up."

"Agreed," Shaw said. "We sent you footage from the security cameras at The Magnolia, right?"

"Yes, it's in the computer file."

"Have you had time to compare that man in the footage to Sutton Davidson?"

"No, I have not," Fisher said.

"Then I'll save you the trouble. They're not the same man. According to Sutton Davidson's DMV information, he's six-four, one eighty pounds, which makes him damn skinny at that height, and the man in the security footage is not that tall. He's also not skinny. And the facial recognition program we use kicked him out."

Fisher sighed. "Well, I guess I should say that's good to know, but it's really not. We already know our killer is willing to hire a hit man, because we have a dead one here on a slab in the morgue."

"Oh really?" Shaw said. "You're sure it was a hire?"

"Yes. A local with a bad rep named Harley Fish. He had a thousand-dollar roll on him and the address of the Travis estate written on the back of a scrap of paper. And…when a relative came to officially identify the body, we learned Harley Fish could read some and knew his numbers, but his handwriting was illegible, which means Fish did not write that address on the receipt himself," Fisher said.

"Damn it. This is like trying to pin murder on a ghost."

"Agreed," Fisher added.

"Okay…so we have another heir to the Travis estate, but we can't tie him to either one of these hits," Shaw said.

"Not yet, we can't," Detective Fisher said. "But we both know shit floats. He'll make a mistake, and when he does, we'll get him."

"Then I wish you luck," Shaw said. "Stay in touch. If you take him down, let me know."

"You can count on that. Thank you for staying in contact," Fisher said, and then disconnected.

Bubba was on his way home early.

The longer he'd thought about the challenge Sahara had thrown out, the more irrational he'd become. The scenarios running through his head were rash, with little chance of succeeding. It would do him no good to kill her if he got caught in the process.

He thought about taking a couple of days off work to find a location where he could watch the house. If enough people left the premises and he was in disguise, he would take the chance on going through her bodyguard to get to her. With a big enough gun, he could take anyone down.

That little trip outdoors through the tunnel of wisteria whetted Sahara's appetite for freedom, which made the impossibility of walking out the front door an insult all over again.

So to stay on the move, she prowled the rooms from top to bottom, looking in places she'd forgotten were even there with Brendan patiently at her side. She showed him a tiny room on the servant side of the house where a slave skilled in sewing would mend laundry and make clothes. She showed him the ballroom on the grand side of the mansion, where Katarina regularly held parties, and a single chair in an empty room that used to be where the gentlemen of the house got their haircuts.

The antiquity of this house along with the historical aspects were impressive, but Sahara's opinion of the place came from her life experiences, not the grandeur. Each place she talked about held a dark memory. Never one of joy. When she'd finally announced there were no more rooms to be seen, he shook his head.

"There's one more room you haven't shown me."

Her eyes narrowed angrily. "I'm not going there."

"It was your bedroom," he said.

"It was my *upstairs* room. I didn't live there. It was for show when guests came for dinner. Katarina made a big deal about putting me to bed there, which made everyone comment on what a great mother she was. Of course, she loved the attention, and after I reached my teenage years, they made me live up here full-time. I didn't know why then, because I missed being down with Mama, but looking back, it was probably her way of splitting us up. She didn't love me, but she expected me to acknowledge her as the dominant woman in my life."

"Do you mind if I look at it?" he asked.

The question startled her. "Why would you want to do that?"

"I saw where you lived with Billie. I would like to see where you lived the lie."

She shoved her fingers through her hair, digging them into her scalp in frustration.

"God, McQueen, whatever…knock yourself out. But I'm not going inside."

"That's okay," he said.

She frowned. "I thought you didn't want me out of your sight."

"Then come with me," he said, and held out his hand.

She sighed. "You tricked me."

He led her up the stairs, stopped at the first door on the left and walked inside.

For Brendan, seeing the opulence in this room was shocking. Furniture, carpet, draperies, bedspreads, pillows, even the walls were either snow white or as brilliant as Midas's gold. The walk-in closet was almost as large as the room itself, and the bathroom was spaworthy and gilded to boot.

"Wow," he said, and then realized Sahara hadn't said a word.

What he didn't know was that she was speechless.

From her standpoint, it was a shock to see everything exactly as she'd left it, considering she'd literally been thrown out of the house.

"I do not get it. What the hell?"

She was obviously angry. Thinking he'd forced something that was going to be a mistake, he quickly reached for her hand.

"Sweetheart, what's wrong?"

"Nothing in this room has changed except that." She pointed to a portrait of her hanging over the bed. "That portrait is less than four years old and is from a movie I was in. I can't begin to imagine how they even knew it existed, or how they got their hands on it. Who does this?" she cried. "They kicked me out of the house and then turned my bedroom into a shrine. Now I'm back, they're dead, and I own the damn place. Again, who does this?"

"Looking at this mess as an outsider, I can say that it's far easier to claim a connection to someone without investing in them. Kind of like your fans. They love you so much, and yet you wouldn't know one of them if you passed them on the street, right?"

She was listening, but he could see she wasn't sold.

"So for them, the emotion is all from one side. From what you've told me, Leopold and Katarina were more in love with the idea of a child than the actual child herself. And once you became an adult, your physical presence beside her would be aging her on sight. People would see a lovely young woman and then her. Like the fairy tale… Mirror, mirror, on the wall. Who's the fairest of them all?"

Sahara gasped. "Oh my God! I never thought of it like that, but knowing Katarina, that is *exactly* why I was ejected from this house. So I would not be a reminder that they were growing old."

She stepped back, looking at the room with new understanding. It wasn't for her. It had never been for her. It had all been for them, playing at being parents without any of the risk—and certainly without any of the love. When she became a vivid reminder of what they were losing—their youth—she was discarded like worn-out shoes.

"Thank you, Brendan. Thank you for making me come back in here and face the past. I have never been able to come to terms with that night. The rejection from Katarina and Leopold, and then believing Billie had rejected me, too, was all-encompassing. I've always felt like something was wrong with me, that there must be something deeply unlovable about me. It nearly destroyed me."

He stroked a finger down the side of her face. She was so much more than the face her fans adored. He would be forever grateful he'd taken this job.

"You're the easiest person to love in this entire world, Sahara. One day this will all be over. And if you still feel the same way about me—about us—then I'm taking you home to Wyoming and showing you what real families are like."

"What do you mean...if I still feel the same way?"

"Right now, I am your lifeline to survival. You have no idea how you'll feel when it's over, and we both need to know this thing between us isn't all based on your fear."

Her eyes welled with tears, but she didn't budge.

"Fine. You are so wrapped up in your opinion of my feelings, you refuse to acknowledge what they really are, but there's something you need to know. I cannot count the number of love scenes I've filmed, or the number of astoundingly handsome men who have made passes at me, claiming their undying love for me. But I can tell you I have been in love only once, and it's with you. I never gave my heart away to anyone but you. So if you reject me, too, Brendan McQueen, then I am done with love. I am done with an emotion that doesn't really exist."

"It does exist and I'm holding you to this, because I damn sure don't want to lose you."

He kissed her there, beneath a shimmering candelabra in a room of garish gold, banishing the last of her fears that she would always be alone.

Lucy landed in LA, and the moment the plane touched down, her thoughts began to stir, thinking of the task ahead. Even though Sahara's life revolved around make-believe, Hollywood was the city where magic was made. She couldn't wait to get back to her apartment and unpack, and she still needed to call Harold and tell him what Sahara had sent her to do, then contact Adam and make sure he would be able to get her into the penthouse.

So much to do and so little time.

But first things first.

She had to make a quick call. The phone rang twice, and then Wiley picked up.

"Hello, baby. Please tell me you're back home," he said.

She sat down on the side of the bed and kicked off her shoes.

"I'm home, and I came alone. No duties for tonight, and light ones tomorrow until I'm able to get into the penthouse."

"I'm still on the job, but I want to see you. I'm going to be late, though."

"Whatever time it is doesn't matter. I can't wait to see you again."

He chuckled, and the sound rolled through her like wildfire.

"Then I'll see you later," he said. "Welcome home."

"Thanks," she said, and then disconnected with a smile.

Brendan had been on the phone off and on all afternoon with Detectives Fisher and Julian. They finally returned his last call as he was waiting for Sahara to get out of the shower.

They were reluctant to go along with the ruse. Frustrated, Brendan challenged them, asking if they were ready to arrest someone for the continuing attempts on her life.

They were forced to admit they were not.

"Then what do you have to lose?" he asked. "Damn it, if ever there were extenuating circumstances, this is it. Two people dead in LA, three dead here, counting Harley Fish. I gave you an heir you didn't know existed, but you can't put enough together to even bring him in for questioning. The longer you wait, the more she's in danger."

"Look, I hear you," Fisher said, "but it's not my call. This will have to come from the commissioner."

"Then you ask him if he's willing to accept the blame for her death after all of the info I gave you."

"Well, hell, McQueen, why don't you say what you really think," Fisher muttered.

"If I haven't heard from you by tomorrow morning, then be aware we will set it up on our own. There are plenty of people in Hollywood who would do anything for her at the drop of a hat. In the world of film, accumulating a squadron of cops with uniforms and cruisers, along with a believable bad guy, is a simple fix. It's your call," Brendan said, and disconnected.

He could still hear the water running and was glad she didn't know the police in her hometown were dragging their feet.

A few minutes later she came out wrapped in a bath towel and went straight to the walk-in closet to dress. She emerged wearing a knit shirt and slacks, both in a soft shade of blue, and then went to check the cell phone she'd left charging. A big grin spread across her face when she picked it up.

"It charged!" She began searching contacts and email and was elated to find everything intact and functioning. "I can't believe it! My phone still works!" she crowed, and began scanning the hundreds of messages that had accumulated since the initial attack.

Brendan looked over her shoulder. "Are you going to answer all of those?"

"Not all of them, but a few."

He grinned. "Now I am about to find out if you're as manic about your cell phone as other people are."

"Hey, that's not fair," she said. "Did you once see me freaking out about it?"

He laughed. "Just kidding you, honey, and no, I can't say that I did."

"Okay, then," she said, and tossed it on the bed. "See. It stays behind. Let's go down to dinner early and see if Mama needs any help."

"Good idea," Brendan said, and then patted her firm little backside as she sauntered past. "Nice slacks," he said.

She looked over her shoulder and grinned. "You don't give a damn about my slacks, and we both know it."

He laughed out loud and followed her from the room.

Instead of a solitary dinner at home, Bubba went out with friends. One phone call with the invitation was all it took to send him out the door. He joined them at the bar while they waited for a table, and by the time it was ready, he was three drinks to the good and feeling no pain.

He sat with his back to a wall, giving him a clear view of the patrons, and realized he knew at least half the people in the room. That's what comes from being successful, he thought, and when one of them saw him and smiled, Bubba raised his glass in a toast and smiled back.

A waiter came with menus, then came back later for the orders. By that time Bubba was on his fourth drink and the room was beginning to tilt just a little bit to the right. He was saved from making a fool of himself with the arrival of a bread basket. Once solid food hit his stomach, he began to level off.

The conversation hit a momentary lull, and when it did, he heard himself asking, "So, what do you think about all the drama going on with Sahara Travis? It's like something out of one of her movies."

They stared at him for a few moments, a little surprised by the change of conversation, considering it had all been about their NFL football team, the New Orleans Saints, for the last hour and a half.

"Yeah, I guess," one of them said. "I haven't really kept up with it."

"All I know is both her parents are in the morgue and someone keeps trying to put her there, too," another said.

Bubba nodded. "Can't imagine what she's been going through and I heard the cops haven't got a clue," he said.

The only married guy at the table rolled his eyes.

"So what else is new?" he drawled, everyone laughed and the moment passed.

But for Bubba, it was eye-opening. No one at this table seemed to give a shit about what happened to her. That took a little of the joy out of his goal, then he remembered the mass turnout at the gates when they thought she was already dead. There were plenty who would care. They just weren't sitting with him at this table.

Their food came, and the more he ate, the more sober he became. By the time they parted company, he was stone-cold sober, regretting he'd ever mentioned her name and determined that tomorrow was the day he began his stakeout. All he had to do was to call in at the job tomorrow and tell them there'd been a death in the family and he'd be out of town for a few days.

It wasn't exactly a lie; it was just a little premature.

Nineteen

Billie was in her room lying down when Sahara came looking for her. She saw the darkened room and the wet cloth over her mother's eyes and remembered.

Migraines.

"Mama, do you need anything?" she whispered. "Did you take your pill?"

"Yes, took it. Need nothing," Billie whispered.

"Then you rest," Sahara said, and pulled a coverlet up over her mother's shoulders and backed out of the bedroom straight into Brendan. She closed the door and turned around.

"Migraine," she said softly. "She took her medicine. She'll have to sleep it off."

They slipped out of her rooms, then back through the short hallway to the kitchen.

"So, we're on our own tonight. Let me see what's already thawed and in the refrigerator," she said, and opened the door.

"I'm good with omelets," Brendan said. "We can

make them without making too much noise and making Billie's misery worse."

Sahara looked at him then, leaning against the counter with his hands stuffed in his pockets, watching her with that calm, steady gaze.

"Brendan McQueen, that might have been the kindest, most thoughtful comment I've ever heard. Have I ever mentioned how very much I love you?"

He smiled. "Not nearly enough."

"Then I will do better," she said. "Now, there are lots of things here we can put in an omelet, but you need to tell me what you don't want in it."

"You can skip the onions," he said.

"Good call," she said, and began pulling out ham, cheese and eggs.

But when she reached for the jar of sliced jalapeños and a bottle of Louisiana hot sauce, he whistled softly.

"Now we're talking," he said, as he saw the spicy condiments she was accumulating.

She shrugged. "What can I say. I was raised on Cajun and Creole cooking. Sliced bread, bagels and English muffins are in the bread box. You pick what you want to eat with yours. I'd like a toasted English muffin with mine."

She began breaking eggs into a bowl, but he couldn't bring himself to move, and the longer he watched the tall, leggy beauty, the movie star she'd become began disappearing before his eyes.

This was the real Sahara, the child who was bartered to a vain and hateful couple for a better place to live—the girl who fell beneath the cracks and crawled out of them on her own.

The love he had for her swelled to the point of pain. Whatever fate had in store, he would not be the one to doubt and betray her again.

He swallowed past the lump in his throat and went to the bread box. By the time she was turning omelets out onto their plates, he had a plate of toasted bread and muffins on the table, as well as the butter and peach preserves he'd gotten from the refrigerator.

"I didn't make coffee," Sahara said, as she carried their plates to the table.

"I'll take a Pepsi," he said.

She danced a little two-step on her way to the refrigerator.

"And I choose ginger ale."

He got the glasses and iced them while she got the bottles of soda. He watched her pouring ginger ale into her glass, then quickly take that first sip to get the full effect of the fizz. Another facet of the real Sahara was revealed, seeing such simple joy.

They ate together as if they'd been doing it for years, talking about the charade they intended to play out.

"What if he doesn't take the bait?" Sahara said. "We'll have given the media more fodder to relay false news."

"It's the chance we take, but if you want to call this off, I'm good with that. If you're having second thoughts, all you have to do is say so."

She shook her head. "No. I want this over. I want to do it."

"Okay, then," he said.

They finished their dinner and cleaned up the kitchen as quietly as they could, then went up to bed.

"I'm going to call Lucy and make sure she arrived safely," Sahara said.

"And I have a few emails to return," Brendan said.

"Turning down more jobs because of me?" she asked.

"Turning down jobs is part of my job. I can't ever take them all, and don't sweat it. I'm right where I want to be."

She blew him a kiss, then plopped down on the bed and reached for her phone. Just having it back made her feel connected to normalcy again.

She made the call to Lucy, expecting her to answer on the second or third ring just as she always did, and then frowned when the call went to voice mail.

"Uh...Lucy, it's me. I wanted to make sure you got back okay and to tell you I have my old phone again and it works...so let me know what's going on when you get a chance." Then she disconnected.

"She didn't answer?" Brendan asked.

Sahara shook her head, frowning.

"Don't worry," Brendan said. "All kinds of reasons why. Remember the time difference, too."

"You're right," Sahara said, and stretched out on the bed. "Will it bother you if I watch TV?"

"Not a bit," he said, and went back to work.

* * *

Lucy was in bed when her cell began to vibrate, but she ignored it for the glorious climax washing through her and the sweaty man inside her.

"You like that, baby?"

"Oh my God, yes, yes," she moaned.

He grinned and drove deeper and harder.

Their little orgy lasted until well into the morning. Wiley slipped out of their bed and left her sleeping so he could get home in time to shower and clean up for work. He would have liked to stay, but at least she was back. She was his life.

Lucy woke up the next morning, sad that Wiley was gone, but glad to be home. When she picked up her phone to check messages, she remembered the call from last night and was shocked to see it was from Sahara's phone. She listened to the voice mail and then sent her a quick text.

Sorry I didn't hear your call last night. I was so tired I went to bed early. Glad you have your phone back. I'll keep you updated on what's going on from this end, and say hello to Billie for me.

She put in a call to Adam at The Magnolia to let him know what she'd been sent home to do, and then called Harold out of courtesy. Then she got up to shower and dress. Today would be hectic, to say the least.

Lucy's text arrived midmorning on Sahara's phone, leaving her relieved. She was in the foyer with her mother, who was letting in the cleaning crew. Except for what she called a drug hangover and exhaustion, Billie felt better.

The crew barely made it over the threshold before Brendan lined them up and, one at a time, did a complete pat down. Then he went through the cleaning supplies they brought in before he let them go.

It was the first time the cleaning crew had been there since Sahara Travis's arrival, and they were intimidated by the presence of a woman of such fame and the bodyguard with her. But it was Billie who got their attention when she lit into them for doing shoddy work.

"Just because there's no traffic in and out of certain rooms in the house does not mean I want dirt, spiders and rodents setting up house there!" she said. "Mr. Travis's office was a disgrace."

"Yes, ma'am. We're sorry, ma'am. We'll be more thorough," they said, speaking over each other.

"See that you are. This time I'll be checking every room in this house when you're gone, and if it's not up to my standards, your boss will hear about it. If Mr. Brendan is satisfied with you, then you're free to go."

"They're good," Brendan said.

They scattered to the different floors to do their jobs, heads ducked in embarrassment by the dressing-down they'd been given.

Sahara stayed silent until they had dispersed, and then she shared her news.

"Lucy's fine. She just went to bed early, and she said to tell Billie hello."

Billie smiled. "She's a sweet girl. I enjoyed her company."

"Yes, she is." But Sahara was eyeing her mother closely. "Mama, why don't you go rest while they're here?"

"Oh, they'll be here for hours. I can't lie down that long. Besides, the ground-floor crew always starts in my rooms."

"Well, after they're gone, you can lie down if you want. There's no one left to tell you what to do here. It's basically your house now. Live it like you own it," Brendan said.

Billie paused a moment, then slowly smiled. "I never thought of it like that, but you're right. There's no one expecting anything out of me anymore, is there?"

"Certainly not us," Sahara said, and hugged her.

"What about lunch?" Billie said.

"What did you always do on cleaning day?" Sahara asked.

"I picked up food to go from wherever they wanted."

"So today, when you feel like it, you pick up food from wherever *you* want it. I would give anything to be able to get it for you, but I don't dare," Sahara said.

Billie patted her daughter's cheek. "I don't want you taking any kind of chance. And I will get some food later…for all of us. I have a debit card from the household account. I'll use it like I always do. As soon as they're through in my place, I believe I will lie down for a bit, but don't let me oversleep. If I'm still asleep around eleven, wake me up. Getting food during the noon hour takes forever."

"Yes, ma'am, I'll do that," Sahara said.

Billie left them on their own.

"Now what are we going to do, since the house has been invaded?" Sahara asked.

"We don't have enough privacy for what I had in mind," Brendan said.

She laughed. "You are outrageous."

"So I've been told. Anyway, we'll just go where they're not, and if they come in, we'll move."

Bubba had been up for hours. He had a headache from overindulging in liquor last night but was ready for this shit to be over with. He'd already been to Baton Rouge and back again and was all decked out with a rental car and a magnetic sign he'd stolen from a car there. He was wearing a uniform of sorts. Khaki slacks, a navy blue double-breasted blazer and a navy-colored cap. Posing as a courier was a good way to get the door open, and then he'd shoot as many as he had to, to get to Sahara.

He was all hyped up as he turned the corner and headed up their street, only to see two vans from a cleaning service parked in the front drive.

"Well, hell," he muttered.

They'd be in there for hours, which meant this wasn't happening today, and maybe this was a sign. Mama had always been big on signs, so today wasn't meant to be.

The hours dragged throughout the day. By the time they finally had the house back to themselves, it was late. They opted for sandwiches and cheesecake from the freezer for dinner, and again Billie chose an early time to retire. It was barely past 8:00 p.m. when she got ready to leave the kitchen.

"I've had all of this day I care to observe," Billie said. "If you two don't need anything more, I think I'll go to bed."

"If we need anything, we'll get it ourselves. Good night, Mama," Sahara said, as she hugged her. "Sleep well."

"You, too," Billie said, and left to go to her rooms.

Brendan and Sahara left the kitchen hand in hand, walking toward the stairs.

"Movie marathon?" Brendan asked, as they reached the staircase.

"A marathon for sure," Sahara said.

He grinned. "Damn, woman, but I do like how you think."

She ran her finger down the inside of his arm as she leaned closer, whispering near his ear, "It's because I love you, and I love this pretty skin and all these muscles, and the way you laugh, and the way you say my name when you come. I just can't seem to get enough."

The smile died on his face as he swept her up in his arms.

"Hang on," he said gruffly. "I'm about to go up a flight of stairs faster than I've ever done before."

She wrapped her arms around his neck and did what she'd been told.

Once he reached the upstairs landing, he paused long enough to set the security alarm. Moments later they were in the bedroom tearing off their clothes. He locked the door. She stretched out on the bed.

The marathon was on.

Bubba was parked at the far end of the block watching lights turning off inside the house. He already knew there were motion detector lights all over the grounds and wondered what would happen if he were to get caught under one, but he was afraid to find out. He needed to survive this unidentified and unscathed, or all of his effort would have been for nothing. So he put his car in gear and drove away. Tomorrow he would put the signs back on the rental car and arrive at the gates as a courier.

He was about six blocks from home when he began hearing sirens and looked up in the rearview mirror at the fire truck behind him. He pulled over and stopped to let it pass, and moments later had to pull over for a second one.

"Damn," he said, wondering where they were going.

It wasn't until he drove three more blocks that he began to panic. Flames were shooting up into the sky a good twenty feet above the rooftops. Someone's house was on fire. Someone close to where he lived.

He accelerated, his heart pounding, feeling like he needed to pee. He turned the last block and saw fire trucks and police cars everywhere, including the building with the flames shooting through the roof.

He pulled over to the curb to park and jumped out running.

His neighbors were on their porches. He could hear them calling out as he ran past.

"Sorry, man!"

"If you need a place to stay—"

And then a cop stopped him from going any farther.

"Let me go!" Bubba cried. "That's my home!"

"I'm sorry, sir, but it's gone," the cop said.

Bubba sank to his knees in shock.

"It's a sign. I see it, Mama, but it's too late to turn back."

He rocked back on his heels and watched in silence as the apartment building was engulfed in flames. He was still there, watching the fire crew dousing out hot spots, when the sun came up.

Brendan was asleep when his cell phone rang. He rolled over, reaching toward the nightstand, answering without bothering to look at caller ID.

"Hello?"

"McQueen, this is Detective Fisher. The commissioner gave us the go-ahead. If you're still up for all this, we have it set up for this morning before eleven, so be prepared for a break-in. Our guy is one of the undercover officers. He's about five-ten, stocky build and has long blond hair. He'll be in jeans and a T-shirt with the sleeves cut off. His gun will have blanks. Detective Julian is on his way over there bringing you a gun with blanks and some balloons of fake blood to tape to your body. You'll both need to look all shot up if this is going to be convincing. Our cops and the ambulance will arrive a couple of minutes after the security alarm goes off and take you and all the fake evidence away."

"Remember to tell them they need to let me out at that alley," Brendan said.

"Yes, they know. We've gone over it with everyone twice. The killer's body will supposedly go straight to the morgue and you to the hospital, but no one will know which hospital, so when you don't show up at one, they'll all assume you're somewhere else. That's as good as we've got."

"Much appreciated," Brendan said.

"What's happening?" Sahara said.

Brendan was already up and grabbing his pants and a shirt.

"The commissioner went for it. The break-in is happening at eleven."

"Today?"

"Yes, ma'am, and Detective Julian is on his way over here with props. Get dressed."

She flew out of bed and ran into the bathroom, then came out a couple of minutes later with her hair brushed and tied back, and ran to find a pair of shorts and a T-shirt as Brendan slipped his gun in the holster, then went out into the hall to turn off the alarm on the security system.

"I'm ready," she said, as she came running out of the bedroom.

He looked at her feet and frowned. "Did you run out of shoes to wear?"

She poked him on the arm and headed toward the stairs with him beside her.

Billie came out of the kitchen wiping her hands and was surprised to see them already up and in the hall.

"Detective Julian just buzzed the gate. What's going on?" she asked.

"I'll tell her. We'll be back here," she said, and pulled her mother into the formal living room.

"Not out of sight," Brendan said.

"No, just here beneath the arch, okay?" Then, as the doorbell rang, she began explaining to her mother what was happening.

Satisfied with their location, Brendan answered the door.

"Good morning," Detective Julian said. "Are you ready for your close-up?"

Brendan's smile was a shade on the grim side. None of this was funny to him.

"Come in."

Julian glanced at Sahara and tried not to stare, but it was confounding to be up close and personal with a woman of such fame.

"Good morning, Miss Travis. Miss Billie."

"Morning," Sahara said.

Billie shook her head and walked off.

"She's not happy about this," Sahara said, as she moved closer to Brendan.

"None of us are," he said. "So, Detective, show me what you brought."

"I have orders to do this right, so peel off your shirt," Julian said.

Brendan pulled the shirt over his head, revealing a rock-hard six-pack and massive shoulders.

"Damn," Julian said, eyeing Brendan's bare chest and then the size of the fake blood packs he had. "These are balloons filled with tomato ketchup for blood. Real fake blood from movie sets stains a lot of stuff, so we didn't go there, and we're not using the squibs they use during filming to make them detonate to look like a gunshot, since no one is going to see it go down except the ones in on the ruse."

"Then how will we bust them open?" Sahara asked.

"He can bust the ones on his chest. You can bust the ones I tape on his back before he lies down."

"Awesome," she said, watching as Julian taped two bags to Brendan's chest and then three across the back of his shoulders, then handed him a handgun.

"This one is loaded with blanks. It'll make all the noise you need to make. You answer the doorbell. Everything needs to happen just here in the foyer. You're too good to be tricked into letting someone get all the way into the house."

"But the gates…you have to be buzzed in. How does he get through the gates?" Sahara asked.

"He will have a remote that reads the gate code, then bypasses the system in place," Brendan said.

She was horrified. "What keeps everyone from having something like that? What good are doors and locks if technology continues to find a way to bypass human safety just for the sake of being able to do it?"

"I know. It makes our jobs harder, too, but the good part about one of those things is they're not cheap, and the average thief doesn't have access to that kind of thing," Julian said.

She was beginning to realize that being safe was no longer a choice, just a state of mind.

Brendan could see she was rattled.

"Don't think about it right now," he said. "We need to concentrate on today."

"Yes. I'm fine," she said, not wanting him to know how this had unnerved her.

"Okay, that's it for me," Julian said, as he taped down the last bag on Brendan's back. "Remember, set your security alarm, but don't lock the front door. That way when he comes in, it'll still set off the alarm."

"Will do," Brendan said, and let Julian out, closed the door, then set the security alarm from the panel in the niche.

He glanced at the time.

"It's almost 9:00 a.m. We have time to do breakfast before all this starts, and I need to remove padlocks so I can get back into the house."

Sahara walked into his arms. "This sets the trap, doesn't it?"

"Almost as good as some of the rescue missions I've been in on," he said.

"And this time you're rescuing me. God, I hope this works."

"It's an open invitation he won't be able to resist. If he thinks you and Billie are alone in this house, he'll come. He needs to gloat. He needs to tell you why this is happening."

"If this *is* Sutton, I cannot tell you how pissed and hurt I'm going to be."

"Well, he's going to be hurting more than you before I'm through with him, so hang on to that thought, my love."

"I am so tired of this house. All we do is eat, sleep and dig through Leopold's ugly life."

"And make mad, crazy love," he said softly, then brushed a kiss across her lips.

"You are the saving grace in the madness," she said. "I don't know what Billie and I need to do as this goes down, but we need to be told."

"A lot of panic and screaming, and more crying when the cops come."

Then they heard Billie calling them.

"Breakfast is ready, I do believe," Brendan said. "Don't want to make the cook mad. Let's hustle."

Billie was carrying pancakes to the table when they walked in.

"Honey, would you pour coffee?" she asked.

"Yes, Mama," Sahara said, and went after the carafe.

"Brendan, would you please get the bacon?"

"Yes, ma'am," he said, and picked up the plate of hot, crispy bacon sitting on the warming shelf.

They all sat down together, served themselves from the platters of food and began buttering and pouring syrup, then passing it around.

"Mama, when all this stuff starts happening here this morning, you and I are going to have a part in the charade."

Billie frowned. "What do I have to do?"

"Just a little bit of acting. We're going to scream and cry and be believably upset when the cops arrive. We'll be the only people still upright, so you can just go in and out of the doorway as if you were watching for the cops, and I may be visible from the doorway, down on my knees beside Brendan's body."

Brendan paused as he was about to take another bite.

"That's good directing, honey."

"Plenty of experience," she said, and winked at her mother.

"If it would save Sahara, I'd dance naked in the street," Billie said, which made the other two laugh.

Billie blushed, but she was giggling a little, too.

As soon as they finished, Brendan went upstairs to leave his gun in the room and slipped the one loaded with blanks into the holster. He pulled out one of his rifles, checked the scope and then loaded it while Sahara watched. When he was finished, instead of putting it away like everything else, he left it lying on the bed.

Sahara looked back as they were leaving the room.

"You're going to leave it out?"

"I need to be able to get to it quickly."

She shuddered. He put his arm around her as they moved toward the stairs. She was beginning to panic, and he knew it.

"I love you, baby."

With four simple words, he centered her world. She looked at him and felt the blessing.

"I love you, too, Brendan McQueen."

They went straight to the butler's pantry, opened the secret passage and walked down the stairs.

Brendan unlocked the padlock in the house, then Sahara stood at one end of the wisteria tunnel, watching as he ran to unlock the other.

When they were as ready as they were going to be, the three of them sat down in the white room, the one nearest to the foyer.

Billie waited with her hands folded, her head down as if in prayer. Sahara sat beside her, waiting, and Brendan stood at the window, watching.

Time felt heavy. It wasn't passing, it was dragging its feet.

Sahara watched him, taking her cue from his body language. Then all of a sudden it changed as he turned away from the window and pulled his gun.

"He just opened the gates."

Billie's head came up as Sahara slid to the edge of her seat, ready to play her part.

They jumped when the alarm suddenly went off in a shrill, siren-like scream that echoed what Sahara was feeling.

Brendan bolted out of the room as the intruder came over the threshold. With the alarm still shrieking, they began to trade shots.

Sahara ran into the foyer with Billie behind her, both screaming as they ran.

The intruder gave them both a thumbs-up, staggered backward against the doorjamb to pop the balloons on his back and then stumbled forward, bursting the ones taped over his heart, as he dropped to the floor.

Sahara hit the ones taped to Brendan's shoulders with her fists as he broke the ones on his chest, and then he staggered toward the open doorway before sprawling awkwardly where he fell, the gun lying loosely in his palm. Blood was spreading across the center of his chest while the balloons on his shoulders began pooling more on the floor beneath his body.

"Scream, Mama," Sahara said, and then let out an ear-shattering scream while Billie sidestepped the body in the doorway, screaming as she ran.

The continuing shriek of the alarm added to the panic as people on both sides of the streets came running out of their houses. Even traffic on the street outside the property was slowing down as the shriek of the security alarm blasted the area. Once people realized they could see bodies just inside the open door, the phones came out capturing video and sound, and the stories began to spread.

"I hear sirens," Sahara said, as she dropped to her knees beside Brendan.

He gave her hand a quick squeeze but said nothing.

Billie was standing in the doorway, crying and wringing her hands, and then ran back inside. Soon the cops came flying through the open gates. When Billie ran back outside, Sahara ran with her, her hands and shirt covered in Brendan's blood.

The drama of what went down was already on social media before the ambulance arrived.

Cops set up a perimeter to keep people away from the gates while others came out of cruisers with their guns drawn. They piled into the house and didn't come out.

When the ambulances arrived, a couple of cops led them inside.

The undercover cop who'd portrayed the killer was photographed lying in the pool of blood, then photographed from every angle, while Brendan was loaded onto a gurney and taken out to a waiting ambulance. It took eight men to get him down the stairs. The moment they had him loaded, they drove away with lights flashing and sirens screaming. Only then did Billie shut off the security alarm.

The moment the ambulance began driving away, Brendan was off the gurney and getting ready to jump out.

"You okay, buddy?" one of the paramedics asked.

Brendan gave him a thumbs-up, bracing himself as the ambulance took a quick right turn.

"Almost there. Get ready," the driver shouted.

As it began to slow down, Brendan moved to the back of the ambulance. Then he felt it braking.

"Now!" the driver cried.

Brendan opened a door and jumped down on the run. An EMT grabbed at the door as it swung back; Brendan was already in the alley. He reached the veil of vines in seconds, pushed them aside and hit the door with his shoulder. It swung inward on silent hinges. He began to breathe easier knowing he was back on Travis property and safely hidden inside the tunnel. He paused long enough to padlock the door, then ran back through the tunnel and into the house.

He replaced the last padlock, then stripped off his shirt and began pulling off the balloons from his body and rolling them up in the shirt before going upstairs.

He could hear voices from all of the cops still in the front of the house and hoped that they stayed there. He didn't want anyone to know there was a secret passage in this house.

He found plastic bags in the butler's pantry, dumped the bloody shirt and everything else inside it, slipped through the kitchen to the garbage can in the utility room and then went the back way up the servants' stairs to the second floor. Sahara hadn't been out of his sight since that day in the emergency room, and he didn't like the distance between them now. He paused to send her a text.

Upstairs. Now.

Then he slipped into their bedroom and quietly closed the door.

Twenty

Sahara was sobbing, standing close enough to the open door so people could see her. It wasn't hard to lock into that emotion because the thought of losing Brendan was enough to take her there.

Billie was beside her, holding her in her arms as if to console her as they waited for act three of this ruse to play out.

After the chaos of gunshots, the piercing blast of that security alarm, and the sirens of police and ambulances, the relative silence and the pools of blood left everyone with an eerie, unsettled feeling.

A short time later Warner Nelson, the medical examiner, showed up. By then the crowd across the street from the estate was large and spilling out into the streets.

Nelson was less than pleased to be participating in the charade and he made no bones about it, glaring at Sahara, muttering beneath his breath about overpaid actors and pseudodrama as he went through the motions on the so-called body.

It startled Sahara, then hurt her feelings, then it made her mad. She pushed out of her mother's arms and went for him, stopping just short of where he was kneeling.

"Hey," she said.

He looked up, startled that she was on his heels.

"We haven't been introduced, so I have no idea what to call you except rude. It's obvious my existence means shit to you, although I've been trying to stay alive for days now. Back in LA, someone poisoned my food on set, and someone else ate food meant for me and died. I narrowly escaped being blown up in an elevator, had to be rescued from the rooftop of my apartment because of the smoke and fire. My mother was murdered. A bomb was planted in my own plane. A man at the airport was murdered because of someone's need to see me dead. A cottonmouth was delivered to my house in a vase of flowers and nearly bit me. My father's body turned up dead in an abandoned building, and a hired gun got onto the grounds and tried to take me out. There are cops in two states trying to figure out who's doing this, and none of you are coming up with shit. I am so sick of this I could scream. I challenged the bastard on air, and now this event is, for all intents and purposes, removing the last obstacles he might have to getting to me. I have set myself up as the sitting duck, and if things go wrong, you get to recover my body, so maybe that will make up for your current dissatisfaction. I don't know what's wrong with you, but do not glare at me again. You've been working with dead people too long, you've clearly forgotten how to treat the living with a little respect."

She turned on her heel and strode out of the foyer without looking back. She was almost to the stairs when she felt her phone vibrate, signaling a text. She glanced down and saw Upstairs. Now.

"On my way," she muttered, and ran.

Brendan was already stripping and moving to the shower when she rushed into the room.

"Did everything go okay?" Sahara asked.

"Yes. Exactly as we planned, and just so you know, both doors are once more padlocked. I'm going to get in the shower."

She cupped the back of his head and kissed him.

"I had to do that," she said. "All of that stuff on you is scary. Just wanted to assure myself you're still okay."

"The fake stuff on you is scary, too," he said. "Wash it off and change your shirt. It looks too real." And then he headed for the shower.

Sahara followed him into the bathroom, took off her shirt and began washing her hands as he stepped into the shower.

Dear Lord, the chaos they had created, and this day was just beginning.

Back in the foyer, Billie moved into housekeeper mode.

"Are you gentlemen nearly through here?" she asked.

The ME was still reeling from his dressing-down.

He felt small for behaving as he had, but he wasn't a man used to apologizing to women for anything.

"Yes, ma'am," he said shortly. He directed the body to be put on a gurney, then covered it with a sheet from head to toe so the gathering crowd would assume the person was deceased.

When the body was rolled out of the house and down the steps, a wave of voices moved through the crowd, all with the same message…*someone was dead.*

And then the cops began leaving. As soon as the last one passed through the gates, Billie reset the bypass and the gates swung shut. Now she was left with the aftermath of their mock attack. Fake blood was everywhere, and while she would love to call the cleaning crew to wash all this up, it wouldn't take but seconds for them to know it wasn't real. So she went for a mop and cleaning supplies and did it herself.

Bubba was in a motel room cutting tags off the new clothes he'd purchased and still waiting for a call back from his insurance company. He was reaching for another shirt when a news flash interrupted the show he was watching. As soon as he heard the name Travis, he grabbed the remote and turned up the sound, watching in disbelief.

"Wait! What just happened? That's someone on a stretcher! Oh shit, that's the bodyguard! What happened there? What the hell happened?"

He kept watching, seeing Sahara running out of the house and then back inside again.

"So she's still alive and kicking. What's going on?"

He got on his phone and checked Facebook and Twitter to see if this news had already broken on social media and if any fans had more information, which of course, they did. There were dozens of uploaded clips of what onlookers had witnessed at the estate.

He saw enough to know that the bodyguard was taken away in an ambulance, and that the cops were claiming the man who'd been stalking Sahara Travis was dead.

At first, he could only stare, and then the ramifications began to sink in. A copycat killer had just set the stage for Bubba's final entrance. It was the first smile he'd managed today.

He lowered the volume again and began taking the underwear out of the packaging and tossing it into the suitcase he'd purchased. A few minutes later, his phone rang.

Finally. It was the insurance company returning his call. Once he learned they would pay for his lodging for up to a month until he could get a new place, he began to relax. They also informed him that an adjuster would be out at a later time to look at the property, assuring him that it was just procedure.

He didn't care. He'd just bank the insurance check when it came, and for the time being find a furnished apartment for rent. When all of this was over, there would be a big empty house just waiting for occupancy.

On the plus side, his disguise and handgun had been with him in the car—two very important things he wouldn't have to replace.

Tomorrow he was ending this war, and ending it his way.

* * *

Lucy was in the penthouse at The Magnolia, trying to figure out where to begin. The cleaning crew had obviously been here. Everything was gleaming. But beneath the clean scent of lemon that Sahara preferred, the scent of smoke was overpowering.

She opened the sliding doors off the kitchen to let in fresh air as she moved from room to room, mentally writing off all the furniture and draperies as ruined.

She went all the way back into Sahara's bedroom suite and frowned as she opened the door. It smelled like an unemptied ashtray in here. Furnishings were a total loss. At least Sahara could afford to replace what she wanted. A quick glance into the closets and then Lucy backed out of there, as well. The clothing reeked of smoke.

Dishes, awards and trophies were salvageable. All they needed was a good cleaning. She took out her iPad and began making notes as she went. She'd been there about an hour when her cell phone rang. She saw the caller ID and promptly answered.

"Hello…What? Really? Yes, okay. I'll try to get a flight out as soon as possible."

She hit Save on the notes she was making, closed and locked the sliding doors again, and then began looking for flights back to New Orleans. To her relief, the last one for the day flew out at 4:00 p.m. She still had time to get home and pack. The thought of leaving Wiley behind again made her sad, so she booked two tickets to New Orleans instead of one.

He was going to love it there.

* * *

Marcus was at his flower shop when he began hearing stories from customers claiming that the man stalking Sahara Travis had broken into her home. At the time, all he kept hearing was that one person was dead and another one taken away in an ambulance. He dropped the flowers on which he'd been working and went to his office to make a quick call. The phone rang several times, and just as he feared it would go to voice mail, the call was answered.

"Hello."

"Miss Billie! This is Marcus. I just heard some most troubling news. Is everything all right there?"

Billie frowned. "Just a minute, please." She put her hand over the phone to whisper, "Sahara, it's Marcus Beloit. He wants to know if everything is all right. What do I say?"

"Let me," Sahara said, and reached for the phone.

"Careful what you say," Brendan whispered.

She nodded, then took a deep breath and slid into character as easily as putting on shoes.

"Marcus, it's me," she said, her voice shaking.

"Sweetheart! What's happened? I heard gossip. I didn't want to believe it was true."

"I don't know what you heard, but the news here is bad and good. Brendan killed the stalker who'd been after me, which is such a relief, but he was shot in the process. He's injured badly and in intensive care. They don't know if he will make it or not."

"Oh dear! I am so sorry," he cried. "What can I do?

Do you need anything? Can I drive you to the hospital? Just tell me."

"You know what my life is like. I can't show up just anywhere like a normal person. I would be mobbed. The police advised me it was best to stay here rather than cause a ruckus at the hospital and make trouble for so many others."

"Yes, that makes sense. Still, I'm stunned. Did they identify the man who was stalking you?"

"No. I didn't know who he was." Then she choked on a sob. "I can't talk about it anymore. Thank you for calling."

"Of course. Remember, let me know if I can be of service."

"I will," she said, and disconnected.

The moment she turned around, the tears were gone and so was the dejected tone in her voice. She looked first at Brendan, and then at Billie.

"I am so tired of this. I'm either a damn good actress or a consummate liar. The only times I feel like I can be myself is with you two."

Billie hugged her. "It will be over soon. You'll see," she said.

"Come sit with me," Brendan said, and pulled her into his lap.

She tucked her head against his shoulder, loving the deep rumble of his voice as it reverberated against her ear.

"Don't worry, love. We'll all see Sutton coming a mile off, and if he's hired someone else, then the simple fact of a stranger on the doorstep will be warning enough," Brendan said.

"Okay. I called Harold a few minutes ago because I knew he would see the stuff all over the news. I felt I owed him the call, but all I said was that it was over. I'll have to explain it again when it's really over," she said.

Quiet settled between them like a welcome friend, until she realized Billie was mopping tears.

"Mama, what's wrong?"

"I don't know what to do next. My life here…this job… It no longer exists."

Sahara slid out of Brendan's lap and into the chair beside her.

"I own this house now, but you know that I have no desire to live in it. If you want it, it's yours and the money that comes with it."

"Thank you, darling, but no, I don't want it, either. This place…staying in it was my penance—my jail— for what I'd done to you. I don't care if I never see it again."

"Then what? Where do you want to live?" Sahara asked.

Billie's voice was shaking. "Somewhere close to you, if you would be open to it. I lost fifteen years of your life already. I don't want to lose you again."

Sahara took her mother's hands. "Will you come back to LA with me?"

Tears began rolling in earnest. "A thousand times yes, but only if there's a small cottage on the property for me. I want to be close, but not in your business. You and Brendan need privacy, and I do, too."

Brendan stood up. "Both of you, come here," he said, and opened his arms and hugged them to him. "Where I come from, family sticks together. What's hers is mine, and what's mine is hers, and that includes people."

Sahara had never felt so safe—so loved—as she did standing between these two people.

"Think you can handle this, Mama?"

Billie could only nod.

"Then we're good," she said. "You're going to love California. The weather is beautiful."

"But they have earthquakes," Billie said nervously.

"And they have hurricanes here," Sahara countered. "Safety isn't a place, Mama. It's just a state of mind, and you and Brendan are my safe place to fall."

The next morning as they were cleaning up the kitchen after breakfast, Brendan walked up behind Billie, reached over her shoulder and took the dishcloth out of her hands.

She looked over her shoulder and grinned. "I'm not through with that," she said.

"I need you to leave the house today," Brendan said.

Billie looked startled and then began to panic when she realized why he'd asked.

"No. I can't leave. You might need me. Sahara might need me."

"It's going to take all of my skill and attention to keep Sahara safe today. I don't want you to become collateral damage to whatever may go down."

"And neither do I, Mama," Sahara said. "You will

actually be helping. If the man who's after me sees you leaving, he is going to assume I am here alone, and that's what we need him to think."

"I don't like this," Billie said.

"I don't like any of this, either, but I want it over," Sahara countered.

Billie was outnumbered and she knew it, but she gave them both a parting shot.

"If anything happens to either one of you, I will never forgive myself for leaving." Then she ducked her head and covered her face, trying to hide her tears.

Brendan took her by the shoulders. "Billie, look at me."

She lifted her head.

"If you had to kill someone, would you?"

She gasped. "I don't know. I think I could if Sahara was threatened."

"That's honest enough, but hear me. I *know* I would, and that's the difference between me and you. Let me do my job. I will leave bodies all the way to the door to keep her safe. Sahara has been through enough lately. If something went down and you were hurt… Let's not even make that a possibility."

Her lips parted, but after that, she'd run out of arguments.

"It won't take me long. I need to change clothes and shoes. I'll leave and won't come back until one of you calls me."

"Thank you," he said, and gave her a quick hug.

"Thank you, Mama, it will be all right."

Billie's arms tightened around her. She wouldn't

let herself even think it could be the last time she saw them alive.

"I love you, too. See you later," she said, and left to go change.

They waited to see her off, then locked the kitchen door behind her as she went to the carriage house to get her car.

"Now we wait," Brendan said.

"Where?" she asked.

"I think stay close to the front door, maybe that formal living room."

"The white room?"

He nodded.

"And where will you be?" she asked.

"Don't worry about me. If Sutton is buzzing the gate to be let in, then we'll buzz him in, but when he gets to the door, first look to see if his hands are empty. If they are, then you can let him in. He has to make a move before we know for sure he's behind all this. Just know that you will never leave my sight."

She began to shake. "I play roles like this, but reality is a bitch."

"Come upstairs with me a minute. I want to get the rifle, and I have an earpiece you can wear. Your hair will hide it, and I can give you guidance without anyone knowing it."

It was a small measure of comfort.

"You'll be my director," she said.

Once upstairs, he secured the earpiece on her and then slipped one over his own ear, tucking the battery in his back pocket and fastening the mike to his arm.

"Wait here," he said, then closed the door behind him as he walked into the hall. He walked a few steps from the door and then lowered his voice to just above a whisper and spoke into the mike. "Can you hear me?"

Sahara jumped at the sudden sound of his voice in her ear.

"Yes, I hear you," she yelled.

He jogged back to get her and the rifle.

"Then we're good to go. Let's go back down."

They took seats in the white room. Sahara far away from a window and Brendan hidden within curtains, looking out.

The wait felt endless. An hour passed. Brendan knew the wait was taking its toll on her and started talking to get her mind focused on him instead.

"Waiting is a bitch, isn't it, baby? When I was still active duty, sometimes we'd be out on a mission and have to wait out a target's arrival."

"What's the longest you ever had to wait?" she asked.

"Forty-two hours."

"That's almost two days!" she cried.

He grinned. "Yeah, I know."

"Oh my Lord…how did you stand it?"

His expression blanked. "It mattered greatly that the mission succeed."

"Oh," she said, and could tell by the tone of his voice that was all he was going to say, and let it go.

Silence grew between them again. A clock began to chime down in the library.

"It's eleven," Sahara said needlessly.

He started to speak and then stopped, eyeing the car pulling up to the gates.

"There's a black Ford Taurus at the gates," he said, and they both bolted toward the kitchen to see the video feed and buzz him in.

"It's a courier," Sahara said. "See the sign on the door?"

"I see a sign but not much of his face. Tell him to look toward the camera."

She nodded, then pressed Talk.

"State your business," she said shortly.

"Nationwide Courier service, ma'am. I have a packet of papers for you. Signature needed."

"Look up at the camera, please," she said.

"Oh! Sorry," he said, took off his cap and looked straight up into the camera.

"One moment," she said, and buzzed him in.

They watched the gates open and the car approaching the house.

"Do you recognize anything about him?" Brendan asked.

"He sits tall in a seat like Sutton, but he looks older and heavier."

"When he rings the doorbell, let him in and don't let him past the foyer. Don't let anyone past the foyer. You won't see me, but I swear to God if he goes for a gun, I'll drop him where he stands before the gun is in his hands. And one other thing, Sahara. If you hear me tell you to drop, you need to hit the floor immediately. Not a second of hesitation. Understood?"

"Understood."

"I love you." He kissed her quick and hard. "So much," he added, then took off running up the stairs just as the doorbell began to chime.

Sahara moved toward the door, praying as she walked.

Twenty-One

Bubba rang the doorbell, then took a deep breath to calm his nerves. This day had been a long time coming, although it was *not* how he wanted it to go down. He hadn't wanted to watch Sahara die. But she'd challenged him, called him out in front of the world. He couldn't let that pass.

He shuffled the envelope and clipboard from one hand to the other and wiped sweat from his brow as he waited for Billie to answer. He still hadn't decided what he was going to do about her. On one hand, she'd become caught in Leopold's trap just as his mother had. But on the other, they'd let her live here. It didn't matter that she'd been turned into a servant. She'd been under this roof, not suffering hunger or evictions, never worrying about paying utility bills or going without clothes.

As for Sahara, they'd chosen her to keep. There was no way for him to explain how deeply that knowledge had hurt once he'd learned the whole story. Just because she'd been born beautiful, and Katarina had wanted a beautiful child, his own father had thrown him away.

Then he heard a lock turning and gave his face a quick pat, making sure the stage makeup wasn't melting off his face in this damn heat. He slumped his shoulders, patted the gun in the back of his pants, then held the envelope and clipboard against his chest.

The door swung inward, but it wasn't Billie, it was Sahara standing before him. He stuttered. "Uh…packet for Sahara Travis."

"I'm Sahara Travis."

"You'll have to sign for it," he said, and then pretended he'd left the pen in the car. "Oh, I'm sorry, I must have dropped the pen. I'll go—"

"No, I have one just over there," she said, pointing to an ornate antique desk against the wall. "Please step in out of the heat."

"Yes, ma'am," he said, and pushed the door shut but didn't let it catch as he followed her.

Sahara picked up a pen and then held out her hand for the clipboard.

The front door swung inward as he handed it over.

Sahara looked up and stifled a gasp. "Lucy! What are you doing here?"

"I needed to tell you that the furniture and clothing in the penthouse are ruined."

Sahara frowned. "You could have just called."

A stranger stepped up behind her. Lucy took him by the hand.

"I also wanted to introduce you to someone very special. Sahara, this is Wiley Johnson…my boyfriend.

I thought now was as good a time as any for you two to meet."

Sahara's gaze darted from the couple to the courier, who seemed to be patiently waiting for her to sign. Was she reading this wrong? What should she do?

And then she heard Brendan's voice.

"Move a few steps to the right."

She casually stepped to the right as she acknowledged the introduction.

"It is a pleasure to meet you, Wiley."

"Thank you, ma'am. Lucy is my sweetheart. I'd do anything for her."

They came inside, but instead of bypassing the courier, they stopped beside him.

Sahara's heartbeat stuttered. "What's going on?" she asked, then heard another car coming through the gates.

"Shut up," the courier snapped, and dropped the envelope to the floor. "We can't start this party until all the guests have arrived."

Lucy giggled. "If he hadn't been late, he could have arrived with all of us. He's always the slowpoke."

"Wait, baby. Someone else is coming. Don't worry, I've got you."

She wrapped her arms around herself so they wouldn't see her shaking.

"Lucy? What is going on? Are you part of this? Please God, tell me you're not."

"If I said that I wasn't, then it would be a lie," Lucy said, and snuggled back against Wiley, who just stood there grinning, now holding a gun.

When Marcus Beloit walked in the door and sauntered up to the others, Sahara moaned. Her knees went out from under her as she staggered to catch herself.

"I got held up in traffic and feared I'd be too late." Marcus made a sad face. "Poor little rich bitch. I think we've shocked you."

Sahara looked from one face to the other and back again, unable to believe what she was seeing. She'd been expecting Sutton, but Marcus? Lucy? She felt utterly sick and completely betrayed.

"Are you all…responsible for what's been happening to me?"

"Ta-da," the courier said, and grinned as he pulled a gun from behind his back.

That was when she recognized him.

"Sutton?"

"What? Is my makeup melting already? Damn hot soupy day today, but a good day to die."

Her voice began to shake. Her heart was beating so fast she felt like she would faint.

"Lucy? Marcus? I thought you were my friends. Sutton, we grew up together. Why are you—"

"Why? I'll tell you why!" Sutton shouted, hammering his fist against his chest. "We're Leopold's children, too. But he didn't keep us. He threw *us* away and kept *you*! You had everything and we had nothing."

"That's not true and Lucy knows it!" Sahara cried.

Lucy shrugged. "I know he left you everything…as if you didn't already have too much. If it hadn't been for that pig of a girl on set, you would have had your last lunch ages ago and none of this would be happening."

Sahara gasped. "*You* poisoned the food!"

"I sure did. It would have been so easy."

"You're okay, baby. Just keep them talking. The cops are on the way, coming quiet. No sirens."

Sahara took a deep breath. Unwilling to let them know how scared she was, she transformed into the role she knew would make them angry and defensive, throwing back her head and putting her hands on her hips.

"Okay, that explains the cyanide. Which one of you has the hots for bombs?"

Wiley Johnson raised his hand. "That would be me, because I have the hots for Lucy. I'd do anything for her."

"If we'd taken my jet when we left California, you would have blown her up," Sahara snapped.

Lucy frowned. "They didn't count on me going with you," she said.

"So Sutton said," Sahara drawled, pointing at him. "But there would have been one less heir."

He flushed.

Sahara waved her hand as if pushing them aside.

"So that takes care of the LA failures. Who killed Leopold and Katarina? I'm guessing Sutton because Marcus wouldn't want to get his hands dirty."

When Marcus screamed out an epithet, Sutton laughed.

"And you'd be right. Brother Marcus doesn't like ugly."

Sahara turned her head slowly, centering her gaze on Marcus.

"That means you're the snake in the grass who sent the snake in the vase. So who hired Harley Fish? Either you or Sutton. I'll bet that pissed you off when you figured out the cops had your thousand dollars and I was still alive."

Marcus shoved past Lucy and Wiley and would have gone after her but for Sutton, who grabbed him by the back of the shirt.

"No, brother. You have to go find the security system and get rid of the evidence that we were here."

"I'm not looking for anything until I watch her die," Marcus shrieked.

"Then stand back," Sutton said, and started to reach for his gun.

"I brought my pretty pink pistol, too," Lucy said.

Marcus pulled out a box knife, shoved the blade into the cut position and began waving it toward her face.

"Just so you know, that beautiful face is going to look like a patchwork quilt after you're dead. There won't be any glorious Hollywood send-off for someone who looks that gruesome."

When Sahara grinned, they stopped, staring in disbelief.

"You think this is a joke?" Sutton shouted.

"If it is, then the joke is on you. What in hell made you think that showing up after I'm dead would get you anything?"

"Because we're blood kin. Because we're Leopold's bastards just like you."

"Except I was adopted. And they named me their heir, and I outlived them, which means all of this now belongs to me," Sahara said. "And my will already names the people who will inherit my fortune, none of whom are you, you or you," she drawled, pointing at her siblings. "So, it doesn't matter how dead I am. You won't get shit."

"You don't have a will," Lucy growled through clenched teeth. "I checked."

"Oh, little sister, yes, I do, as of a few days ago. And why? Because Brendan already found out Sutton was my half brother and found records naming all the women Leopold had paid off. I'm not stupid. When it became obvious I could have siblings who were behind this, I made damn sure they wouldn't get a dime."

Lucy screamed and went for her gun.

Sutton was cursing her with every breath as he started to take aim.

But it was Marcus who was closest, and who was already coming at her with the box cutter when Sahara heard Brendan say *"DROP."*

She hit the floor facedown just as Brendan fired four shots in rapid succession from somewhere above and behind her.

She heard one thud, then another as Marcus and Sutton hit the floor without a sound. They never saw this coming.

Lucy's scream was cut short as her shot went wild. A bullet went right between her eyes and plowed a rut through her brain.

Wiley dropped like a rock on the cold marble floor.

Sahara's head was still down, her eyes were closed, and she was screaming Brendan's name.

All of a sudden she was in his arms, and he was walking outside with her face pressed hard against his chest.

"Don't look, baby, don't look," he kept saying. "It's over, it's all over now."

Policemen exited cruisers and came running up the steps with their guns drawn, passing Brendan and Sahara as they ran inside.

He carried Sahara all the way to the top of the steps and then slowly lowered himself onto the porch, still holding her in his arms.

She couldn't stop crying.

"They hated me," she sobbed. "My own sister and two brothers, and they wanted to be rich bad enough to kill. Oh my God, Brendan, oh my God. They hated Leopold, but they turned out just like him…greedy, selfish, liars."

"I know, baby, I know, but it's over. They can't hurt you anymore."

An unmarked cop car pulled up.

"The detectives are here," he said.

She groaned.

Fisher and Julian came up the steps on the run.

"There were four of them?" Fisher asked.

Brendan held his gun up by the barrel.

"Three other heirs and a boyfriend. The female on the floor brought the bomber with her from LA. He said he loved her. Said he'd do anything for her. This is my gun. I have permits and a license to carry, and I want it back when you're done with it. My rifle is on the second-floor landing. I didn't use it."

Julian dug an evidence bag from his pocket.

Brendan dropped the gun in, and Julian fastened the bag and tagged it, then squatted until he was eye level with Sahara.

"Miss Travis?"

Sahara opened her eyes. The cop was blurry, but she recognized him as he touched her arm.

"I am so sorry for all that has happened to you here. You should have been welcomed into our city and able to focus on laying your family to rest. Your bodyguard is ace at his job. So glad you are okay."

"Thank you," she said.

Fisher also touched her arm briefly as he passed, and then they were inside.

"One of us needs to call Detective Shaw in LA," Julian said.

"I'll do it. You start with the bodies," Fisher said.

Outside, Brendan reached in his pocket and handed her his phone.

"Call your mama."

Sahara did as he asked and then waited as the phone began to ring. Billie answered breathlessly.

"Hello?"

"Mama, it's over. They're dead and neither one of us was hurt."

"Thank the Lord!" she cried, and then realized what Sahara had said. "What do you mean 'they'?"

"There were three of them, Mama. Three more of his children and a boyfriend who loved enough to kill."

"Who? What?"

"Just come home, Mama. We'll talk about it when you get here."

"I'm on my way."

Sahara disconnected, then put the phone in Brendan's hand.

"A crowd is gathering again," he said, looking toward the gate.

"For once, I don't care," Sahara muttered. "I'll have to give a public statement after we get back."

"I won't be part of it. Will you be okay with that?"

Her heart sank. "Do you mean you're still leaving me?"

He hugged her and kissed the crown of her head.

"No, never. What I mean is that I don't publicize what happens to my clients, even though you turned into far more than that. You can say anything you want about me. But I need to stay out of the public eye. A bodyguard can't become the target, too."

"Oh," she said, but amid all of the surrounding chaos, she got very quiet.

"Are we okay here?" he asked.

"We're okay."

"Are you still going to come to Wyoming with me to meet my family?"

She sat up, needing to see his face.

"Yes. I would love to meet your family. Do you think they'll like me?"

He smiled wryly. "When my mom finds out I'm coming home with a woman, regardless of who she is, she'll be mentally planning a wedding before we can get there."

Sahara managed a shaky smile. "Really?"

"Yes, really."

"Are we planning a wedding, too?" she asked.

Brendan glanced around at the cop cars and the noise, thought of the four dead bodies in the house behind them and thought, what the hell.

"I think I need to ask you first, but never in my wildest dreams would I have imagined proposing to the woman I love more than life itself in the middle of such a clusterfuck. However, let's just consider this something we can tell our grandkids someday, okay?"

Imminent joy rolled through her.

"Okay."

Brendan took both of her hands, kissing freshly bruised knuckles she'd gained from hitting the floor, then held them against his heart.

"I love you, Sahara Travis, more than I believed it was possible to love, and faster than I ever thought possible to fall this hard. I will never betray you. I will spend the rest of our life together honoring you and protecting you, and I will never leave you behind until God calls me home."

Sahara's gaze was locked on his face, on his eyes and on his lips, watching the changing expressions on his face as he promised her a lifetime of allegiance. The ache in the back of her throat was so big it hurt to breathe as she waited for those four little words.

"Despite the fact that we are in the aftermath of hell, will you marry me?"

She was laughing through tears as her arms went around his neck.

"Yes, yes, yes, I will marry you. Thank you for loving *me*, not the famous me with the ugly secrets and crazy life."

The first kiss was little more than a brush of lips across her mouth. The second kiss was with intent, lingering longer. The last kiss was urgent and deep, with promises of so much more to come.

"Get a room," Fisher said, as he passed them on the way back to his car.

"I'm about to put a ring on it," Brendan said.

Fisher stopped and smiled. "Then let me be the first to congratulate you both," he said, and continued down the steps.

"We'll get a ring together back in LA, before I take you home to Wyoming," Brendan said.

She cupped his face and kissed him, and then kissed him again before she paused.

"I'm trying to come to terms with the worst day of my life and the best day of my life happening at the same time. As for a ring, I like simple. Even if my life is glitz, I'm not. I can't wait to go with you to Wyoming, but Lucy said everything in the penthouse was ruined. This will be the first time I can honestly say I have nothing to wear."

He was laughing when he saw Billie's car at the gates. She was looking for a way to get around all the traffic to get to the carriage house.

"There's your mama," he said. "She can't get past the cop cars."

"She sees us," Sahara said, and watched her mother stop behind the last car and get out running.

"Go," Brendan said, and turned her loose.

Sahara went down the steps two at a time, then slowed to a walk, unable to believe that she was outside and safe. The midday sun was hot and the air was thick and close, but it didn't matter because her mama was coming for her. The closer she got, the faster she went, until she was running into her mother's arms.

Brendan stood, leaning against a stately white column with his hands in his pockets, watching them embrace and thinking about how long they had been forced to live a lie.

Today wasn't just about endings—it was new beginnings, and he didn't like the distance between him and them.

He took his hands out of his pockets as he went down the steps, moving past cop cars and ambulances toward the rest of his life.

Epilogue

Three weeks later

The private jet landed safely at Cheyenne Regional Airport, then taxied to a stop out on the tarmac.

"We're finally here," Brendan said, kissing Sahara and then her hand, near the square-cut, two-carat diamond she was wearing. It was anything but simple, but it was hers.

"I'm so excited, and at the same time feeling a little guilty about leaving Mama behind," Sahara said.

"You heard her," Brendan said. "This visit is for you alone. She'll come another time. And after that makeover you gave her last week, I don't think she's going to be on her own for the rest of her life."

Sahara grinned. "A little hair color. A stylish cut and some new clothes...yes, Billie Munroe was looking good when we left."

"Harold was looking pleased, too," Brendan said.

"It was nice of him to have her as his guest while we're gone."

Sahara rolled her eyes. "Harold wasn't just pleased. He was smitten. He could very well become family for real."

Brendan laughed.

Sahara glanced out the window. Her pilot was lowering the stairway. She got up, smoothing out the wrinkles in her very short dress.

"Do I look okay? Not too wrinkled or messy? Should I do something to my hair?"

"You are a knockout. Stop worrying. Oh, look! See that wild crew waving like fools on the far side of the security fence?"

She bent down and looked through one of the windows.

"Yes, I see!" She stood up. "Is that them? Oh, Brendan, you do have a big family. I am finally going to belong…really belong to a big family."

Her pilot entered the cabin.

"Sorry to interrupt, but you can disembark now. I'll get your luggage."

Nervous all over again, Sahara reached for Brendan.

"You've got this, my love. Enjoy it."

He gave her a quick pat on the backside and then took her by the hand.

There were shouts of hello, catcalls and whistles when they appeared at the head of the stairway.

"You first, baby. I wouldn't want to hide one single inch of those long, beautiful legs from the viewing public. Give 'em the full Hollywood strut. You can be your sweet self later after we're home."

She grinned, her eyes glittering from the excitement of the moment as she took a step forward, looking out with wonder at the vast open sky and the backdrop of mountains. As she did, the Wyoming wind caught her hair, lifting it up and whipping it about her face. Even the wind made her welcome. She threw her head back and laughed.

The McQueens were dumbstruck by the stunning beauty of the tall, leggy woman coming down the steps. They'd seen pictures that did not do her justice. The turquoise minidress she was wearing was hugging every curve, and she was laughing as she descended with that wild mane of black hair blowing in every direction.

And there was Brendan coming down behind her, as always, making sure he had someone's back, but with a look on his face they'd never seen.

"He's in love," his mama said, and started to cry.

"So is she," his daddy said, and cleared his throat.

They reached the gate.

Brendan opened it to let her pass, and as he did, Sahara was engulfed. Hugs, kisses, oohs and aahs over her ring, hugging her again because of the grief she had endured, promises of the years of joy to come. The broken bits of her were filling up so fast.

She looked over her shoulder to see where Brendan had gone. He waved, still standing at the gate and watching her over the crowd with that look on his face that never failed to make her shiver.

He spoke, and while the words were lost in the noise, she read his lips.

He'd just told her, welcome home.

* * * * *

New York Times bestselling author

SHARON SALA

weaves a tale of a murder in Eden...

Before he dies, Stanton Youngblood manages to leave a single clue to his killer's identity: the word *Wayne* scrawled in his own blood. This floors his widow, as Leigh Youngblood was once Leigh Wayne, who left her family behind thirty years ago after falling in love—a betrayal they could never forgive. Now she publicly vows to discover which of her siblings is responsible for her husband's murder.

Back in town to find his father's killer, Brody Youngblood finds his own search for justice comes with an unexpected ray of light. The torch he has always carried for Talia Champion reignites upon his return, as this time it's *Talia* who needs *him*, and it isn't in him to deny her anything.

But the killer still has a score to settle, and that may mean spilling more blood...

Available now, wherever books are sold!

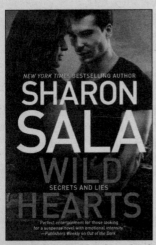

New York Times **Bestselling Author**

SHARON SALA

There's only one way to keep secrets buried...

If only something else had brought Lissa Sherman and Mack Jackson back in touch after so many years—something other than the murder of Mack's father...

Thirty-five years ago, four friends went for a joyride that ended in a terrible accident, leaving one dead and the others with no memory of that night. Now two of them, including Mack's father, have been murdered, and if the lone survivor knows why they're being targeted, she's not talking.

Even in the midst of tragedy, Lissa and Mack find themselves drawn together. Then someone comes after Lissa, too, and the mystery deepens. Is the danger to her tied to the other deaths, or are two killers at work? Now Mack has to fight an unknown attacker as well as his feelings for Lissa, and it may be that he can't win either battle.

Available now, wherever books are sold!

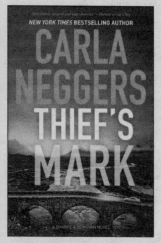

Get 2 Free Books,
Plus 2 Free Gifts –
just for trying the Reader Service!

STRS17R

SHARON SALA

32792	TORN APART	___	$7.99	U.S.	___	$9.99 CAN.
31997	RACE AGAINST TIME	___	$7.99	U.S.	___	$9.99 CAN.
31968	FAMILY SINS	___	$7.99	U.S.	___	$9.99 CAN.
31877	DARK HEARTS	___	$7.99	U.S.	___	$9.99 CAN.
31659	GOING GONE	___	$7.99	U.S.	___	$8.99 CAN.
31592	GOING TWICE	___	$7.99	U.S.	___	$8.99 CAN.
31342	DON'T CRY FOR ME	___	$7.99	U.S.	___	$9.99 CAN.

(limited quantities available)

TOTAL AMOUNT	$ _____
POSTAGE & HANDLING	$ _____
($1.00 for 1 book, 50¢ for each additional)	
APPLICABLE TAXES*	$ _____
TOTAL PAYABLE	$ _____

(check or money order—please do not send cash)

To order, complete this form and send it, along with a check or money order for the total above, payable to MIRA Books, to: **In the U.S.:** 3010 Walden Avenue, P.O. Box 9077, Buffalo, NY 14269-9077; **In Canada:** P.O. Box 636, Fort Erie, Ontario, L2A 5X3.

Name: _____

Address: _____ City: _____

State/Prov.: _____ Zip/Postal Code: _____

Account Number (if applicable): _____

075 CSAS

mira

Harlequin.com

MSS1017BL

*New York residents remit applicable sales taxes.
*Canadian residents remit applicable GST and provincial taxes.